TAKE YOUR CHARMING SOMEWHERE ELSE

A Hollywood Lights Novel

The Hollywood Lights Series
Book 5

KATIE ROSE PRYAL

Blue Osprey Books

Pryal, Katie Rose Guest 1976-.

Take Your Charming Somewhere Else : A Hollywood Lights Novel / Katie Rose Guest Pryal.

ISBN Paper: 978-1-947834-86-6

ISBN Ebook: 978-1-947834-87-3

1. California—Fiction. 2. Los Angeles—Fiction. 3. Love—Fiction. I. Title

813'.6

Updated Blue Osprey Books Edition, 2025
First Blue Crow Books Edition, 2021

Blue Osprey Books

Published by Blue Osprey Books,
a division of Pryal Consulting, Inc.
Chapel Hill, NC
blueospreybooks.com

Also by Katie Rose Pryal

NOVELS

Entanglement

Chasing Chaos

Fallout Girl

Take Your Charming Somewhere Else

NONFICTION

Life of the Mind Interrupted: Essays on Mental Health and Disability in Higher Education

The Freelance Academic: Transform Your Creative Life and Career

Even If You're Broken: Bodies, Boundaries, and Mental Health

A Light in the Tower: A New Reckoning with Mental Health in Higher Education

Your Kid Belongs Here: Parenting Neurodiverse Children

Praise for the Hollywood Lights Series

Entanglement is an evocative story of enduring friendship, rivalry, and the ties that bind. A heartfelt, fabulous novel!

Bestselling author Diane Haeger for *Booktrib* Magazine

"*Entanglement* is a rich romance that had me hooked until the last page. Pryal's characters sparkle with charm and wit—I devoured the whole series!"

Lucy Day, award-winning author of *My Star-Crossed Summer*

Women and men, love and obsession, need and want: *Entanglement* has it all!

USA Today bestselling author Ann Garvin

Equal parts heartbreaking and heartening, *Entanglement* shines a light on the interior lives of two flawed and fascinating women.

Washington Post bestselling author Camille Pagán

Poignant and thoroughly entertaining, *Love and Entropy* is a novella you won't be able to walk away from and you'll think about long after the last page. Fantastic read!

New York Times bestselling author Kristy Woodson Harvey

Love and Entropy is utterly captivating ... Pryal writes with a rare understanding about the complexity of new adulthood and what it means to be a true friend.

In *Chasing Chaos*, Pryal pierces L.A.'s film industry veneer to find complex and relatable characters and then winches the ties between them, pulling the reader right into the fray. The result is as psychologically astute as it is engaging.

As glamorous and mercurial as Hollywood itself, *Chasing Chaos* is a novel that glitters.

In *How to Stay*, engaging characters lead the reader through a poignant and layered narrative about the universal desire for something so elusive—a safe place to fall.

How To Stay is an intelligent romance. The central tension isn't whether the girl will get the guy, it's whether she will let herself–something all readers can relate to and enjoy.

Modern, fresh, and entirely credible, *Fallout Girl* is a love story wrapped inside a heart-rending struggle for personal freedom.

Fallout Girl is a dangerous, sexy, motorcycle ride of a story, which pulls off the feat of being both humorous and heartbreaking at the same time.

Sandra Block, author of *What Happened That Night*

Fallout Girl is compelling story of friendship, family, and love with a honest look at mental illness that doesn't shy away from the painful realities so often hidden beneath the surface.

Susan Bishop Crispell, author of *Dreaming in Chocolate*

A gut-wrenching journey through darkness to redemption, one that proves that love, and family, can conquer anything. *Take Your Charming Somewhere Else* is her best yet. Do not miss this emotional tour-de-force—or anything Pryal writes.

Washington Post bestselling author Kelly Harms

For MAE,
for standing by me through this journey, and for the terrible, wonderful
puns.

Author Note

S ome people, like me, need content warnings to allow us to fully engage with and appreciate our world, including books.

This book contains flashback scenes of child abuse and neglect by parents, of attempted killing by poisoning, and of self-defense killing by gun.

Charlie, the protagonist, struggles with PTSD and alcohol abuse.

Los Angeles, Autumn of 2008

Chapter One

Charlie George didn't expect to have his mother's death cause him so much trouble that Wednesday. After all, three years had passed since she'd died, and he'd been fine. At least he'd become fine, after a while.

But sometimes events from the past exert an unexpected pull. And sometimes they knock you off course entirely.

Mid-morning on Wednesday, Chalkley Bogart, known as Chalk, entered Charlie George's office without knocking. Charlie George, annoyed by the interruption, looked up from behind his desk. In his late twenties, Charlie was a senior associate, a top-flight attorney, and next in line for partner. Chalk was only a second-year associate, just two years out of law school.

In Charlie's estimation, Chalk was not a bad attorney, but he was far from top-flight. And Chalk was only not-bad if you were willing to overlook his flaws.

Chalk's flaws included his inability to knock, his inability to properly use punctuation in legal documents, and his inability to act like a human being with a conscience.

Chalk was carrying a case file in his hands as though he'd just found oil on some worthless land in Texas—jittery, eyes wide. His pale blond hair needed a trim, its ends curling around his ears. He looked sloppy. Charlie hated sloppy.

But Charlie knew that Chalk, while sloppy, was also dangerous.

Not only because he made reckless decisions, but also because he didn't care whom he hurt. Everything Chalk did—from reaming out a paralegal for a small mistake and causing the kid to quit in the middle of a case, to making bad plea deals for Charlie's clients without running the deals by Charlie first—had terrible collateral damage. Worse yet, Chalk seemed to revel in the damage he caused.

Charlie knew that Chalk both admired Charlie and also constantly looked for ways to take him down. Chalk would take pleasure in knocking Charlie off his throne.

Charlie glanced at the case file while keeping one eye on Chalk.

The file was thin. Thin meant it was a new file, one that had just landed in the office. Somehow it had been deposited directly into Chalk's unclean hands, and that was unusual.

"You got a minute?" Chalk said.

Sighing loudly, knowing it would needle Chalk, Charlie said, "For you? Precisely one minute."

Chalk bristled at the implication that he wasn't worth Charlie's time, but he shook it off. Waving the case file, Chalk said, "You're gonna love this one."

Charlie knew that he should interpret Chalk's words to mean the precise opposite. Chalk only loved the absolute worst cases: Wives beaten till their teeth fell out. Kids left in dumpsters to die. Horrible stuff. The stuff that turned even Charlie's bullet-proof stomach. Chalk reveled in the misery of others, and he delighted in the most gruesome details.

Chalk was, without a doubt, a psychopath.

"What would give you that idea?" Charlie said, shuffling through papers on his desk, not bothering to hide his disregard for his fellow associate.

Charlie worked at an elite law firm in Los Angeles. The firm paid Charlie a lot of money to defend criminals who could afford the firm's outrageous fees, and he would never let a rookie like Chalk Bogart put his career at risk. Every chance he had, Charlie made sure Chalk knew just how beneath him he was in the firm's pecking order.

Chalk grinned, his teeth too large for his mouth, not at all put out by Charlie's disdain. That was unusual: Chalk was always put out by Charlie's disdain.

Suddenly, Charlie was on alert.

"The defendant in this case is a kid who shot his parents," Chalk said. "He just cracked one day and shot them both right in the chest over breakfast." Chalk dropped the file on Charlie's desk, a cracking sound shattering the quiet air.

Chalk seated himself in one of the leather chairs that Charlie kept for clients. Charlie felt the urge to tell Chalk to stand because he didn't want the younger man to be comfortable in Charlie's space. But that would reveal the surge of anger Charlie felt.

The surge of panic.

Chalk hadn't stopped running his mouth. "I don't know why Birch wants you to take cases like this. Probably because that pretty face of yours could convince any jury that some murderous teenager is innocent."

Romeo Birch, their supervising partner, decided who tried which cases. Obviously, Chalk wanted this one for himself. Probably so he could see someone suffer up close.

"Will you let me second chair?" Chalk continued, talking too fast. "What do you think, bud?"

"Don't call me *bud*." Charlie glared down at Chalk. "Grow up. This isn't a frat house."

Chalk sucked in his breath. Charlie's words had struck a nerve.

Good.

Because Charlie worked at a high-dollar defense firm, he usually worked white-collar crimes. But occasionally the work was gruesome. Stuff like O.J. Simpson and the Menendez brothers, although neither of those cases had come through their firm. And most of Charlie's cases—like most criminal cases, period—ended in a plea, with no trial and no jury.

Charlie eyed the case file in front of him—it was so thin. Why hadn't anyone in the firm done any preliminary work on it yet? There was only one explanation.

"Is this a pro bono case?" Charlie asked.

"Yeah." Chalk rolled his eyes. "Kill me now, right?"

Chalk often complained about the firm's commitment to pro bono cases. He didn't understand why the California State Bar strongly suggested that every attorney provide fifty hours of pro bono work each year. But Charlie knew why he and Chalk and every other associate in the firm had to do the pro bono work: The partners wanted the firm to look good, which meant the associates' had to make the firm look good. Charlie was next in line for partner because he understood his job, and he did it well.

Charlie didn't have a bleeding heart. He didn't think they should represent every sad sack off the street, but he took his work seriously, and just because a case was pro bono didn't mean he would do shoddy work.

He took pride in his work, no matter what. Appearances mattered. Reputation was everything. Charlie was an excellent attorney, and the entire firm—the entire criminal bar in Los Angeles—knew it.

He looked at the thin file again. The fact that the case was a pro bono referral explained why there hadn't been any significant intake yet. Charlie would remedy that problem right away. He pulled the file toward him and opened it. As he flipped through the pages, he found a police report and a statement by the defendant upon arrest. Charlie was going to have to start from scratch.

At the thought of real legal work, of the research, the interviews, the negotiations, the rhythm, the push and pull, Charlie's panic and anger subsided. He could do this. It was just a case like any other.

It had to be.

An image flashed in his mind: the defendant with a gun. Firing it at his mother, then his father.

Another image took its place. In this one, Charlie's hand held the gun.

Charlie swallowed hard, determined not to give Chalk the satisfaction of seeing his panic. Chalk might be subpar in a lot of ways, but he could sniff out fear. Sadists were like that.

Charlie drummed his fingers on the desktop. "Anything else you're forgetting to tell me?" he asked, sounding bored.

Chalk reached across Charlie's desk to the case file and flipped to a page near the back. "How could I forget?" He tapped the page with his finger. "This is the best part. I've got a great defense for you. The kid says that his parents abused his little sister, so he shot his parents to protect her."

At Chalk's words, muscles in Charlie's shoulders, and all the way down his spine, tightened.

His body was as rigid as a drawn bow.

His emotions surged again. The fear clawed up his throat like acid. Anger at Chalk filled him, a grenade with its pin pulled.

But he revealed none of this to Chalk. Charlie was an expert at revealing nothing. Growing up in his family, revealing nothing had been a survival skill. His surface was smooth, perfect, like his two-thousand dollar suits.

He flipped the case file closed. "I'll take it from here," he said to Chalk, dismissing him.

"Everything all right, man?" Chalk asked.

Charlie looked fine. He knew it. He would never show weakness in front of this animal. Charlie ignored him.

Chalk didn't give up. He was digging for something, his eyes bright, his grin too wide. "You don't look so good."

"Nothing that your absence won't cure," Charlie said, nodding at the door.

Chalk inhaled sharply, but he didn't take the bait. He stood. "I was just wondering, you know, since your mom bit it while you were in law school. Didn't know if this case cut too close to home."

With those words, Charlie was certain that Chalk was baiting him on purpose. But to what end? Was Chalk just feeding his desire to make someone else suffer? Or was Chalk actually gunning for Charlie this time?

Charlie reached into his reserves, into what made him Charlie George, and pulled out the strength he needed to shut down Chalk. He stood, towering over the shorter guy, and leaned forward, resting his hands on his desk. "Birch gave this case to me because he knew you'd fuck it up. So why don't you go make coffee? Surely you can do that properly."

Nervous in the face of Charlie's attack, Chalk took a step back. His jaw tensed, and, for a moment, Charlie thought he might make another comment to try to get a rise. But Chalk gave him a curt nod and turned to leave.

Charlie definitely did not want Chalk as his second chair on this case. Birch believed he and Chalk made a great team, and Charlie understood why. Chalk would do things that Charlie would not.

Although Charlie was cutthroat—he'd go for the kill like every other lawyer in this firm—one thing was also true: Charlie had lines he wouldn't cross.

Unlike Chalk, Charlie actually cherished the dignity of the law. He was a bloodthirsty shark who worked at a firm full of bloodthirsty sharks. But the difference between him and someone like Chalk was respect for the law. Chalk, and lawyers like him, didn't respect anything but himself. He only cared if he won, but he didn't care how, and he didn't care whom he hurt while he was winning.

For Chalk, being a lawyer wasn't about serving his clients. It was about Chalk. But Chalk's selfishness was the reason why Chalk only second-chaired cases. Chalk couldn't be trusted to speak properly to judges. And he made jurors nervous—they never liked him, and they never trusted him.

It wasn't Charlie's pretty face that won over judges and juries. It was his respect—for them and for the law. Charlie, unlike Chalk, wasn't a monster.

Chalk reveled in his clients' misery. The more miserable, the bloodier, the better.

Like the miserable, bloody case in front of Charlie right now.

Charlie opened the case file once more. *Michael Dunworth*. He remembered the name. Not too long ago, the media splashed the news of the Dunworth case everywhere: a Beverly Hills brat shot his parents dead, and the brat was charged with murder.

Charlie read on. At the time of the shooting, the kid was only twenty, home from college for spring break. His little sister, not a defendant but a key witness, was a minor when the shooting occurred. She was eighteen now—just turned—living alone somewhere in North Hollywood. She should have had her parents' millions to spend, but she seemed to be keeping a low profile.

Charlie felt the emotions rise inside him. He knew from experience that all the money in the world wouldn't bring a family back.

According to the defendant's statement, the father had been

sexually abusing the sister since she was ten years old. Worse, the mother knew about the abuse—the daughter had told her—but the mother hadn't stopped it because she didn't want to leave Beverly Hills. The mother had signed a prenup that meant she'd lose everything upon divorce, and she was willing to sacrifice her kids rather than be broke.

The brother only found out about the abuse, and his mother's knowledge of it, when his sister was a senior in high school. According to his statement, he confronted his mother and father separately. His mother said she was helpless. His father denied it despite confirmation from both his wife and daughter. The defendant told him to stop, and the father didn't. So, the son killed them both.

Charlie would have to interview the defendant and his sister to verify the story. He'd see if his sister Miranda would assist him on this case—she was his paralegal when she felt like it, and a third-year law student at UCLA. Best of all, she was a walking lie detector, even better than he was.

Charlie stared into space, meditating on the facts. His mind hooked on the defendant's mom and wouldn't let go. What an idiot she'd been. Any good lawyer could have blown that prenup to hell with allegations of child abuse. All she had to do was care, just a little, about her kids. But she hadn't. Now her kids were fucked up for life, and she was dead—but good riddance to her and her husband.

Charlie had grown up rich, just like the defendant in this case. And Charlie's mother had died when he was in his early twenties. But Charlie's mom hadn't been an enabling, selfish idiot like the mom in this case. She'd had her struggles, but she'd loved the hell out of him and Miranda.

His dad, on the other hand, was questionable. Charles George, Sr., was still alive but, thankfully, out of his life. Best of all, his dad sent him and Miranda a lot of money every few months—to keep them happy and to keep them quiet.

Chalk, with his predator's sixth sense, had somehow figured out that this case cut far closer to home for Charlie than the facts on paper revealed. Charlie's mother was dead, but she hadn't committed suicide like the papers reported. That's not what had happened at all.

Charlie had a lot more in common with the defendant in this case than Chalk should have been able to find out. But something in the details had caught Chalk's attention, and Chalk must have done some digging.

Charlie had worked hard to bury his secrets. The last thing he needed was someone like Chalk unearthing them.

Standing, tucking his hands in the pockets of his Italian suit, Charlie stared out of the tall windows of his office. The firm took up an entire floor of their building in Century City. The parking garage had a detail shop that spruced up his M5 every week. The first floor had a gym, a coffee shop, a dry cleaners—everything he needed to get his errands done. He liked working here. The work challenged his mind, and the prestige of the firm reminded him that, despite everything that had happened, he was successful. He was worth something.

He could do the work he loved at a firm that was just as prestigious as the one he'd turned his back on. Although Romeo Birch's firm wasn't George Law, the firm his mother had founded back home in North Carolina, Charlie had found a new home, a new career, a new life, here. And Charlie could never go back home to George Law, not ever. That door was closed forever.

He checked the time on his Patek Philippe. The watch was one of three that his parents had given him over the years. Two had belonged to the men in his family, his father and grandfather, and one had been new, just for him, when he'd graduated from college. The new one was the only one he wore because it had been a gift from his mother.

Eschewing diamonds and flashy gold, the watch was made of platinum with a black enamel face. Like his mother had been, it was fine, yet understated.

The day his mother died, he was wearing this watch. After the ambulance and the police, after everything, he soaked it and scrubbed it to remove her blood from the crevices. The original leather band had been destroyed by the bloodstains. Later, for months after she'd died, he kept imagining he saw dried blood where the crystal met platinum around the dial.

He still saw the blood sometimes.

Setting his black leather brief bag on his desk, Charlie opened the top flap and slid in the Dunworth case file along with his laptop, then snapped it closed, locking the troubles of the Dunworths away until he got home.

At that moment, Chalk returned with fresh coffee from the office espresso machine and sat back down across from Charlie.

"Heading out?" Chalk asked, sipping his coffee. He eyed Charlie like a reptile, eyes twitching and cold.

"Yeah. I'm gonna work on this one from home."

"Gonna get your foxy sister to do some research?"

Charlie took a deep breath in lieu of answering. Hearing Chalk talk about his sister Miranda might push him over the edge.

Chalk stood. "I'll walk with you to the elevators."

"Great," Charlie said, even though he felt the opposite. "You can carry my mail to Betty." He nodded at the small stack of outgoing mail on the corner of his desk.

"Seriously, dude?"

Charlie chuckled, a sound he knew would get under Chalk's skin. "Make yourself useful. See what it feels like."

"I brought you coffee." Chalk all but whined.

Charlie eyed the coffee with distaste. "I changed my mind. Give it to someone else." Then he strode from his office, not waiting for Chalk.

Chalk snatched up the mail. Strolling beside Charlie, Chalk said, "Do you think the kid will take a plea?"

If Charlie had had doubts about Chalk's intentions before, they were gone now. Chalk was coming at Charlie like a cruise missile, and the Dunworth case was his warhead.

"Since I haven't met with my client yet, and I'm not a mind-reader, it's difficult to say." Charlie put all of his disdain in his voice, and Georges invented disdain. "You do realize that actual legal work must occur at some point in this case, right?"

"You don't have to be such a dick," Chalk muttered.

"But how will you ever learn?" Charlie replied. "I have to speak your language to get through to you since you didn't bother learning the rules of evidence."

Chalk groused, "I took evidence in law school."

"Outstanding," Charlie said jovially. "Then you should know that you don't even think about pleas before seeing discovery."

Charlie turned at the printers and headed toward the lobby. Chalk trotted to keep up.

"Fine, your highness. Have it your way. Can you *speculate* whether he would take a plea?"

Charlie heaved a sigh. "The only plea I would advise him to take is one with no jail time."

Chalk laughed. "You think you could get him off a double homicide? You're a cocky bastard."

Charlie didn't bother to reply. He wasn't cocky. Well, he was, but not about this case. "Based on the facts as they appear in the case file? Any first-year law student would say the same. That's not cocky, it's close reading and issue spotting. Do you need a skills review? I'm sure one of our law school interns would be glad to help you."

"You're hilarious," Chalk said. He pressed on, undeterred by Charlie's insults. "Good of you to take the case, though, given your family history."

At the words *family history*, Charlie's spine stiffened again.

Chalk continued. "Let me know how it goes with the client interview. I mean, what kind of person does it take to put a cap in his own mom, right? What kind of cold-blooded bastard could pull that off?" Chalk shook his head.

The fear and anger Charlie had felt earlier returned with renewed power. Charlie squeezed the handles of his bag so tightly the leather squeaked. He thought about how much time he'd spent scrubbing his wristwatch clean of blood.

"Even if it was in some kind of self-defense or defense of another theory, I just don't know." Chalk was watching Charlie closely now. "I don't want this kid walking the streets."

Charlie kept walking, focusing on the elevators.

"He sounds like a nut job, right?" Chalk's voice grated on him. "Executing your own mom, point blank? When she's just sitting there? Unarmed?" He laughed. "I'd like to see inside that guy's head."

Charlie came to a stop in front of the elevator bank. He eyed

Chalk. Chalk eyed him back. That's when Charlie realized—Chalk must know his secret.

Charlie dropped his bag, pulled back, and punched Chalk clean in the jaw. Chalk fell back. Back and back and back, until he hit the marble floor, unconscious.

Chapter Two

When Charlie arrived home at the condo he shared with his sister Miranda, it was lunchtime. He'd left Chalk on the floor of the firm's foyer and stepped into the elevator as though nothing had been amiss.

He'd turned off his cell phone before getting in his car, and left it off. He didn't want to know what the consequences of his actions would be. Not yet.

He called out to Miranda as he shut the door behind him. He needed to explain what happened at work. Hell. He just needed to talk to her. His older sister was the only one who would understand the rage and fear he felt. His racing heart.

The blood on his watch.

"Miranda?" he called again when she didn't answer right away.

"Back here!"

Striding through their expansive apartment, his leather shoes tapping across the wide-plank wood floors, he passed the immense dining table and into the sitting area. He set his brief bag on the low, tufted leather couch. The walls of the entire condo were painted a soft gray, which Miranda found *soothing*, she said. The living room furniture, the long couch and matching chairs, were brown leather with chrome legs, in the throw-back, mid-century style so common in L.A.—and so different from their parents' colonial style back home in North Carolina.

Miranda liked things clean, with neat lines and straight edges. Charlie liked finer things, like the Italian suit he wore and the Givenchy briefcase he carried. Fine things reminded him who he was and where he came from, even though he'd lost so much when his mom had died. Miranda wanted to erase everything having to do with their old life, but he clung to those memories, to his legacy, like a lifeline.

But sometimes their tastes overlapped, like when they'd decorated the condo. He ran his hand across the back of the couch, upholstered in the smoothest leather. Simple enough to suit Miranda, and fine enough to suit him.

He entered the bedroom Miranda used as a home office. He remembered years back when they'd first moved in, when she'd sat in there for three weeks straight to study for the Law School Admission Test—as though she'd needed to study for it. Mostly she'd wanted to beat his score, a 175, and she had, rolling in at a near-perfect 178.

Now, she used the office when she was doing her homework for law school, or when she was working from home for him. A third-year law student at UCLA, about to graduate early in December, she also earned course credit as an intern at his firm. The firm was willing to hire her for more hours if she wanted them, and sometimes she agreed. The third year of law school was hardly rigorous, not compared to 1L year, and she wanted the work experience.

Miranda certainly didn't need to work for the money. Just like Charlie, she had plenty of money coming in from their father, Charles Senior. But just like Charlie, she didn't trust the source of the money one bit. At any moment, Charles Senior might cut them off because of some imaginary demand that they failed to meet.

At least they owned their home outright.

Between them they owned two cars, this apartment, one and a half law degrees, and some savings—because Miranda insisted they be prepared for the day that Charles Senior left them high and dry.

Correction: Miranda owned the condo because she'd tricked their father into buying it for her. Charlie was just her roommate. But Charlie never worried about having a home. Ever since they were small, he and Miranda had been an unbreakable team.

———

THE LAST TIME CHARLIE SAW HIS FATHER, ABOUT THREE YEARS AGO, Charles Senior had come out to L.A. from North Carolina to "sort things out" with Miranda. She'd just moved into the W Hotel with Charlie, after having a near-breakdown and running away to L.A. soon after the death of their mother, Sorcha.

It was early summer, and they swam in the hotel pool, ate room service, and worked. Charlie had just graduated from law school and was studying for the California bar. Miranda had already decided to take the LSAT that fall, but in the meantime she was working with her boyfriend, John, writing web copy for his clients—John owned a web design company with clients all over L.A.

After what Charles Senior called Miranda's "escapade," he decided to come out uninvited and exert some control. Miranda had never taken it well when Charles Senior tried to boss her around. The only reason she'd ever tolerated him at all was because of their mother Sorcha. With Sorcha gone, she had no use for their father.

Charles Senior arrived at the W Hotel on a Friday evening and took a penthouse suite. He'd only given them twenty-four hours' notice of his arrival. Saturday morning, he called and demanded their presence at breakfast in the hotel restaurant. Charlie had received the call on his cell while he and Miranda were having their morning coffee in their suite.

"His Majesty requests our presence at breakfast."

Miranda was furious to hear that their father had dared invade her new domain. "I'm going to stay with John. Don't tell him where I am."

"That's the wrong move," Charlie advised her. "Don't hide from him." Like all predators, Charles Senior would give chase.

"I'm not hiding. I'm avoiding."

Charlie raised his eyebrows. *Bullshit.*

"I don't have anything to say to him," she said, her voice revealing the fear underneath her anger. "He comes to my city with no notice, and without invitation. You know he's going to try to take me home, as if he could throw me over his shoulder and shove me into the back of his town car."

Miranda was probably right about their father's goal. He would indeed try to force Miranda to go home.

But Charlie knew that their father was, on some level, afraid. He'd lost his wife that year, and he'd nearly lost his daughter too. Miranda's "escapade," as he called it, was the kind of downward spiral that typically ended with a funeral. Charlie, once he'd figured out what was happening with his sister, had followed her to L.A. and intervened in a way that Charles Senior could never have done: because Charles Senior had little compassion, and not nearly enough heart.

But now Charles Senior was here, once again inserting himself into their lives, trying to "protect" them from bad decisions—that was, any decisions Charles Senior didn't approve of.

But Charlie could see what motivated his father. Spotting motivations was one of his special powers. Charlie knew that on one bloody afternoon six months before, Charles Senior's entire life had fallen apart: his wife had died, and he'd almost lost his children. Now, his children had moved across the country, wanting nothing to do with him. One day, Charles Senior's life had been in perfect order. The next, it had burned to ashes.

Charlie blamed his father for a lot, and he knew his father deserved that blame. But unlike Miranda, Charlie empathized with him, too. The man had nothing left except a law firm with his wife's name on it. Charlie understood their father's real motive: to protect his legacy, no matter what the cost.

He touched Miranda's hand. "He won't make you go back if he believes that you're all right."

She slammed her fist on the table, revealing how much their father's arrival had upset her. "I am all right." She paused, then whispered, "Things were dark there for a minute, but I'm all right now."

"I know you're all right," he said. "You're amazing. We just have to convince *him*."

She looked to the side, unable to meet his eyes. "You know as well as I do how hard it is to prove a negative."

Charlie took charge, bringing strength because he knew his big sister felt fragile. "You don't have to prove that you're sane, Big Sis.

You only have to show him that you're upholding the family name."

Miranda peered at him through narrow eyes. "You have a plan."

He nodded. "Get your laptop. I think we can get a lot more out of this breakfast meeting than a détente."

"We're going to squeeze him."

He nodded. "A lot."

Miranda smiled. "Should we wager on a dollar amount?"

"No thank you." Only a fool bet against Miranda, and Charlie wasn't a fool. He was, however, relieved to see that she'd regained her spirit.

Before heading down for breakfast, Charlie helped her log onto the website for the Law School Admission Council. She paid her fees, started her law school applications, and registered for the LSAT, the admission test for law school. Miranda printed out the proof of her registration, folded up the paper, and stuffed it in the back pocket of her jeans.

Half an hour later, they joined Charles Senior in the dining room of the hotel. From his father's pinched facial expression, Charlie could tell the place wasn't up to Charles Senior's standards. His father wore a dark suit and navy striped tie, impeccably dressed as always. His dark hair was recently trimmed and neatly combed, and his eyes raked over Charlie and Miranda, taking in their jeans, flip-flops, and t-shirts. He frowned.

Appearances matter, no matter what. His father had drilled that rule into Charlie for as long as Charlie could remember.

"What's the matter, Charles?" Miranda said, launching into attack mode, per usual. *Strike first.* Another rule they'd learned from their father.

Miranda flopped down into a seat next to their father at the four-top table.

"Why aren't you staying at the Beverly Wilshire?" Charles Senior asked, clearly miffed by everything around him, including the flatware.

"We can't afford the Beverly Wilshire," Miranda snapped at him. "It's ten times as expensive as this place."

Charles Senior visibly clenched his jaw. "You absolutely can afford the Beverly Wilshire."

Miranda smiled. "No, Charles. *You* can afford the Beverly Wilshire. In fact, I have a great idea." She snapped her fingers. "Why don't you go there right now?"

Shaking his head in exasperation, Charles Senior turned his attention to Charlie. "How is the bar studying going?"

Charlie took a deliberately appeasing tone. "I'm taking BarBri at a local law school." BarBri was a bar prep course that most law students took to prepare for the bar exam. "I've encountered nothing unexpected." Charlie spoke in his father's language, using cold words that created distance between people, distance that Charles Senior interpreted as respect.

As he'd planned with Miranda prior to coming down, Charlie's job at this meeting was to appear to be a civilizing influence on Miranda.

Charles Senior nodded, satisfied with Charlie's answer. He turned back to Miranda, the tension returning to his face. "You still have no future plans?"

Miranda shrugged. "Who needs plans? I'm enjoying a life of leisure. I make enough money to get by."

Charles Senior's jaw clenched again. "Georges don't *get by.*"

"This one does." Miranda sipped coffee from her mug, her relaxed appearance making their father even more upset.

But Charlie knew that the more upset their father became, the more willing he would be to capitulate. Charlie had planned every step of this Good-Child, Annoying-Child negotiation.

Charles Senior spread his fingers on the white tablecloth, tension evident in every tendon. "You're coming home with me today, Miranda."

"Did you bring henchmen?" Miranda glanced around, then cracked up at her own joke.

He leaned in toward her, his voice laced with threat. "I'll cut off your stipend."

Charlie had to restrain himself from rolling his eyes. He'd expected this. Charles Senior always tried to control Miranda with money, and it never, ever worked.

Miranda shook her head at Charles Senior's words. "Remember when you had to steal my bank account number in order to sneak money *into* my account because I refused to take it from you?"

It was true—just a few weeks ago Charles Senior tried to bribe her. It didn't work.

Charles Senior's jaw visibly clenched.

Miranda laughed. "You think I care if you stop sending it?"

For a moment, Charlie allowed himself to feel a twinge of panic. Because Charlie would care, a lot, if his father cut off his own stipend. Fortunately the threat hadn't been leveled at him.

Miranda continued. "I have five different people willing to take me in and give me a home. I have a job. I don't need your money." Looking bored, Miranda flagged down a server and ordered a mimosa.

Charlie was entranced by his sister's act. If he hadn't known what she had in her back pocket, and if he hadn't helped her stage this play, he would never have believed what was coming next.

Charles Senior rubbed his hand over his face in frustration. There was no lever big enough for him to make Miranda do what he wanted, not since Sorcha died. The poor guy—Charlie almost felt sorry for him.

"You can't just do nothing with your life." He nearly growled.

Charlie smiled. Miranda was really getting under their father's skin.

Miranda glanced back at their father. "Look, why don't you just tell me what you want instead of gnashing your teeth? You can't take me back to North Carolina and lock me in the attic. You must have a plan."

"You're a George. You should be in law school."

Miranda nodded thoughtfully, as though she actually found their father's argument convincing, as though being a George were a reason a person should do something, and that Miranda agreed with that reason. "There are worse fates than law school." Miranda tapped her finger on the table. "I'm prepared to entertain offers."

Charles Senior's eyebrows slowly raised. "You're serious."

"If your offers are serious. Do you have paper? A pen?"

"What for?"

She gave him a withering look. "A contract, of course."

Charles Senior returned her look. "I didn't bring my brief bag to breakfast, no."

"I did," Charlie said. "I thought I'd work by the pool after we ate." A fabrication, one that allowed him to come to breakfast prepared.

Reaching into his bag, Charlie pulled out a legal pad and a Montblanc pen his mother had engraved with his name when he'd finished high school. He pushed them over to his sister.

"Thank you, Charlie." She slowly unscrewed the cap of the pen, then just as slowly screwed it onto the pen's base.

Charles Senior watched her deliberate movements. "You're prepared to apply to law school?"

She eyed him. "Slow down, sir. We're just talking."

Charles Senior frowned, testy. He wanted to get his way. "You'll get your monthly stipend. A car." He paused, considering what else he might dangle in front of Miranda to bend her to his will. "And a three-year apartment lease, pre-paid in full."

Miranda tapped her bottom lip, considering his offer. "You want me to give up three years of freedom to study for a career I don't want. Have *never* wanted—and you know that."

Charles Senior nodded thoughtfully. Miranda had complained about lawyers their entire lives; there was no doubt that Charles Senior knew he was asking Miranda to do something she hated.

Or so he thought.

Charlie had coached her through this negotiation twice before they'd come downstairs.

Miranda leaned back in her seat. "Counteroffer. Stipend arrives quarterly, not monthly—in advance. The car is of my choosing. And you purchase me a condo of my choosing, titled in my name, no strings attached."

Charles Senior's face revealed nothing while he considered her demands. "Counteroffer. Agree to quarterly stipend. Agree to car, with the stipulation of net price capped at one hundred thousand dollars. Agree to condo purchase, with the stipulation of net price capped at three million."

Miranda frowned. "Charlie's car cost more than a hundred thousand. That's not fair."

Charlie suppressed a smile. Miranda had gone off-script about the car. But cars had always been her weakness.

She said, "Counteroffer: All terms acceptable, except net price of car capped at two hundred thousand."

Charles Senior nodded. "All terms acceptable, except, if you fail to graduate from law school or if your GPA drops below 3.0, stipend will be withdrawn and title of condo reverts to me."

Miranda rolled her eyes. "Oh jeez, Charles. Do you think I'm going to break my word or lose brain cells?"

"Do we have an agreement?"

Miranda picked up the pen and swiftly wrote down the terms. Looking up at Charles Senior, she held out the pen to him.

Charles Senior didn't take the pen.

Charlie held his breath.

Charles Senior nodded at the contract Miranda had drawn up. "I'll need proof of good intention before I purchase the car or the apartment."

At these words, Charlie smiled.

Miranda nodded in agreement. "Once you have proof of good intention, you'll put the money into my account?"

Charles Senior scoffed. "I'm not putting anything into your account. I'll put the money into my local attorney's escrow. And I would do it today if I were certain you were serious."

"Today?" She snorted, as though she didn't believe him.

"Today." Charles Senior said, believing his words were a dare.

Miranda added that statement as a clause to the contract, then held out the pen again.

Charles Senior took the pen and signed. Miranda signed beneath him. Charlie signed as witness.

Miranda snapped a photo of the signed contract with her phone.

"Pleasure doing business with you, Charles," she said. Standing, she pulled the folded piece of paper from her back pocket. She smoothed it flat on the table, then handed it to their father.

The paper showed all of the work she'd done upstairs: that she was registered to take the LSAT in October. That she'd already begun her law school applications. That she'd paid the fee to the admissions organization. It was all there, on that piece of paper. "There's your proof of good intention." She sat down again. "What's your attorney's phone number?"

When Charlie saw the emotions flash across his father's face—surprise, then anger, then satisfaction, the anger again, he remembered yet another rule his father had taught them. *In negotiations, there are no winners.*

By the end of the day, Miranda and Charlie had hired a real estate agent, and Charles Senior was on his jet back to North Carolina.

Chapter Three

S tanding in Miranda's home office, his hand starting to throb from the punch he'd thrown at Chalk, Charlie smiled at the memory of that morning three years ago. He and Miranda had always made a great team. Her dramatic flair, his cooler head— together, they could do anything.

Miranda had decided to go to law school before that breakfast confrontation, but Charles Senior hadn't known that, and so he'd been willing to put down the cash in exchange for making his daughter obey him.

But Miranda had needed Charlie to help her see all of the angles. To help her see that Charles Senior didn't really care about the money.

No, the fight had never been about money. Charlie had clearly seen what each player's endgame was, and he'd set up the pieces on the board so that his sister would win. Their father's desperate need for control versus Miranda's desperate need for freedom. Charlie had ensured his sister would win by handing his father the thing he valued second-most in the world: the family's good name. Charles Senior had been miffed, sure, but in the end he'd been satisfied. Miranda would go to law school, and she would graduate. And so Charles Senior had left, and they hadn't heard from him since. The deposits landed in their accounts at the beginning of every quarter like clockwork.

In return for winning her freedom, Miranda had given Charlie a place to stay, gratis, for as long as he wanted it. And Charlie did want to stay with her, but not because he needed to save the money. Hardly. No, Charlie had his own reasons for wanting to live with his big sister. At first, those reasons had had a lot to do with the dried blood he'd kept seeing on his watch. He'd had nightmares about the day his mother had died, and he hadn't wanted to be alone. The nightmares faded as the months went by, and now, after the years had passed, neither of them could imagine living separately.

Memories rushed back, of Chalk lying on his back in the foyer of his law firm.

He shut his eyes and breathed deeply. He needed to talk to Miranda.

Now, Charlie was the one in need of help.

He'd expected to find Miranda reading a casebook for one of her classes, or a client file for work at his firm. She only worked the cases that Charlie pulled specifically to interest her strangely bleeding heart.

He did not suffer from that particular affliction. Indeed, he found Miranda's desire to help the indigent and disadvantaged abjectly weird.

Thinking about the file he'd brought home, he managed a smile. Miranda was actually going to love the Dunworth case.

But, Miranda wasn't at her desk. He glanced through the open sliding door to the balcony, and saw Miranda sitting on one of the low-slung chairs, with a friend to her right. He could smell the pot from where he stood.

He smiled, shaking his head. His sister was comforting in her predictability. And she very predictably loved marijuana.

She looked over her shoulder at him. "Hello, Little B," she said, using her childhood nickname for him. After a moment, her eyes narrowed in suspicion. "Why are you here? It's barely lunchtime." The marijuana might have eased her a bit, but it did not dull her sharp mind.

Draping his suit jacket on her desk and rolling up his sleeves, he stepped out onto the balcony. The condo was on the twentieth floor of a plate-glass high-rise in Marina del Rey. Miranda had picked the building because of the pool and tennis courts—tennis was a bloodsport for the George siblings—and because it was as far away from the supposed hipness of Hollywood as they could get without being in Orange County or the Valley.

Neither George sibling could stand Hollywood. They lived in Los Angeles for two reasons alone. It was a continent away from their father and anyone else who might know them from their old life. And, they'd made some good friends here, real friends, people they actually cared about.

It was a strange feeling for Charlie, really caring about people. His whole life, he only ever cared about Sorcha and Miranda. Even his buddies from school weren't real friends. They never really knew him. They certainly never came over to his house. But now his darkest family secrets were out in the open. Without terrible secrets to hide, he found he had friendships that mattered. It was an unsettling, but not unpleasant, feeling.

He sat in the third balcony chair and reached out for the joint.

Miranda narrowed her eyes as she held it out to him. "Your hands are shaking."

He looked down. It was true. He squeezed his hands into fists, hoping to stop the tremors. His right fist ached.

"Are you sick?" a voice asked from his sister's right.

Charlie was not only startled by the question, but also by the person asking it. He'd already forgotten that someone else was out on the balcony, and he hadn't noticed who it was. It was so unlike him to fail to notice his surroundings. Situational awareness was another George family survival skill. The confrontation with Chalk must have shaken him up more than he realized.

Sitting on the other side of his sister was Tory Murphy, an emergency medicine doctor and his sister's best friend. The four of them—Miranda, Tory, and Miranda's college friends Greta and Daphne —made up the heart of Miranda's circle of friends in L.A. That his sister had a circle of friends at all should have made Charlie happy. Miranda had been a loner growing up. He'd been the one surrounded by people —people who didn't know him well—but people nonetheless. To see her smiling, just smiling, should have made him happy.

And it did.

But his hands were shaking. And inside, he felt like his ribcage was getting crushed. He felt like he couldn't breathe, like his heart was going to stop beating at any moment. Either that or his heart was going to explode through his chest. He had no words to explain what was happening to him. No logic. He couldn't stop thinking about blood. And his watch. And the Dunworth case.

And his mother, Sorcha.

He'd tamped down his feelings about Sorcha for so long, he'd forgotten how much they hurt. And the images that flashed through his mind—they were gruesome. Heartbreaking.

Paralyzing.

He didn't want his sister to worry, and he didn't want to embarrass himself in front of Tory, so he hid what he was feeling, and he was very good at hiding what he was feeling.

Turning to Tory, he said, "Not sick. Just tired."

Then he reached out to Miranda. "Pass me the joint, snotface."

"Harsh, little brother." She smiled, handing him the joint.

He took it and inhaled like his life depended on it. He leaned back in his chair, looking through the glass panel below the aluminum tube railing, out over the marina below, where the yachts were tiny white dots, the condos along the marina were Lego bricks of gray and brown. Past them, the Pacific met the clear sky, the smog of L.A. blown away by the ocean breeze.

Miranda's voice cut into his thoughts. "Spill. Why are you home from work?"

Exhaling, he could already feel the pleasant prickles of the drug moving down the back of his neck, down his shoulders, down his arms. His heartbeat slowed. "I'm on leave."

"The hell you are. You must be sick." She put her hand on his forehead. "You don't have a fever." She looked over at Tory. "Does he have a fever?"

Leaning over Miranda to touch him, Tory placed her cool palm against his cheek, touching his face here and there, meeting his eyes with her own. For a moment, he fell into her big, brown eyes, crinkled at the corners with her smile. He was entranced by the freckles sprinkled across her nose, by her pink lips.

Suddenly, he felt raging hot, all the way down his spine, and it wasn't because of the weed.

Tory's effect on him wasn't unusual. He just tried to ignore it. Sleeping with Tory was not an option, as much as he wanted it to be.

She said, "He doesn't have a fever."

He shut his eyes and exhaled slowly, chuckling as he did so. "Maybe not. But if you keep your hand there a minute longer, I'll need your medical attention." Then he opened his eyes and smiled at her, the smile he reserved for friends. Because that's what Tory was. A friend. No matter how much they flirted, no matter how gorgeous she was, she'd only ever be his friend. He could ignore how he felt about her forever if he had to. He didn't have a choice.

Tory quirked her mouth to one side, then returned to her seat. He grinned at her. She grinned back.

Miranda gave him an assessing look, one that told him she knew precisely how much of their exchange had been harmless flirting on his part and how much had been sincere—more than he wanted Tory to know, that was for certain.

Charlie first met Tory at the home of Alexander Martin, *the* Alexander Martin, he of the multiple Academy Awards and prestigious film career and the even more respectable real estate portfolio. Somehow, Greta Donovan and Daphne Saito, two ordinary North Carolina girls his sister knew from college, had befriended Alexander—*Sandy*, they all called him—and then Miranda had as well.

In fact, Miranda had befriended Sandy a little *too* well for Charlie's comfort. One night, mad as a bull that the man had taken up with his sister—Charlie had wrongly believed that Sandy was taking advantage of Miranda, as though such a thing were possible—Charlie crashed a party at Sandy's house and made a scene too melodramatic to win any Oscars. Charlie blew in like a hurricane and taunted his sister into a fight in front of all of her new friends. Miranda, although mortified, didn't back down. They stood toe to toe in Alexander Martin's living room, hurling insults like grenades.

And right in the middle of it all was Tory, not the least bit concerned by Charlie's ridiculous tirade. Of all the people who were present that night, Greta, Daphne, Daphne's boyfriend, even Miranda herself, who ended up just as angry as Charlie, Tory remained the most unfazed. Sipping her drink, she looked at Charlie not like the intruder he was, but like he were a delicious item on a buffet laid out just for her.

When he laid eyes on her, he found her both disconcerting and wildly attractive. Her level of cool, even more than her athlete's body, had caught his attention and kept it over the years.

Tory was a good person. She was a doctor. She'd stitched up Daphne when Daphne had gotten hurt. Then she turned around and stitched up drug dealers and gangsters—she didn't judge any of the patients who landed in her emergency room.

But he and Tory were nothing alike.

He might defend bad guys, but he didn't do it because of some belief that all people rich and poor deserved a fair shake or some horseshit like that. No, that was his sister's gig, and Tory's. He did it because there were rules, gorgeous rules set forth by the law.

And to win within the parameters of those rules?

The rush. There was nothing like it.

To win the way Chalk did, and the other dirtbags like him? By hiding discovery from the opposition, "losing" important evidence, encouraging your clients to lie or take terrible plea bargains? That wasn't winning. That was cheating. Charlie knew he belonged at the top; he won to prove it to himself and to everyone else.

Unbidden, the memory crashed into his mind—how his knuckles spread as they made contact against Chalk's jaw, how Chalk's jaw gave, how Chalk's teeth slammed against each other, how Chalk's eyes shut, how the tension left Chalk's muscles as Chalk fell back, unconscious.

Charlie was struck by a sudden fear. What if he had ruined everything he'd worked for? What if he lost his job—what would he do then? Who would he *be* then?

No one. He would be no one. Everything his mom had worked for and had wanted for him would be gone. Everything that made him Charlie George, snuffed out.

He felt himself spiraling. His heart racing again, his lungs squeezing.

He looked around, desperate for a distraction. The boats below, the tiny people on the walkways. Then he eyed Tory and realized he wasn't the only one home at an odd hour. "Shouldn't you be at work?" he asked her, forcing his voice not to shake. "What's Miss Doctor Perfect doing getting high on a weekday afternoon?"

God, and she was perfect—thick brown hair that she usually wore in a ponytail. Brown eyes nearly as dark as her hair. Pale skin with freckles across her nose like a little girl's. When she wore a sleeveless shirt—or a cutout tank like she wore right now—her fit shoulders and arms made his mouth water.

After he first met Tory, Miranda told him that Tory was a runner—and then Miranda had made gagging sounds. Miranda thought running—as in, on purpose, not while being chased by a bear—was completely unhinged.

Tory ran a lot. One year ago, she'd run the L.A. Marathon—she'd said she wanted to do it before she turned thirty. All that training, even while working long shifts in an ER? That level of dedication? Charlie couldn't help but admire her. Charlie also admired her lean body, her long legs—kicked out in front of her right now in cut-off jeans.

Then there was her big smile that she never held back, the one she was giving him now. Charlie had been with lots of girls. Too many. But he'd never been in love. And he had never felt anything like what he felt when Tory Murphy smiled at him.

"I'm a free woman." Smiling that ruthless smile, she reached for the joint. Their fingers brushed when he handed it to her. As he felt the rush after their touch, he wondered if she felt it too.

Her eyes met his, and then she took a righteous drag.

Yeah, she'd felt it too.

After all these years, Tory still looked at him like he was something she would drink through a straw, sucking him right up.

Lots of girls thought Charlie was hot. But Tory was different because Tory knew he was an arrogant pain in the ass and, for some strange reason, she wanted him anyway. That placed her in dangerous territory. Because there was one fantasy that Charlie never allowed himself: that someone would see beneath his façade and still want him.

If Tory could see what was really beneath his veneer, even she would turn away. If she knew why he still got nightmares sometimes, she'd hate him.

"Tory quit her job yesterday," Miranda said.

"You quit your job at the hospital?" Charlie was surprised. "I thought you loved it there."

Exhaling, Tory handed the joint to Miranda. "I used to love it there. Then I didn't. So I quit."

"You just quit?" he asked, flabbergasted.

"You might enjoy hundred-hour work weeks," she said, "but I have someone at home who misses me now, so I have to think about more than just myself."

Miranda coughed on her inhale, laughing.

Charlie felt a flare of jealousy. In all the years he'd known Tory, she'd been as single as he was. Now she'd moved in with someone? And he hadn't known? He shouldn't be jealous—he had no hold over Tory. Only in his imagination that he allowed to run wild now and then.

Like, every day.

He glared at Miranda. She should have warned him. Miranda knew what he felt, even if they'd never spoken about it in direct terms.

"How is Daisy?" Miranda finally said. "Has she filled out since you adopted her? I need to come see her again and we can take her for a walk."

He felt a rush of relief so profound he almost fell off his chair. Tory had adopted a dog.

He glared at Miranda again. She blinked her lashes, all innocence.

Glancing down at his right hand, Charlie flexed his fingers. His knuckles had started to swell, turning red and purplish.

"Whoa." Grabbing his hand, Miranda pulled it toward her. "What happened? Did you close it in a car door?"

Tory leaned forward to examine it as well. She raised her eyebrows. "How does the other guy look?"

Of course Tory would know what had caused his hand injury. There was no lying his way out of this situation. Charlie turned to stare at the ocean again, the pristine blue surface smooth and unruffled. The opposite of what he felt.

"Charlie." Miranda put her hand on his knee. "You got in a fight?"

"Not exactly."

"Yes, exactly," Tory said. "Unless you punched a wall." Turning to Miranda, she said with fake concern, "Does he typically punch walls?"

Before Miranda could make some snide reply, he said, "I punched Chalk Bogart. I left him unconscious by the elevators. That's why I'm home early from work."

Miranda's eyebrows raised, her mouth falling open.

"Interesting," Charlie said. "If I'd known punching Chalk Bogart would get you to shut up, I would have done it months ago."

Tory suppressed a laugh.

"Okay, butthead." Miranda stood. "Enough jokes." She grabbed his hands and pulled him to his feet. At six-four, he was much taller than she was, even though she was five-ten. She turned him around and pushed him from the balcony and into her office. "Go," she ordered. "Living room. Sit."

"How are you so bossy even when you're stoned? Isn't there some sort of rule about that?"

She narrowed her eyes at him, pointing in the direction of the living room.

As he headed toward the living room, he heard her murmur to Tory something about seeing her the next day at dinner. Right— Miranda's graduation party.

Dropping onto the couch, he rested his head back and stared at the ceiling.

Tory stopped by him on her way out, resting her hand on his shoulder. "Whatever happened, I'm sure he deserved it." She gave him a half-smile that made her dark eyes sparkle.

Her hair, loose around her shoulders instead of in its customary ponytail, looked so soft he wanted to bury his hand in it and pull her down into his lap. But he didn't. He couldn't destroy his friendship with Tory. If things were different—if *he* were different—he would ask her out to dinner, find out something she'd always wanted to do— knowing her, it would be something like skydiving—and they would do it together. He would meet her family. He would be part of her life, a real part, not just her best friend's brother.

He looked at his swollen knuckles again. "He did deserve it. Massive douchewicket. Economy-sized."

He glanced up. Tory was still looking at him like he would taste delicious. And perhaps she was right. Perhaps the two of them would have a blast—for a night, or a week, or a month. And then they would fall apart. She would deserve more, and he wouldn't be able to give it to her.

She gave him that half-smile again, and then she left, closing the door softly behind her.

Meanwhile, his sister was banging around in the kitchen, slamming doors and setting glasses on the granite countertop with a little too much force.

"I know you hate to cook," he said, "but you don't have to take out your anger on the cabinets. They're custom-built."

"That means they're well made and can tolerate a little abuse." She yanked two liquor bottles from a lower cabinet and slammed it closed with her knee.

"They're sensitive. You might hurt their feelings."

Some people might mistake Miranda's actions for anger. He knew better. Miranda was worried.

She hefted a rocks glass like she wanted to toss it at his head. "Will you shut up about the cabinets?"

A few minutes later, she emerged from the kitchen with two drinks. A scotch and soda for him, and a greyhound for her. Neither of them gave a shit that it was barely noon.

Sitting next to him on the couch, she tucked her bare feet underneath her cutoff sweatpants. "Cut the crap. Tell me what happened."

He pulled the case file from his bag and handed it to her. She scanned the documents quickly, her brows drawn together. His sister was two kinds of brilliant: plain old brilliant and legally brilliant. He was going to need both kinds to help him get out of the mess he was in.

She started firing off questions. "Chalk brought you this case?"

"Yes. He said Birch told him to."

"Was Chalk lying about that?"

Charlie thought back. "Perhaps. He only implied that Birch assigned me the case." He took a sip of his drink.

"There's an angle there."

Charlie nodded. "Agree."

She kept skimming. "Did he say why he brought you the case?"

"He said I would love it."

Miranda snorted. "Ass. Anything else?"

Charlie rubbed his hand on his face. "Honestly, Mir, after I looked at the file, I started to feel…panicky."

"So you distracted him."

Charlie nodded. "Chalk brought it to me just to get a rise."

"It obviously worked." She flipped through the file, skimming every page until she reached the last one. She paused, reading the details of the little sister's abuse.

"Chalk knows about Mom." Charlie hated how the panic sounded in his voice.

Miranda scoffed. "Chalk knows nothing except that our mom is dead." She set the file on the coffee table, then took a sip of her drink.

She chewed a piece of ice, the pop-popping sound echoing in his ear as loud as a gunshot.

"Chalk knows." Charlie squeezed his hand into a fist, even though doing so hurt his sore knuckles.

Miranda raised her brows. Her brown eyes, identical to his own, were full of skepticism. "Fine. I'll play. How could Chalk Bogart, the most inept attorney at your firm, possibly know anything about our mother's death?"

"Speculation: He pulled the coroner's report from our mom's death and read it. He drew some possible conclusions. I then confirmed those conclusions with a punch to the face."

"Counterpoint: Does Chalk even know how to pull a coroner's report?"

He would have laughed if his gut weren't tearing him up. "Miranda, you're not helping."

"At least admit that none of this is about Chalk Bogart. It's about you, and mom, and your guilt."

He dropped his face into his hands and groaned. Miranda was right. Miranda was always right. "It's about me, and mom."

Miranda waited, tapping her finger on her glass.

"And my guilt."

She sighed. "Conclusion: Even if Chalk did con a paralegal into pulling a report from some faraway jurisdiction, and he was somehow able to read about our mother's death, all he was able to read is what Dad cleaned up after you moved here to take the bar exam. There's nothing for him to *find*, not anymore."

"He could find out the truth."

"That's what I'm saying. The truth can't hurt you anymore, Charlie."

Charlie shook his head at his sister's words. Although they were logical, he knew that the truth could still destroy him. Years ago when their mother had died, their father had covered up the truth of what had happened to preserve the George name. Everything for Charles Senior was about the George name. But even Charles Senior knew that the State Bar examiners might look a little closely, might find some reason to deny his son his bar license. So his father had gone back and pulled more strings, explained that he'd only tried to protect his children's mental health, and wiped away the old coverup of what Charlie had done.

Miranda was right—there were no more lies.

But the truth itself was still too much for him to overcome. His nightmares proved that much. He didn't tell his sister what he knew: that no matter what he did, he could never atone for the death of their mother. He didn't argue the point though. They'd only reach a stalemate. "There's still the matter of the punching. Birch is going to fire me for it."

"If Birch has any sense, he's going to fire Chalk, not you. You're a much better lawyer." She closed the folder. "However, we can't rely on people to have sense. Therefore, you are going to get Chalk in trouble and save your job. He's an idiot and doesn't deserve to work there anyway." She tucked her hair behind her ear, dark blond hair the same color as his. Even though she was two years older, people often mistook them for twins. "What do you have on him?"

Charlie smiled at her words. They were so, so alike. Of course he had a file on his nemesis. "I have enough."

"Good. Get Chalk fired, and then go save the Dunworth kid."

At Miranda's words, something fired up inside of him. Saving the Dunworth kid, someone so like himself, energized him more than any case had in months, years even. Electrified with his renewed sense of purpose, Charlie turned to face his sister. "Miranda George, do you agree to officially assist me on a case?" His tone of voice, suddenly serious, let her know he needed her to say yes.

"As a paralegal at your firm, I agree."

"Do the intake with me? I need to know if the kid is telling the truth about his parents."

She nodded. "Get your job back, then tell me when."

————

AFTER THEY FINISHED SMOKING THE JOINT, THEY WATCHED THE MOVIE *Aliens*—which they agreed was by far the best in the franchise—and ordered food in.

Miranda bitched a little bit about some reading for class she needed to finish and how she couldn't work on it because she had to take care of her mopey little brother, but Charlie knew she wasn't really concerned about school. She just wanted him to owe her a favor.

They went to bed in their adjacent bedrooms. Each had a plate glass window overlooking the marina and the Pacific beyond. Miranda had really scored with this corner unit. The entire living area and all three bedrooms had balconies.

But that day three years ago when they'd manipulated their father over breakfast, Miranda hadn't known what kind of home she wanted. All she'd known was that she wanted a retreat from the chaos her life had thrown at her. She'd found it.

Charlie only wished that he could find the same. But his retreat wasn't from the world outside. No, he needed to escape what was inside of himself.

Charlie stood at his window, shirt off, hands in his pants pockets. After a while, he realized he was afraid to go to bed. The fear was an old one, familiar. Before, when the death of his mother had been new, he'd gotten nightmares so bad that he wouldn't go to bed unless he was drugged or blind drunk. When he and Miranda had moved in together at the hotel, and then later, after they'd moved into this condo—he'd realized having her around had soothed him. Knowing she was safe. Alive.

He'd told her about the nightmares, and she'd understood. She'd had her own demons to battle, after all. She'd never judged him or thought him weak.

Eventually, as the months—years—had passed, the nightmares had subsided. The fear and the guilt had faded enough for Charlie to go on with his life, and he believed he was all right. He carried a secret that he couldn't share with anyone but those closest to him, but most people had secrets. Someday, maybe, the weight of the secret wouldn't be so heavy.

Right now, though, as he stripped off his pants and climbed into bed, he had a feeling of doom lurking just over his shoulder, doom that he couldn't escape, like a curse. He knew this feeling. It had haunted him for months after his mother had died.

And now it was back.

Dear God.

He fell asleep.

He fell into the bright, many-windowed room in his parents' house, again.

Miranda, falling to the floor, eyes cracked open, unblinking, liquid leaking from the corner of her mouth, again.

His mother, staring at Miranda, fascinated, holding a gun on Charlie, again.

Charlie leaping forward, snatching the gun from his mother's hand, again.

Charlie firing. Again.

Chapter Four

Around eight o'clock Thursday morning, Charlie sat up, putting his feet on the hardwood floor. Even his teeth felt tired. He opened and closed his mouth a few times, stretching his tight jaw muscles.

After he'd woken from his nightmare, he'd only been able to nap the rest of the night, slipping in and out of light sleep, jerking awake, afraid the horror would return.

After pulling on an old pair of jeans, he sat on the edge of his bed. He reached for his phone where it was charging on the night stand. On top of it lay a note.

Little B-
I headed to the firm early to get more info on the Dunworths. Then I have to go to class. I'll be home around five, in time for the stupid dinner party. Get your job back so I don't have to quit working for you.
-M

Picking up his phone, he turned it on. He ignored the text messages and voicemails that pinged. None of them were important. Just gossip-hunters from the firm. There wasn't a call from the person who really mattered.

He took a deep breath and exhaled. It was time to call Romeo Birch to see if he still had a job.

Dialing Birch's direct office line, he prayed the man would pick up. He did.

"Hey Birch. It's Charlie George." Standing, Charlie started pacing around the apartment, unable to sit still while his future was on the line.

There was a long pause before Birch spoke. "You left a little early yesterday."

"Yes sir. Given the circumstances, I thought it best I work from home the rest of the day."

"You're probably right about that."

Romeo Birch was forty-two years old, a solid guy, someone Charlie admired and liked working for. He was smart, and a great lawyer. He worked just as hard or harder than the lawyers who worked for him. He never asked the attorneys to pull a long weekend if he wasn't willing to do the same. Plus, he was charismatic; when they went out for a client wine-and-dine, every lady in the place wanted to talk to him. But you couldn't be jealous of him, because he made every one of his friends feel like they were just as smooth as he was.

Not that Charlie ever felt jealous. He was the only other lawyer in the firm who could hold his own with Romeo Birch. That was why Birch always made Charlie come to the client wine-and-dines.

But Birch had one flaw: he tolerated Chalk Bogart, using Chalk's moral laxity to the firm's advantage. Charlie always knew that one day, things with Chalk would blow up in Charlie's face. Luckily, Charlie played a long game. He'd saved up evidence of Chalk's more egregious misdeeds over the past year, the ones that Birch wouldn't be able to ignore. Charlie figured he might need the evidence someday.

He needed it today. "I imagine you've heard about some goings on by the elevators yesterday."

"I wouldn't want to run into you in a boxing ring, I guess."

Charlie couldn't get a read on Birch's tone yet. So he went straight for what he wanted. "I'd prefer it if I weren't fired, sir."

"Then I guess you'd better tell me your side of things."

Relieved that Birch was going to give him a chance, Charlie spun his side of the story. "Chalk brought me the Dunworth case yesterday.

He said you assigned it to me." Charlie paused. "I'm not sure if you know he did that."

Birch paused. "I do now."

Charlie smiled. He now had one point in his favor. "Did you instruct him to bring me the case?"

Another pause. "No."

He and Miranda had been right—Chalk had lied about Birch assigning Charlie the case. Chalk's lie would make this call go much easier for Charlie.

Charlie continued. "Chalk has a pattern of behavior that I've been working hard to rein in. I should probably have come to you about it sooner. I'm sorry about that." An exaggeration, and a false apology—Charlie had done nothing to rein in Chalk. He'd let Chalk dig his own grave, and Charlie was tossing Chalk into it now.

Birch responded, "Go on."

"He's been agreeing to pleas against our clients' interests. And by the time I'm made aware of the deals, it's too late for me to fix them. I can't figure out why he'd make these deals." Pausing for effect, Charlie let Birch consider what Chalk's motives might be. Preparing for a lateral employment move? Sabotage? Laziness? "The Dunworth case was the last straw. He brought me the case, telling me you assigned it." Charlie emphasized Chalk's lie once again. "When I suggested a plea in our client's favor after a cursory review of the file, he told me that the plea would be way too difficult to negotiate. Then he suggested that I go for the easy win—a less favorable plea—one that would require little work on the firm's part." Charlie paused, letting his words sink in.

Charlie knew that although Romeo Birch was an equity partner in the firm, he still worked more than sixty hours a week. No afternoon tee times for him. And because he worked hard, he expected everyone around him to do the same. At any whiff of lax behavior, Birch blew his top.

"I see. Tell me about the plea."

"I'm not sure what you know about the case."

"I know a little."

"Given the circumstances, I think we can get a manslaughter plea with some legwork. Chalk insisted that was impossible. Told me a pro bono case wasn't worth the time." Charlie knew he was embellishing a bit. But only a little. "When Chalk refused to let the argument go, I lost my temper. If this incident had been the first of its nature," Charlie paused again, "perhaps our argument would have had a different outcome. But he's done it before. Many times."

"You can give me case names with the bad pleas?"

"Naturally. I wish I could have prevented them. The least I could do was keep track in case there was an opportunity for a habeas petition. Or…" he trailed off deliberately.

"What, George? Are you talking malpractice?" Birch sounded furious—a little bit at Charlie for even mentioning such a thing, and a whole lot more at Chalk.

"I hope not," Charlie said in a soothing tone.

"You still have the Dunworth case file on you?"

"I do."

"Work from home. Interview our client and the key witness. The sister, right?"

"Will do." Charlie felt a wave of relief. He was in the clear.

"Email me the list of cases with the bad pleas."

"You'll have it within the hour."

Birch heaved a sigh. "Don't punch people, George. Not even him."

"I apologize, sir. Won't happen again."

Hanging up the phone, Charlie stopped pacing and leaned against the kitchen counter, suddenly boneless. Everything he'd worked for, everything he *was*, would go up in smoke if he no longer had that glass-plated office, that wide desk, those leather chairs. He didn't need the money, but the fancy salary told him that he was valuable. That he was carrying on his mother's legacy. He owed her that much after everything he'd done.

He checked the time on his watch. It was just before nine a.m. He had plenty of time to get started on the Dunworth case.

He examined the watch more closely, the one he couldn't seem to look at without seeing his worst nightmares.

In his bedroom, he opened the top drawer of his dresser, pulling out his wooden watch case. Inside were his other two watches and the empty spot for the one he wore. He picked up his father's watch, his least favorite of the three, holding it up to the light. Looking at it, he felt nothing. No memories, fond or otherwise. He took off his mother's watch and slipped it inside the case, and put on his father's instead. Returning the watch case to its place inside the drawer, he slid the drawer shut. He rested his hands on top of the dresser and dropped his head to his chest.

Maybe now the nightmares would stop.

Charlie brought his work bag to the dining table, a long rectangle of walnut that would seat sixteen. Miranda had chosen it because she liked to spread out when she was working, and because there was room enough for her and Charlie to work together. Once again, he was grateful that his big sister had welcomed him into her home so readily. He knew he was lucky to have Miranda. When he'd moved to L.A. three years before, he'd been lost—just as lost as she'd been, honestly. He'd left behind his mother's firm, his only anchor in the world.

Now he knew just who he was. He was a litigator. And he liked it.

Charlie pulled out his laptop and the case file. Turning on his laptop, he opened a document where he'd stored the case names, file numbers, dates, and pleas that Chalk had overseen over the past year, the final nail in the coffin of Chalk's career at Birch's firm. He dropped the document into an email to Birch and sent it.

His legal career preserved, Charlie opened the Dunworth client file, spreading the meager paperwork across the table. He opened a new document on his laptop for note taking, and began the slow yet satisfying process of unfolding a new case.

———

AROUND TWO IN THE AFTERNOON, CHARLIE HEADED OUT ON FOOT TO A bar in Venice Beach called The Typhoon's Widow, his favorite place to unwind.

After law school, Charlie tried to explain to Miranda how much he needed to be near her, how having her close kept away his inexplicable fear and the images that jabbed into his brain every time he closed his eyes: of Miranda falling to the floor, eyes half-closed, of his mother, covered in blood. Then there was the unshakeable feeling of death looming over Miranda like a black shadow. He felt so helpless, and being close to her helped. After a while, the images faded, the nightmares became more rare, and the sense of doom drifted away.

He'd had two years of peace.

Until now. When Chalk Bogart had dropped the Dunworth case on Charlie's desk, he'd thrown Charlie back in time. Now, it was as though no time had passed at all since his mother died. Over and over the past twenty-four hours, the thoughts crept into his mind as fiercely as they'd done years ago.

He shook his head, pushing the thoughts away. But they kept coming back.

Why now? He demanded of the universe. *Why now, damn it?* He had everything he wanted. He'd built a life his mother would be proud of. He needed the past to leave him alone. But he couldn't shake his memories. They were now overlaid with the story of Michael and Amanda Dunworth, two people so different from him and Miranda, and yet so much the same.

He kept walking, leaving behind the shadow of their tall building. Back when they first moved to L.A., he and Miranda had their pick of condos—money was essentially no object after Miranda's negotiations with Charles Senior. Even if they found one whose price exceeded their contractual budget, he and Miranda had enough saved to cover an overage.

But while they wanted to move to L.A., they both felt a strong ambivalence about the city. Miranda disliked the impossible beauty standards which she believed she could never measure up to. She disliked how many people in L.A. prized looks over brains—which wasn't surprising considering her massive amount of brains.

They continued to live at the W hotel on the West Side while they house hunted, Miranda perpetually dissatisfied, it seemed, with every neighborhood they visited.

"I'd rather live with happy retirees than those jerkoffs," she said one night when they were having drinks with her friend Daphne. "I just need some tennis courts, a pool, and maybe to be walking distance to the beach. Is there a retirement community that'll take a twenty-something with a bad attitude?"

"You should live in Marina del Rey," Daphne said. "It's where all the retirees live. Basically it's like living on a cruise ship but with more room, plus you can walk to Venice."

So they headed to Marina del Rey to scope out condos, and they found a glass-fronted, high-rise building with a pool and tennis courts. The real estate agent showed them a unit with an immense amount of square feet given the zip code, and Miranda had bought it with their father's money: three bedrooms, two and a half bathrooms, and multiple balconies with an ocean view.

Now, wearing worn jeans, an old NASA t-shirt that he bought on a field trip in high school—it still fit him, albeit far more tightly across the chest and shoulders than it did back then—and flip-flops, Charlie strolled toward Venice Beach while trying to forget about the horrendous afternoon three years ago that changed his life forever. But he couldn't seem to eject the memories from his head.

Some might think that heading to a bar at two in the afternoon was odd, but Charlie George—just like Miranda—had always done his own thing. He needed a drink, and he didn't want to drink alone in his apartment. His sister had warned him about the dangers of drinking alone. So had his mother Sorcha, if unintentionally. And so he was going to the Typhoon, what locals considered an old watering-hole-turned-tourist-trap.

He pulled his sunglasses down to shade his tired eyes from the sun, and he headed down Admiralty Way with the marina to his left. After about five minutes, passing yachts and old houseboats alike, and a few more turns, he turned west on Washington, strolling straight toward the ocean and the heart of Venice Beach. A few minutes later, he entered the Typhoon's covered patio and passed through the propped-open door.

Christmas lights looped across the dark walls and hung from the low ceiling, the only lights on at this time of day. The scarred wood bar ran along the wall opposite the entrance. As he crossed the floor, he could feel the grit of sand beneath his flip-flops. When he slouched onto a rough, wooden barstool, he relaxed, as though all of the strain of the fight with Chalk, of the Dunworth case, of the nightmares, slipped away.

Pulling his phone out of his pocket, he shot Miranda a text: **At Typhoon. Ditch work early and we'll connive**.

A few minutes later, his phone dinged with her reply: **Your conniving has already succeeded. Chalk was just fired**.

Charlie reread her message three or four times before her words penetrated his mind. Relief flooded him. His job was safe; *he* was safe. Chalk, and Chalk's suspicions about Charlie's past, were gone.

So why didn't he feel any better? Why did he still feel haunted? He remembered Miranda's words from earlier: all of this, his worries, his fears—they weren't about Chalk at all.

Charlie signaled for the bartender, who'd been hanging back, giving him space. The Typhoon's bartenders always gave the locals space—it was one of the reasons Charlie liked coming here. Plus, this particular bartender was his friend.

"Hey Lala," he said.

"Hey George," Lala replied. Lala, or Luisa Alvarez, was the bar manager of the Typhoon, a five-foot-two thirtyish total fox who ran the place like Patton. Charlie was alternately terrified of and in love with her.

"Scotch on the rocks, please," he said.

"Pondering something today?" Turning to make his drink, she stood on her toes to pull a rocks glass from a high shelf. Lala was able to read people's minds by their drink orders.

"I'm dealing with a conundrum."

"Where's your viper of a sister? She'll knock that conundrum right out of you."

"Miranda's not a viper."

"It's no insult." Lala poured his drink heavy. "No matter what she does, she has a clear conscience." Sliding his drink across the bar to him, she took the twenty he offered and turned to the old cash register. "That's something to envy."

A clear conscience. What had Miranda gone through to earn that? Charlie wondered. What had she suffered? She was so at peace, now.

Glancing at his watch, Charlie took a sip of Scotch, hoping the drink would clear his conscience too, if only for a little while.

———

"BUT I DON'T WANT TO GO." MIRANDA SAID AS SHE LAY BACK ON HER bed in a man's t-shirt and boxer shorts.

Charlie didn't recognize the clothes, but he figured they belonged to her boyfriend, John. "The party is for you, Miranda. You have to go."

It was five-thirty Thursday night, and he and Miranda were expected at the restaurant in half an hour—the amount of time it took to get anywhere in Los Angeles during rush hour if you were lucky. Miranda's moping on her giant bed was going to make them late.

"I didn't ask for a party." She covered her face with a pillow.

"That's the thing about having friends. Sometimes they want to do things to make us happy.

Miranda scowled at him.

"And sometimes we have to do things to make them happy."

Rolling her eyes, Miranda got to her feet. "Life was so much easier when everyone hated me."

Charlie chuckled. Miranda had done her best to make everyone hate her, it was true. But she'd failed. His sister, despite her flaws, was lovable.

"Besides, celebrating my imminent graduation from law school? Any moron with half a brain can graduate from law school."

Charlie snorted. Miranda had not merely finished law school. She'd attended UCLA on a full merit scholarship—one of the most prestigious law school scholarships in the world. She was graduating with honors in two and a half years, when law school took three years for mortal humans. With highest honors.

Charlie had graduated from law school with honors, sure, but he'd never been as fancy as that.

If he were being honest, Miranda had indeed done something worth celebrating.

"I'm wearing jeans," she said.

"Don't wear jeans. We're going to Rivet. Only douchebags wear jeans to Rivet."

Rivet was an exclusive, high-end restaurant on the west side of L.A. owned by some of their friends. Charlie wore slim cut custom-tailored Hugo Boss black pants, a Prada French blue shirt, and his favorite black leather ankle boots by Valentino. It was a typical night-out getup for him, and he knew he wore it well. Charlie had plenty of money, and he enjoyed spending it on himself. He heard his father's voice in his head, unbidden. *Appearances matter, no matter what.*

"I'm tired. I worked all day."

"You worked till four-thirty. That is hardly all day." To be fair, Miranda worked part-time and went to school full time. It was a lot for anyone.

"You're supposed to be on my side." She started digging through her walk-in closet, which contained far fewer clothes than one would expect given how much money she had in her bank account. It was downright barren compared to Charlie's closet. Miranda had left most of her nice things behind in North Carolina when she'd run away from home after their mother died, and she hadn't bothered to replace them in intervening years.

She pulled a navy blue dress from the rack, then made a twirling motion with her finger.

He turned his back to her just as she was yanking her t-shirt over her head. After some rustling, she said, "All right."

She had the dress on and was pulling gold strappy shoes onto her feet. She ran her fingers through her shoulder-length hair, grabbed a lipstick from her bedside table, and declared, "I'm ready."

"Don't you need a purse or something?"

"Why would I? You're driving, and you're paying. Or they are, or whatever." She strode from her bedroom, her heels clacking on the hardwood floors.

As they waited for the elevator, she placed her hand in the crook of his elbow and eyed him carefully. "Are you okay, Little B? You're looking a little less fresh-faced than usual."

If Charlie were being honest, he was not okay. Even now, looking at Miranda, her blond hair gleaming in the light, her large brown eyes bright and intelligent, her face so alive—all he could see was her eyes deadened, her body falling to the floor. He couldn't shove the awful images from his mind.

But he didn't want to tell Miranda about his troubles, not tonight. He could tell her tomorrow, when it wasn't her night of celebration. "Just worried about the Dunworth case."

Miranda kept eyeing him, even as he led them onto the elevator.

"You're worried about the case, yes." she said. "But you're also worried about something else."

Of course she could tell he was lying. She could always tell.

"Maybe I am." He thought about the nightmares, too, the ones he hadn't told her had returned. How sometimes, from the corner of his eye, he saw his mother's body on the floor, drenched in blood.

"Will you tell me later?" she asked.

And this was the difference between the Miranda of today and the one who'd run away after their mother's death. Before their mother had died, Miranda would have come at him hard, relentlessly, until he'd confessed everything.

Today, she was more gentle.

He loved her for it. "I'll tell you later. I promise."

Chapter Five

Tory Murphy knew better than to even think about Charlie George, let alone look at him the way she was doing right now. But he was just so delicious to look at, like a chocolate truffle that would melt in her mouth.

Yum.

She first met him three years ago, late one spring night when he'd stormed into the Laurel Canyon mansion of movie star Alexander Martin to pick an epic fight with his big sister Miranda.

At the time, Miranda had been schtupping Sandy Martin, which had earned Miranda Tory's eternal respect.

But Charlie had not been okay with Miranda's sleeping arrangement. He'd arrived, tossing Sandy's door open like he owned the place, then raged like a Greek god come to Earth. Tory narrowed her eyes at him in thought. Charlie was like Apollo, all muscled and golden.

He and Miranda had fought—Miranda had won of course—but Tory had been awestruck by Charlie. She'd never seen anything like him, and she'd lived in Los Angeles her entire life. He was six-foot-four of lean muscle, strong jawline, cut cheekbones, and brains.

She'd nearly melted to the floor.

In the years since, Tory had become friends with Miranda. In fact, Tory would call Miranda her best friend, and Miranda would call Tory the same, excepting Charlie, who fell into his own special category in Miranda's life. So Tory had had a lot of time to get to know Charlie, and time and proximity had not done much to ease her crush. On the contrary. Getting to know Charlie had confirmed that he was as arrogant and bossy as he'd seemed that first night, but he was also considerate, especially of women—Miranda, as she often said, had trained him well. He was highly intelligent, so Tory was never bored when he was around, and despite his arrogance, he was also able to laugh at himself, so she teased him constantly.

They also flirted constantly. Harmless flirting, of course, just empty words. Like yesterday. *But if you keep your hand there a minute longer, I'll need your medical attention.* Just words, but he managed to make them sound like he was ready to take her clothes off right there on the balcony. He managed to sound serious—right up until he didn't.

Tonight, Tory sat next to Miranda at Miranda's law school graduation party. They were at Rivet of all places—who would have thought Tory Murphy would ever hang out at this fancy place regularly? She'd been born in L.A., but with her professor parents, Hollywood had seemed like another world.

Directly across from Tory sat Charlie, and even though she saw him all the time, she couldn't keep her eyes off of him. He looked great—of course he did, he always did—but it was more than that. He was chatting with Greta, who was seated next to him, listening to her speak with a focused intensity that showed just how much he respected what she was saying. He was always like that. He could make you feel special just by being near him. It was part of his charm, part of what made him Charlie.

He could probably do the opposite, Tory supposed, make a person feel lower than the bottom of his custom-made shoes. But he'd never done it to her. No, he always made her feel like the only person in the room. In the building. On planet Earth. When she talked, he listened carefully to what she said, and when she saw him days or weeks later, he remembered their conversation, every detail.

Being around Charlie George, for Tory Murphy, was like a drug designed just for her because so much of her life she'd been overlooked. For much of her childhood, she might as well have been invisible. She never knew that a small child feeding herself breakfast and making her own way to school was weird until much later in life. That coming home alone and putting herself to bed without a good-night kiss was strange. Wrong, even. To live in a house with two parents who rarely even noticed she was there.

She shook her head to clear away those unwanted thoughts.

She sipped her cranberry and soda, peering at him over the glass, at his broad shoulders and blond hair shining in the candlelight, a god among mortals.

Apollo, indeed.

Just because their flirting was harmless didn't mean he wasn't the most attractive guy she'd ever met. It didn't mean she wasn't falling in love with him a little bit every day since she'd first laid eyes on him because he made her feel *seen*.

Suddenly, Charlie met her eyes. Holding her gaze, he raised one dark blond eyebrow and smiled, like he'd known she'd been thinking about him.

There was a constant undercurrent of attraction between them, yes. But he'd never acted on it, even as she'd watched him fool around with a never-ending stream of rail-thin blondes with impressive cup sizes. She'd only had to spend a short time with Charlie George to realize that she was very much not his type.

She sighed.

Sometimes she wondered if she only imagined the zap of mutual attraction she felt when she was around him. It wasn't like Charlie George to deny his sexual urges. And she didn't, either—she was just less conspicuous about it.

But it didn't matter. She'd had three years to shake this more-than-crush, and after all this time she knew it wasn't going anywhere. He made her feel special, important. It was entrancing, and it was the most direct way to her heart. Or, well, her panties.

Yes, Tory Murphy knew better than to even think about Charlie George because, when she thought about him, all she wanted to do was rip his clothes off.

And, if she were honest, she wanted something more.

Suddenly, he stood, gesturing to Miranda with his wine glass. "Congratulations, big sister, on your accomplishment, such as it is."

He heaved a dramatic sigh. "Although a bit of a step down for you, a UCLA diploma will do." He lifted his glass in a toast.

Miranda rolled her eyes, lifting her own glass. "I should have expected such gravitas from you."

"I went to UCLA for medical school," Tory tossed out. "I turned out fine."

When Charlie turned his gaze on her again, she wanted to take back her words.

His gaze said, *You turned out fine, indeed.*

The entire table went silent.

Tory wanted to sink into her chair.

The silence stretched. And stretched.

Oh no—she and Charlie were having a *moment.*

It wasn't that Tory was afraid to attract his attention. On the contrary—Tory wasn't afraid of much at all. The problem was that she wanted to toss him on the bar and lick him all over. And now everyone at the table would be able to tell what she was thinking.

She looked away from Charlie, pretending she hadn't been taking in his dark brown gaze, his jawline that could be used as a masonry tool, his long, lean frame. Like his sister, he was so, so tall.

"You turned out great," Miranda said to her, smoothly ending the pause in the conversation. "As have I. And we will endeavor to ignore my brother's snobbery for another day."

"I have to admit, your brother's snobbery has started to grow on me," Daphne Saito said from Tory's left.

"That's not a thing," Miranda snapped. "Snobbery doesn't grow on people. It's revolting."

"His is quaint and adorable." Daphne took a sip of her martini.

Charlie sat, turning to Daphne. "Did you just call me quaint and adorable?"

Daphne nodded. "Like a bichon frisé."

Tory snorted, secretly relieved that the attention had moved on from her and Charlie.

Daphne Saito was the reason Tory knew this group of friends in the first place. Daphne had shown up in Tory's emergency department one night after a horrible car accident. After that, they'd become friends. And becoming friends with Daphne Saito meant being adopted into her entire circle. Daphne and Miranda were friends from college, along with the other woman at the table, Greta Donovan. Not that Tory minded being adopted, not at all. Working long shifts in the emergency department meant that it was hard for her to make friends outside of the hospital, and most of the ED docs were guys who split their time between the hospital, the gym, and the sports bar across the street from work. Befriending Daphne, and then Miranda, filled a hole in Tory's heart, one that she had ever since she realized she would always come second to her parents' work.

Miranda's law school graduation was an event that should have been a non-event given her pedigree and her smarts. But Miranda had been through hell the past few years of her life, so graduating from UCLA Law was a big deal. Her brother's jokes aside, Tory knew that Charlie was proud of his sister.

As was everyone else at the table. Daphne and her fiancé Marlon. Greta and her husband Timmy. Miranda's boyfriend John. And Alexander Martin himself, who sat at the head of the table with his girlfriend Patricia. Tory was still nervous talking to him, like any person with a brain would be. The man basically glowed.

Realizing that she and Charlie were the only two single people at the table, Tory took a big sip of her soda water.

Maybe Charlie would be down for a quickie in the bathroom. Just to take the edge off.

Oh God. Now she couldn't stop thinking of her back pressed against the bathroom wall, her legs around his waist.

Her face turned red. She hated how badly she blushed. She could only pray no one looked her way.

———

Two hours later, dinner was over, and some of the party had dispersed to Rivet's bar. Tory spied Charlie standing at the bar with John, Miranda's boyfriend. John seemed like an unlikely friend for Charlie George just as he seemed like an unlikely boyfriend for Miranda. John was a couple of inches shorter than Charlie, with brown hair and standard good looks—next to Charlie, John faded into the background. But John was kind, and intelligent, and he had a wicked sense of humor that could keep up with Miranda's.

Tory remembered when Miranda had first come to L.A., when she'd been in so much trouble. John had been there for her no matter how hard she'd tried to push him away. She was certain that Charlie remembered, too. And Charlie would be loyal to John forever for what he'd done for his sister.

She was about to sidle over to the bar to flirt with Charlie when Daphne grabbed her wrist.

"He's nice to look at." Daphne shook her head. "Maybe it's better just to look."

"Touching's better than looking." Smacking her lips for emphasis, Tory gave Daphne a grin.

"He's fine to hang out with. He's fine as Miranda's brother and your friend. But I don't want you to get hurt."

Tory snorted. "He won't hurt me. Well, not unless I ask him to."

Daphne rolled her eyes. "Will you be serious for one second?"

"Why, Daphne? You're being bossy. He's just Charlie. We've been flirting for years."

"Something's different tonight between you two."

Tory felt a flare of heat in her belly. So the others had noticed the moment at the table. Tory didn't know whether to be thrilled or embarrassed. "Maybe, but nothing's going to come of it. Nothing ever does."

Daphne's face turned serious, as serious as Tory had ever seen her. "I just want you to be careful. He's not as charming as he seems on the surface. The first time I met him, he got arrested. And the other guy died."

"What are you talking about?" Tory felt a jolt of shock. "Charlie killed somebody?"

Daphne shook her head, flustered. "What? I didn't say that." She paused again, looking unsettled. "I'm talking about something that happened in college."

Tory wondered at Daphne's reaction to her question. Daphne was so rarely unsettled by anything. "Are you trying to warn me away from Charlie?"

"Back in college," Daphne said, "when Charlie was a senior in high school. He came for a campus visit and stayed with Miranda."

"This all sounds not very serious." Tory nearly rolled her eyes. "Get to the point."

"He came along with us to a fraternity party. Charlie and this freshman got wasted, and the other kid died."

"How is that Charlie's fault?" Tory was aggravated now. "I've seen plenty of alcohol ODs. Way too many, actually, and definitely more than you." Daphne was supposed to be friends with Miranda and Charlie. What was going on?

"Don't you ever wonder why nothing ever sticks to Charlie George?"

Tory sighed in frustration. "You're holding something against him that happened when he was in high school. Besides, according to you, you're the one who brought him to that party."

"The important stuff hasn't changed. He's still manipulative and self-centered. He still uses people. He's arrogant. He's obsessed with appearances. He only looks out for himself. Well, for himself and Miranda, but that's it. They're the only two people who count to him."

Angry on Charlie's behalf, Tory said, "Aren't you his friend?"

Chewing her thumbnail, Daphne looked into the middle distance. "I am, I think, as much as Charlie can have friends. That doesn't mean I want him sleeping with you."

"That's my decision, isn't it?"

"Miranda grew up sacrificing herself to keep him safe. But because of her, he grew up with everything handed to him. Charlie isn't like Miranda. She's loyal, trustworthy. He isn't."

Aggravated, Tory felt her anger growing. "I've spent plenty of time with both of them over the years. More than you. Charlie might be trampy, but he has a good heart."

Daphne grabbed Tory's arm and met her gaze. "There are things you don't know, Tory. Things I can't tell you. He might keep it locked down, but Charlie's done things that a person can't come back from. His glossy façade is just that. Underneath it he's...dark."

"If what you have to say is so damn important, why can't you tell me more?"

Daphne shook her head. "All he can be is an acquaintance. A friend's brother. Like…a dangerous pet. Think about what he does for work, Miranda. He's remorseless."

"Jesus, Daphne. He's not a serial killer."

Daphne frowned. "I just really love you, Tory. And as much as I love Miranda, Charlie isn't like her, not in the ways that matter."

Tory looked Daphne over. She was being sincere. But how had Tory never sensed anything off about Charlie after all these years? As she and Miranda had become good friends, she'd spent more and more time around Charlie. He was exactly what he seemed to be— intelligent, hard-working, and fun-loving. Loyal to his sister, just as Daphne said. And really good to his sister's best friend.

No matter how hard Tory thought about it, no matter how many symptoms she examined, she could find no trace of this *dark* that Daphne described.

Until, perhaps, yesterday. She thought of the swollen knuckles on Charlie's right hand. Then there'd been the grim look on his face and, now that she thought about it, the fear.

Daphne shot Tory a pleading look. "Don't get involved."

Tory had had enough. "I wasn't planning on getting *involved*, Daphne. We just flirt a little. No big deal."

Daphne tried a different tack. "But you just said that you're friends. You're friends with his sister. You know what hooking up with someone can do to friendship."

Tory tapped her lip in thought. "True. Do you think Miranda will mind?"

"Actually, she probably won't mind at all. But I'm worried about *you*."

Tory shrugged. "When you're in residency, you have to learn how to hook up and get over it fast. There's a very small pool to choose from, and there's no escaping each other."

Daphne looked doubtful. "But I'm not sure that your hook-up practice has prepared you for Charlie George."

Tory sipped her drink. "I see. You need proof."

Daphne looked at her like she was nuts. "Proof?"

"Follow me."

Tory led Daphne over to the bar, where the bar manager, Quentin, came over and took her hand, kissing each cheek.

"Tory! So good to see you. Can I make you another?"

"Sure. This is just cranberry juice and soda water. I'm not drinking tonight." On Friday mornings, Tory always did her long run for the week, and she didn't want to have a hangover.

"And for you, Daphne?"

Daphne glanced down at her martini glass. "I could use another. Thank you."

As he turned back to mix their drinks, Tory whispered in Daphne's ear. "Three times this summer."

Daphne's eyes widened. "No way."

Tory nodded.

"Who else?"

"At Rivet?"

"There are others from Rivet?" Daphne's voice squeaked.

"It's fun. It doesn't matter."

Quentin slid their drinks across the bar. "Great to see you ladies. Tell Miranda congrats for me."

"We will," Tory said, smiling. She always liked Quentin. He was good-hearted, and generous in the ways that really, really mattered to a woman.

"Sure we will," Daphne said, eyeing Quentin suspiciously, then eyeing Tory as well.

After Quentin turned to another customer, Tory shrugged. "You said you needed proof."

"Proof of what?" A voice spoke from behind Tory. She glanced over her shoulder. Charlie was there, leaning close.

Daphne's eyes grew wide again.

Worried how much he'd overheard, Tory said flippantly, "Just girl talk."

Charlie leaned his hip against the bar. "I love girl talk. Don't stop for me."

Daphne rolled her eyes.

"We were talking about notches," Tory said.

Charlie quirked his head to the side. "Notches?"

"Ladies have them too, you know. Even if we keep them secret from you."

His eyes narrowed, a predator ready to pounce.

"Oh man," Daphne said. "That's my exit cue." She eyed Tory. "Please remember what I said." Then she headed back over to where their friends gathered at their table.

Giving Tory his full attention, Charlie said, "Tell me more about your notches."

Tory looked up at him, admiring, once again, his tall, lean frame, his broad shoulders, his full mouth. If she looked only at his face, he resembled his sister so closely it was eerie. But the rest of him looked so much like someone she wanted to…notch. She shook her head. "No man wants to hear about a woman's notches. Even if he thinks he does."

He leaned closer to her, whispering, "I do."

She smiled. "You don't. Trust me—I'm a doctor."

They held each other's gaze for a moment. Charlie's half-smile nearly broke her resolve, the crinkles at the corners of his eyes making her melt. She tried to hold steady, resting one hand on the bar, refusing to look away first. Then, hearing Quentin's voice as he spoke to another bar patron, Tory glanced over at him. Quentin caught her eye and gave her a grin.

Tory looked back at Charlie. But Charlie was examining Quentin as the bartender poured the patron's drink. Then he nodded thoughtfully.

Damn. She'd slipped up in front of Charlie George. Just like his sister Miranda, Charlie missed absolutely nothing. *Damn, damn, damn.*

"Quentin, huh?" Charlie asked.

Tory pressed her lips together. Miranda had taught her to always keep her mouth shut if she ever got in trouble.

Charlie looked contemplative. "Every woman in this place flirts with Quentin."

It was true. Quentin was very good looking. Plus, he was the bartender, and women fell all over themselves for bartenders.

Charlie's eyes narrowed in thought. "It's probably why they keep him around. For the eye candy."

Miffed, she snapped, "That's not the only reason they keep him around. He's really good at his job. He and Olivia keep the place running as smooth as any operating room at Cedars." Olivia was the floor manager, and she could run a Fortune 500 company, no doubt.

Charlie smiled like a cat. "He's good at his job? Please, tell me more."

Ugh. She'd screwed up again. Charlie had baited her, and it had worked.

She'd thrown one glance in Quentin's direction, and Charlie had figured out her entire relationship with him.

Not that she'd had any real relationship with Quentin.

"Why do you care about my notches, Charlie?" she asked.

He leaned closer to her, putting enough heat in his gaze to melt the ice in her glass. Maybe Daphne was right. Maybe she wasn't prepared for Charlie George.

"Do you care about him?" Charlie glanced in Quentin's direction.

"He's a decent person."

"That," he said, his low voice rumbling all through her, "is not an answer."

She set her drink down on the bar. "It's the only one you're going to get." She tried to keep her voice light, but she failed. Charlie George was acting…jealous, and she didn't know how to feel about that.

He leaned so close that his breath whispered across her temple. "I bet I could convince you to give me a better answer. I have a secret weapon."

She held her ground, even though her head was spinning. His nearness, his unrelenting focus on her, as though she were the only person who existed, nearly undid her. "Maybe you could. But you'd have to fire that secret weapon three, maybe four times before I'd give in."

He laughed, and the deep sound sent shivers all the way down to her toes.

She needed to push him off or she would do something embarrassing, like kiss him. "Besides," she said, "if I tried to keep up with your notches, I'd need a bedpost as long as the PCH."

He nodded, considering her words, and he spoke without a smile in sight. "But what if I don't want just a notch, Tory?"

Her belly hit the floor. She gazed up at him, waiting for the punchline. She waited, and waited, but none came.

He lifted his hand to her cheek, then tucked a piece of hair behind her ear. "I've been wanting to do that since yesterday on the balcony, but I was too afraid."

Tory Murphy, fast-talking ED doc, was utterly at a loss for words. Charlie George, afraid to touch her? "Why?"

He shook his head, his brows drawn together. "I'm realizing some things. And one of those things is you."

Before Tory could begin to process what he was saying, an angry voice called out. "Charles George Junior." Miranda, with John by her side, approached the bar, and she did not look happy.

Charlie whipped his head around—too quickly, apparently—and he stumbled back against the bar, sloshing his drink.

"Oops," he said, chuckling at himself.

Stepping close to Charlie, Miranda raised her voice in aggravation. "You are wasted, you complete ass."

John, Miranda's boyfriend, leaned against the bar and watched. He held a beer and wore an amused expression. This was hardly the first time he'd seen the siblings go at each other.

"Just a little tipsy," Charlie said, holding up his hand and tilting it from side to side, *mas o menos.*

"You're supposed to be my designated driver." Miranda actually stomped her foot.

"That's true." Charlie nodded in agreement. He made no attempt to defend himself. "Too late now. I wouldn't want to put my bar license at risk by getting behind the wheel."

"I can drive you home, babe," John said, touching her elbow.

"I know that." Miranda didn't look at John, poking her brother in the chest instead. "It's the principle of the thing."

"Hoo boy." Charlie released a heavy sigh, his southern accent getting stronger as it always did when he got a few drinks in him. "My sister and her principles."

Miranda leaned closer and bared her teeth. Before she could do any real damage to Charlie, John wrapped an arm around her waist and pulled her back against his chest.

Tory covered her mouth and laughed. She adored Miranda's

relationship with Charlie. Tory was an only child. Not for the first time, she wondered what it would be like to have someone you loved no matter what, even when they were making you bananas.

As John hugged Miranda to him, he said to her, "Your principles are sexy." Miranda wrapped her hands over John's where they were clasped at her waist.

"No," Charlie said. "Her principles are exhausting."

Glancing at Charlie, John shook his head. "And people wonder why you're single."

"And I still can't believe she's dating you."

John smiled. "Just let me know when you want lady lessons. I'm free on Tuesday afternoons."

Charlie scoffed. "What could I possibly learn from you about women?"

Tory's eyes widened as she watched Charlie realize his mistake.

John let go of Miranda and stepped back. "He's all yours, honey."

She stepped toward Charlie, murder in her eyes.

"I'm so sorry." Charlie held up his hands. "I didn't mean it like that. He's got great taste in women."

Miranda's eyes narrowed as she leaned into Charlie's face. "The first lady lesson is this: stay sober when you're supposed to be the designated driver."

Charlie nodded. "Of course."

"The second lesson is to always, always know that you have more to learn."

Charlie nodded again. But he didn't, Tory noted, look like he agreed with her on that point. No, Charlie George thought he knew all there was to know about women.

"I'm going to leave with John," Miranda said to Charlie. "You're on your own, jerkwad."

"Jerkwad?" Charlie said, turning the word over in his mouth. Finally, he nodded. "I deserve that."

Seeing an opportunity, Tory spoke up. "I can drive him home. I came with Daphne, so I don't have a car here."

Turning to Tory, Miranda said, "You don't have to do that. He should have to ride in a stinky cab."

"Consider it a graduation gift for you," Tory said.

Miranda nodded. "A real gift would be if you dented his bumper when you parked."

Looking horrified, Charlie turned to Tory. "You wouldn't."

Tory patted his shoulder. "I would, if you deserved it."

To his sister, Charlie said, "Why would you put terrible ideas in her head?"

Miranda shook her head, disappointment on her face. "Lady lesson number three: We can come up with terrible ideas all on our own."

Slipping her hand through John's elbow, Miranda left.

Tory inhaled deeply, and then let the breath go. Reaching for her drink and sipping the last of it, she leaned forward on the bar. Next to her, Charlie did the same.

Quentin strolled over, giving her a smile. "Ready for something stronger?" he asked, his voice husky, and his words were clearly about more than her drink.

She glanced at Charlie. His easy smile had vanished, and he was eyeing Quentin as though he were sizing him up for a fight.

She flushed. She'd had guys flex around her before, but never Charlie. Charlie didn't get jealous—why would he? He could have anyone. Anyone, anytime, anywhere. Including her. Surely he must know that after all these years. And she wanted him, despite what Daphne said. She didn't find him self-centered or manipulative. He could be arrogant, but his arrogance was funny, not obnoxious.

And he was always, always kind to her. And generous. And respectful.

Too respectful, sometimes. Sometimes, she wished he'd toss her over his shoulder and carry her to his bedroom. A woman could dream.

"I'll just take my check, Quentin," she said.

"Sure thing." He tapped the screen and printed up her ticket, sliding it across the bar to her.

Before she could reach for it, Charlie pulled it to him. "Mine too, if you don't mind," he said to Quentin.

"You don't have to pay for me," Tory said.

Charlie passed his credit card to Quentin. "Let's let the bad guys pay for the good guys tonight."

Tory nodded. "On one condition."

Leaning closer to her, Charlie asked, "What's the condition?"

Tory reached out her hand. "Give me your keys."

He leaned away, eyebrows raised. "Not if you're going to dent the bumper."

Waiting, Tory held out her hand.

He glanced at her, the heat in his eyes burning her up. Without breaking eye contact, Charlie fished for his keys in his pocket. He held them out to her—and then dropped them. *On purpose.*

She watched him. He watched her. Neither of them moved.

Slowly, so slowly, he reached down for the keys.

Tory knelt down so she could pick them up first, her fingers wrapping around the metal ring. But then he was down there with her, his hand wrapped around hers, his breath at her neck.

"Tory," he whispered, inhaling as his nose brushed her skin. He groaned.

She leaned into him, feeling the vibrations of his voice throughout her body. Together, they were still. Another moment stretched on and on.

He stood first, then he helped her to her feet, steadying her. As he did so, she realized that he was way less intoxicated than he'd let Miranda believe he was. His face still close to her ear, he whispered her name again. She knew where this night would end.

Did he set this up? She asked herself, thinking of the fake intoxication, the tiff with Miranda. *Do I care?*

No, she did not.

Chapter Six

Tory had visited Miranda and Charlie's condo innumerable times over the years, but, she realized, she had never been inside Charlie's bedroom. She'd passed by it, glancing inside. She'd seen the king bed, usually unmade, the dark blue comforter rumpled, the crisp, white sheets strewn about.

Tonight, as she followed him in, it struck her as odd that she'd never crossed the threshold.

Glancing around, she noticed that the bed was neatly made, the pillows stacked with precision.

She ran her hand along the top of the comforter, feeling the smooth cotton surface and the plushness beneath.

The rest of his room was spotless as well. Not a sock out of place, not a shoe, the wood floor shiny as though recently scrubbed.

"I don't think I've ever seen your room this neat," she said.

"I clean when I'm nervous," he replied, rubbing the back of his neck.

For a moment, he looked like a young boy. And that innocence made him even more irresistible.

Reaching out, she traced her hand along his jaw. "I'm glad you won the fight. I'd hate to see this handsome face marked up."

He pulled her to him, resting his face against her cheek, whispering in her ear. "But if I'd lost, you'd have to patch me up, doc."

At his words, she felt a moment of panic. If he'd lost the fight, and she'd had to patch him up, she'd be a goner. Tory could never resist a guy who needed her.

She laughed off his words. "You'd use any excuse to get me to put my hands on you."

"Is touching me such a strain?" He ran his hands down her back, pulling up the loose skirt of her dress, taking hold of her bottom, and pulling her against him.

The only thing straining was in his pants.

"Are you kidding?" she looked up at him. "I've wanted to do this for so long."

He cracked a smile. "Me too." Nuzzling her hair, he said, "For like, ever."

"Then why didn't you ever kiss me or something?"

His smile faltered. "It never seemed to be the right time."

She laughed. "Charlie George. There's never a right time. There's only the time we've got."

Hands on her shoulders, he held her back and looked in her eyes, his expression serious. "What do you mean?"

"I mean, if you're always going to wait for the perfect time to do something, then you're never going to do it."

He smiled. "Perfection is, indeed, rare." He still seemed lost in his brain about something.

Time to shake him loose. "So that's it? You made me wait three damn years because you were afraid the time wasn't right?"

"What? Afraid?" He shook his head, pulling her against him again so that their bodies were touching all over.

She grinned. Nothing derailed a man's train of thought like being called a fraidy-cat.

And he felt *amazing*.

She wrapped her arms around his neck and pulled his face closer. "Get naked," she said. "Doctor's orders."

Instead of following her directions, he found the zipper at the back of her dress and pulled it down, slowly.

She wasn't going to make it, and she'd be so embarrassed to wind up in her own former ED.

"I will in a minute," he said. "I'm in the middle of something here."

He pulled her dress over her head in one motion, tossing it across the room.

He rested his hands on her hips, and then, *oh God*, he dropped to his knees. He slid her panties down to her ankles, urging her forward so she stepped out of them, and he tossed them away as well.

And that was it. She was naked with Charlie George.

Charlie kissed her just below her belly button, and she nearly collapsed. He held her up with a tight grip on her hips, his strong arms flexing.

And then he kissed her even more, even lower. And everything was even better than even she'd imagined it could be.

———

Later, Tory lay awake watching Charlie sleep. While his breath was a whisper, she marveled at how quiet it was in his apartment. Where she lived, not even twenty minutes away by foot, the noise of cars and foot traffic could be heard twenty-four hours a day. But not here, high above the water in Marina del Rey. Miranda liked to call the place her retirement home. But Tory knew better; the condo was Miranda's sanctuary.

Now, Tory was starting to wonder whether it was Charlie's too. He didn't have to live here—he made enough money, *had* enough money, to get a place of his own. But he chose to stay. She wondered why.

Tory knew a little about what Miranda went through a few years back, when she first moved to L.A. After Miranda's mother died, Miranda was in a tailspin, and she ran away to Los Angeles and moved in with Daphne. Charlie came out to L.A., desperate to find her and bring her back home. After Charlie helped Miranda unravel the horrible tangle she was in—with the help of their friends— Miranda convinced Charlie to stay with her in L.A. instead of going back east. The way Tory understood it, Charlie George had everything he ever wanted in North Carolina—so what on earth made him leave it behind?

Earlier at Rivet, when Daphne had described Miranda and Charlie's childhood, she'd said that Miranda had protected Charlie growing up. Tory now wondered exactly what that meant. *Miranda grew up sacrificing herself to keep him safe. But he grew up with everything handed to him.* Could two people grow up in the same home but live two entirely different lives? Two people who were as alike as Miranda and Charlie? And how hard had it been for them to turn their backs on their father?

Tory wouldn't know from experience—she was an only child. Tory's parents lived in Los Angeles. It never occurred to her to turn her back on them, not like Miranda and Charlie had done. Daphne and Greta had also left behind parents, and even siblings, when they left their homes to come to L.A.

No, Tory's parents weren't cruel, nothing she would ever complain about. They got lost in their work, and so she'd spent a lot of time alone growing up. But they loved her, even if they rarely said it, and she'd always had everything she needed. She'd had to learn to care for herself too young, but she'd learned independence and life skills. She chose clinical medicine instead of research because treating patients—making connections with actual people— filled a need she had because she'd been alone so much of her life. At least she had the self-awareness to know why she'd made that choice.

She'd quit her job in the emergency department because she wanted work with even more connection. She wanted patients for whom she could provide ongoing care. She wanted to know the people she treated, who they were and what they needed beyond sutures and an I.V. bag.

She knew what drove her. Most people had no idea why they made the decisions they did.

She touched Charlie's hair where it fell across his brow. Around two a.m., he'd fallen asleep, shortly after their final go-round. Passing out after sex was typical dude behavior in her experience. She wished she could sleep like the dead after a night like they'd had. Instead, every time, she stayed awake, running the play-by-play through her head. At least this time the play-by-play was outstanding. Holy crap.

She grinned to herself.

She tugged the comforter up to her chin and rolled on her side to sleep. But before she could drift off, noises woke her.

A whimper. Then another whimper.

Then a word—"No."

She sat up, looking over at Charlie. He was dreaming. No, not a dream—a nightmare.

"No. Miranda." His eyes squeezed shut. "Mom—you're killing her." Thrashing, Charlie moaned. "Mom, give me the gun."

What a horrible nightmare. Dreams about family and violence were the worst kind.

"Mom, let me help her!" He thrashed again. "No." Then, he screamed. "No!"

As his arm tensed atop the comforter, Tory touched his skin. He was drenched in sweat and burning up.

His eyes shot open, and he sat up, a look of horror on his face, tears streaking his cheeks, the moisture reflecting the moonlight through the windows. He turned to her, not recognizing her at all, and grabbed both of her arms in a vise-like grip. "Are you the EMT?"

Oh no, Tory thought. *This isn't a nightmare at all.*

"Charlie, I'm Tory," she said, going carefully through the steps she knew from experience. "I'm a doctor and your friend."

"She's dying. You have to save her. Please." The tears streamed down his face.

"Who's dying, Charlie?"

He sobbed. "I killed her. She's dead. But Miranda, she's still alive —I could feel her heartbeat. Don't let her die."

"Miranda's safe, Charlie. She's with John."

"You have to save her. She can't die, too." He collapsed onto the bed, shaking, sobbing, drenched in so much sweat he looked like he'd stepped out of the shower.

"Charlie," Tory said. "Can you hear my voice?" She waited, counting to ten, watching him shake, knees curled to his chest. "Charlie," she tried again. "You're safe. Miranda's safe."

Gradually, his breathing slowed. His eyes opened.

"Charlie," she said. "Can you hear me?"

He rolled onto his back, staring at the ceiling. "Tory," he said, his voice hoarse.

"Yeah. It's me."

"Shit," he said. "I'm sorry."

"You have nothing to apologize for," she said, pitching her voice low and calm.

She waited patiently as the minutes passed and his breathing slowed to a normal pace. She would wait all night for him, if she had to.

Finally, he spoke, his voice back to normal. "After my mom died, I used to get nightmares all the time. They went away, but they're back now." He shook his head. "I'm not sure why."

Tory recalled Daphne's words at Rivet. How Charlie had done things a person couldn't come back from. How underneath his charming façade hid something dark.

But Daphne had one thing all wrong.

Tory knew what flashbacks looked like. She'd seen plenty of PTSD in the emergency department. From the gang members and the violence they'd lived through to domestic abuse and sexual violence victims. And then there were the homeless veterans the cops brought in. So much trauma, so much PTSD.

Charlie was hiding something behind his façade, and it was painful, and it was dark. But Charlie wasn't remorseless like Daphne had said at Rivet. No. He was haunted.

"It's okay, really." She lay down next to him. "Do you want to go back to sleep?"

"Yeah, sure." But he didn't sound sure at all. He sounded wounded and afraid.

"That was wildly unconvincing."

He laughed, a little, enough for her to see the sparkle return to his eyes. "I probably won't be able to sleep again, not well anyway." He rolled toward her. "Come here."

She nestled her back into his chest and he wrapped his arm around her. "That's better," he said. "Have I told you that you feel amazing?"

"About fourteen times tonight." But she was just as happy hearing it the fifteenth time.

"Good, because I want to be sure I am very clear on the matter." After resting his chin on the top of her head, he said, "Actually, maybe I will be able to go back to sleep."

Five minutes later, he did.

Tory smiled, and followed him off.

Chapter Seven

Friday, the morning after Miranda's graduation party, Tory woke to the sun pouring through the plate glass windows of Charlie's bedroom. The first thing she remembered was the glorious pleasure of the night before. Charlie, dropping to his knees in front of her. *Jesus.*

Then, she remembered the awful flashback that woke him in the night. Sitting up, she turned to him, resisting the urge to take his pulse, to run a quick triage. Her healer senses were on high alert.

Then she remembered the after, how they'd talked, and snuggled, and slept curled together. Peaceful.

He slept now, dark blond hair rumpled, brown lashes brushing his cheeks. Careful not to wake him, she climbed from the bed and stepped quietly around his room, pulling on her panties and one of his shirts, a black concert t-shirt for the band Poison. Charlie had the best t-shirts.

She slipped out of the room, pulling the door nearly closed. Part of her was afraid that closing it all the way would wake him. And another part of her worried that he might have another flashback, and she wanted to be able to hear him if he did.

She made her way to the kitchen—her need for coffee was emergent. After starting a pot to brew, she pulled a mug from the cabinet and the cream from the fridge. She'd been to Miranda's place enough to know her way around the kitchen. It was magnificent, even though the siblings subsisted mostly on takeout.

As she waited for the coffee to brew, she started to worry. Charlie was not okay. And a guy who was not okay…well, he drew her like an electromagnet. If she had a weakness for attention—and she knew she did—there was nothing like the attention she got from a guy who needed healing. It was like a drug. They looked at her like she was some kind of benevolent goddess come to Earth to lay her magic hands upon them. But once they were better, and inevitably they were, things fell apart. They didn't need her anymore. And so she didn't need them anymore.

Fretting, she stared at the door to Charlie's room. She couldn't bear it if the same pattern repeated with him, the guy she'd been dreaming about from the moment she first laid eyes on him. She'd have to be careful.

Just as Tory was pouring her coffee, the front door unlocked. *Yikes.* She wasn't wearing anything but a t-shirt and underpants—whoever was coming in would see all of her business.

Fortunately, Miranda stepped through the door alone, locking it behind her. When she saw Tory, and Tory's state of dress, she raised her brows and smiled. "Cat got your pants?"

Tory covered her eyes with her hand. "Please don't be mad."

Laughing, Miranda said, "Why in the world would I be mad? I hope he was sober enough to make it worth it."

"I don't think I can have this conversation with you. Isn't there like a brother-sister confidentiality clause somewhere?"

Miranda joined her in the kitchen, dropping her purse and leather jacket on the counter. "Fair enough." Miranda poured herself a mug of coffee. "Of course I'm not mad. You two hooking up was bound to happen eventually."

"It was?" Tory was genuinely surprised. Until last night, she'd figured it was never going to happen. But last night, something had changed in Charlie. He'd approached her with interest and an unexpected intensity. She'd expected some harmless flirting. When he'd been jealous of Quentin, she'd nearly spilled her drink in surprise.

"I adore you, therefore you're around here all the time. He's my slutty little brother, and you're a total smarty-pants fox. It was just a matter of time before he realized he liked you."

Snorting into her coffee mug at Miranda's words—*he realized he liked you*—she tried a diversion. "Don't call him slutty. He's just pants-impaired."

"You always see the best in people," Miranda said. "It's one of the reasons I love you. You balance me out."

Tory smiled. "Same. You keep me from falling into unmitigated Pollyanna."

"We're friends for more reasons than that. For example, you're a smarty-pants fox." Miranda raised her mug for a toast, and Tory clinked hers against it.

Suddenly, Charlie's voice called out from his bedroom. "Miranda! You home with John?" There was some banging around, like the opening and closing of dresser drawers, and then he called out again. "Thank God Tory's gone. I'm so relieved she's not a clinger."

Tory's jaw dropped in shock.

Miranda spat out her coffee in the sink.

Tory looked to the side, unable to meet Miranda's eyes. A *clinger?* And—*how could he?*

She was so angry, but also ashamed. All she could think about was her dress. *Surely he could he see her dress?* It was lying on the floor by his bed. She felt the heat rising from her neck to her cheeks. She knew she was bright red. She hated how she blushed. *Hated it.*

She opened her mouth to tell his royal ass-ness that she was still in the apartment, but before she could yell at him, he spoke again through the cracked-open door. "She was hot in bed, but I'm glad I don't have to shake her off since she's your friend and all."

At Charlie's horrible words, Tory gritted her teeth. *Shake her off?* She wanted to run into the bathroom and puke up her coffee. Or throw her mug at his bedroom door. Or march into that room and throw her hot coffee in his smug face. So many feelings at once, and yet she stood there frozen like a stupid deer in the headlights.

Everything Daphne had said last night about Charlie, how selfish he was, how arrogant, how he only cared about himself—all of those warnings—why hadn't Tory listened? She'd expected him to be distant this morning, maybe, but she hadn't expected him to be cruel.

"Charlie." Miranda's voice was diamond-hard. "Shut up."

Pulling his bedroom door open, he stepped out in boxers and nothing else. His eyes locked on Tory. "Oh."

There wasn't a shred of remorse in his eyes.

Again, Daphne's warnings echoed in Tory's ears.

When Tory saw his arrogant face, saw the coldness in his eyes, anger filled her. The anger gave her strength, the same strength that drove her through long nights in one of the toughest emergency departments in the country. Gunshot wounds, abused children, heroin overdoses—all of it, all the time. Nothing threw Tory. Certainly not bratty rich boys like Charlie George.

She leveled her gaze on Charlie, her voice cool and even. "You don't have to shake me off, you asshole," she said. "I don't want anything from you but what I've already received. Next time, of course, I'll shop for it someplace less…high maintenance." She gave him a hard look so he'd know what she meant, and his eyes widened. Hitting him in a weak spot was low, but she didn't care. She was so *hurt*. "And I'm keeping this t-shirt."

"Look, Tory," he said. "I'm sorry. I didn't mean it."

Laughing, even as she hurt, she said, "Of course you meant it. You didn't think I was here."

"Please let me apologize."

Tory snorted. "You don't sound apologetic at all."

"You really don't," Miranda said.

Charlie shot his sister an angry look.

Tory threw back the rest of her coffee then slammed her mug on the counter. "Stay out here while I get my things from your room."

She brushed by him, wishing she were strong enough to knock him aside. But she wasn't, and she only succeeded in hurting her own shoulder.

Once she was alone in his bedroom, she shut the door and took a deep breath. She took another, and another, until her hands stopped shaking and the tears of humiliation that had filled her eyes had dried. Then, she gathered her clothes. After taking off his t-shirt, she pulled on her dress, then she put the t-shirt on over it. Dressed like she was, she looked almost normal for Venice Beach.

Lastly, she went into his bathroom, picked up his toothbrush, and dropped it in the toilet.

Stepping out into the common area again, she ignored Charlie completely. She held up her high heels, asking Miranda, "Can I borrow a pair of flip-flops to walk home in?"

"Sure," Miranda said, still glaring at her brother. "But I'm happy to drive you."

"It's a gorgeous day. I'd rather walk." She knew the half-mile walk would clear her head, but she didn't need Charlie George to know how much he'd rattled her. "I didn't get much exercise last night, you know, so I might as well get some this morning."

Miranda snorted at Tory's words, and left for her bedroom.

"That's some ripe bullshit," Charlie said once Miranda was out of earshot, his masculine honor clearly offended by Tory's words. "You got a stellar workout."

"Whatever, Charlie," she said, her heart racing while she tried to keep her cool. "If you'd wanted to know how you stacked up against Quentin, you probably shouldn't have pissed me off so badly. Now I'm never going to speak to you again, and you'll never find out."

Tory spied Miranda emerging from her bedroom holding flip-flops, but Miranda froze as Charlie stepped closer to Tory, his voice carrying an odd mix of injured pride, and yes, jealousy. "I don't care how I measure up against other guys."

Tory forced a laugh, and it almost sounded genuine. "Of course you care. All guys do. Especially big, bratty bullies like you." Then she snatched the flip-flops from Miranda's hand and dashed from the apartment, slamming the door behind her.

———

After watching Tory leave, Miranda turned her eyes on her brother. "What the hell is wrong with you?"

Dazed, Charlie was still staring at the empty space where Tory had been. "I don't know. It was like my mouth was on autopilot." He dropped onto one of the barstools that lined the kitchen island.

Narrowing her eyes, feeling skeptical, Miranda said, "Bullshit. You're as careful with your words as I am."

"I know. Usually." Charlie glued his eyes to the pale granite countertop, refusing to look at her.

Miranda slapped her hand on the countertop to get his attention. "Well. You've really messed things up now. She was the one for you, and you know it."

Miranda knew that Charlie was never cruel to the women he brought home—quite the opposite, actually. He might not offer them anything long term, but he was really nice about it. She would never have let her little brother act otherwise.

She thought of the shadow that had crossed his face the night before, when they'd been waiting for the elevator. Something had been riding Charlie for days now, ever since Chalk had brought him the Dunworth case.

He finally looked at her. "I had another nightmare last night, a bad one. And she saw it."

"Tory freaked out about your nightmare?" Miranda was surprised —Tory didn't freak out about anything. But she was also worried. Charlie's nightmares had stopped years ago. If they were back, she had more to worry about than an ugly morning-after scene.

"No," Charlie said. "Just the opposite. She was amazing. She talked me through it, and didn't act weird or anything."

"Well that sounds a lot more like her." She glared at him. "That is definitely a reason to drag her through the mud this morning."

"Will you let me finish?"

"I'm still deciding actually. After that performance, do you really deserve to tell your side of the story?"

Charlie snorted. "Probably not."

Miranda waved her hand, *carry on*.

"We went back to sleep—and I was able to sleep, which is a miracle. And when I woke up this morning, I felt so…"

Miranda raised her eyebrows. "What? How did you feel? You might as well be honest with yourself because you can't make things any worse."

"I felt ashamed. I felt embarrassed that she'd seen me so weak. All I could think about was how I could make her leave so that I wouldn't have to face her again."

Miranda rolled her eyes, heaved a deep sigh, prayed for

patience, and then repeated the entire process. Her brother could be such an idiot. "You must know that Tory would never think badly of you because of a nightmare? You burned everything down with the one woman—the only woman that you have *ever* cared for—over this?"

"I'm not talking about the nightmares," Charlie said, his voice barely above a whisper. "What if she found out why I'm having them?"

That's when Miranda realized that something was off, way off, with her brother.

"Charlie, what is the matter?" She took in the black circles under his eyes, his pale skin.

Charlie reached out to her, palm up. "I think something is really wrong with me."

And then he told her about the bloody watch, about why he punched Chalk, about the things he couldn't stop seeing whenever he closed his eyes, and about the nightmares that maybe weren't nightmares at all.

————

Carrying her heels and her purse, Tory took the elevator down from Miranda's apartment, walked out through the tall steel-and-glass lobby, and opened the doors into the bright morning sun. She didn't have sunscreen with her, so she walked quickly, down Admiralty Way, cutting over to Washington toward the water, then up Pacific to the house she shared with her landlord in Venice Beach. One block from the ocean, Tory's apartment was on the first floor of the home of a former prime-time star named Honoria. To everyone in the neighborhood, Honoria was called Ms. Honey.

In the 1980s, Ms. Honey had leading roles in two police procedurals, once as a feisty lieutenant, once as a cop's long-suffering wife. Although she played tough characters on screen, Ms. Honey was a softie in real life. She was no more than five-foot-one and still slender—and she didn't look anywhere near her real age, which was somewhere in her mid-fifties. Her hair remained raven black. Her light-brown skin was unlined. Her French last name that had appeared on screen was apparently her real name, and so was her Louisiana accent—which she'd learned to camouflage on film.

Ms. Honey never had kids, and when Tory showed up a few years ago as she was finishing medical school, answering Ms. Honey's ad for a tenant, Ms. Honey promptly adopted her. *You clearly need someone to look after you, chérie,* she said.

Tory hadn't thought she needed adopting, given her parents' proximity. They told her they were happy to have her live at home during residency. Tory could believe it—they hardly noticed she was there most of the time.

Tory moved into Ms. Honey's apartment just as she was starting her residency. Her parents—the Doctors Murphy—were legends at the UCLA Medical Center long before Tory attended medical school there. They were researchers—not clinicians—and Tory's entire life was spent listening to them discuss their research over dinner, watching them spend late nights in their shared office while she sat just outside of it, reading. Watching them go to work together while she walked to school alone. She knew their work saved thousands of lives. Everyone told her so, frequently.

Ms. Honey's apartment had been a blessing, one made of ocean air and room—one of her own. Then there was Ms. Honey herself, who noticed when Tory got home. Who asked her about her day. Who was, really, a nosy landlady, but one with a big heart. Ms. Honey had known all along just what Tory needed—someone to notice her and care about her. Soon, Tory realized she'd been wrong, and Ms. Honey had been right. Tory had needed adopting after all.

After her twenty-minute stroll home, leaving behind Miranda's condo and Charlie's awful words, Tory typed in the code on the gate's keypad and entered her yard. Ms. Honey was outside tending to her plants. Daisy, Tory's dog, lolled around in the grass.

Daisy was a rescue from the local animal shelter. She was a forty-pound mutt, with dark brown dapples and heterochromia: one brown eye and one blue. When Tory had been looking for a dog, she'd had only two requirements: the dog had to love all of the people Tory loved, and she had to be a great runner. Daisy met both requirements —even if she had been horribly malnourished when Tory first brought her home.

Ms. Honey looked up from her oleander and took in Tory's outfit. Chuckling, she said, "I know the walk of shame when I see it. But usually you don't look so angry when you get home."

Plopping down in the Adirondack chair next to Daisy, Tory filled in Ms. Honey about the pleasant events of the evening, and the disastrous events of the morning.

"You've been friends with this boy for how long, now?"

"Years! That's why I'm so annoyed. I feel like I should have seen this side of him by now."

Ms. Honey tapped her chin. "Why do you think you haven't?"

"Because I haven't slept with him before?"

Ms. Honey didn't look convinced. "There could be another reason."

Tory shook her head. "That's the only logical answer."

"Or, maybe it could be, in all the years you've known him, something's changed recently to make him act out. You usually have a good sense about things. You wouldn't have gone home with a boy you thought was bad for you."

Tory nodded. Ms. Honey was right. Tory did usually have good sense, at least about her flings.

She'd never really had a relationship. For a long time, she blamed her singlehood on residency and working long hours in the ED. Before that, she blamed it on medical school, and the hours she had to spend studying. And before that, on the hours she spent studying in college in order to get into medical school. She'd always had an excuse for why nothing ever lasted long—she met plenty of wonderful guys. But when they pressed her for more, she declined. *Too busy*, she'd say. *I have work. Long hours.*

It's just not a good time for something serious.

It wasn't until recently that she realized it had never been a good time, ever.

She hadn't been a nun. With all of her experience, she was pretty good at selecting her friends-with-benefits. All morning, she'd been blaming herself for making such a bad decision with Charlie the night before. But what if Ms. Honey was right? What if she'd read Charlie correctly all these years—and something new was wrong with him, now?

She thought of the awful nightmare—no, flashback—she'd witnessed the night before. His thrashing, the desperation in his voice.

"I'm going running," she said to Ms. Honey. Looking down at Daisy, she said, "Come on, girl. Let's hit the road."

After throwing on her running gear and snapping a leash on Daisy's collar, Tory dashed out the gate full-speed, heading north. Her route took her from Venice through Santa Monica, a hard pace. If she ran anything slower than a six-minute mile, she felt, well, like a failure. She needed to feel her lungs ache. She needed to feel her legs burn. She needed to feel alive, *real*.

Her loop took her about seven miles. As she walked the final quarter of a mile, cooling off, Daisy looked ready to go another seven. The vet thought Daisy was part Australian Shepherd, the source of both her heterochromia and her endurance. Once they again stood outside the gate of their home, Tory leaned down and kissed Daisy's head. Daisy looked up, meeting her eyes, panting lightly.

"Well, Daisy," she said. "If I can train myself to be a runner, I can train myself to do anything." She punched in the gate code. "I can find a nice, normal guy. Get a nice, normal job that doesn't require twenty-hour shifts." She stepped through, into the yard. "Have two and a half kids and a picket fence." After shutting the gate, she unclipped Daisy's leash. "I already have the dog. The rest is easy."

Chapter Eight

After breakfast on Friday, Charlie and Miranda dressed like lawyers and headed to the Los Angeles County Jail. Charlie handed Miranda the Dunworth case file to read as he drove.

"I don't understand," Miranda said as he headed downtown. "Their parents were rich." Flipping through the file, she shook her head. "Why didn't he pay to stay in the Beverly Hills Jail? It's only a hundred dollars a day. He should never have been transferred to County. I understand that the judge didn't give him bail given the severity the crime, but County? Why?"

"Look at the sister's address."

Miranda flipped through the pages, then she blew air out through her teeth. "She lives in a dump in North Hollywood? Where's all the money going?"

"Something isn't right." Charlie intended to find out what.

Once they passed through security at the jail, they waited in an interview room for their client to be brought in. Miranda had her laptop out for note taking. Charlie had the file open next to a notepad, pen, and audio recorder.

A few minutes later, their client shuffled in wearing a jumpsuit and shackles. Charlie raised his eyebrows at the guard, nodding at the cuffs. The guard shook his head.

Ridiculous, Charlie thought.

Awkwardly, their client took a seat across the table. Nodding at him, Charlie switched on the recorder, then spoke the date, location, and the names of the people in the room.

Next, speaking to their client, Charlie said, "I'm Charlie George. This is my paralegal, Miranda. Do we have your permission to record this meeting?"

Michael Dunworth looked up for the first time, meeting Charlie's eyes first. For a moment, Charlie couldn't breathe. The kid looked no more than fifteen years old.

"Sure." He even sounded young, his voice high-pitched and soft.

Charlie stayed focused as best as he could. "We're your legal team. Our firm took your case pro bono."

Michael nodded.

"That means we're representing you for free."

Calmly, Michael said. "I know what pro bono means."

The kid didn't sound sullen or angry, or even bored. He sounded like today was just a normal day in his life, like meeting with a lawyer about his homicide case was an ordinary thing for him to be doing.

"Great," Charlie said. "I'm required to give you that information though. I'd like to review the facts of the case with you. The file we have on you is really thin."

"Sure." He sat still in his seat, calm and ready. His small build made him seem younger, Charlie realized. Where Charlie and Miranda were built like Vikings, Michael Dunworth looked small-boned, even fragile.

Charlie glanced at Miranda to see what her take on this kid was, but she was watching Michael intently, tapping away at her keyboard.

"You were home from college for spring break when the shooting occurred?"

"I shot my parents when I was home from spring break, yes."

Charlie wanted to groan at the kid's words. Charlie had used the passive voice on purpose. "How old were you when the shooting occurred?"

"I was twenty."

"Who was present?"

"My mom, my dad, and my sister, Amanda."

"Your sister, Amanda Dunworth, was seventeen, and a senior in high school?"

"Yes."

Glancing at Miranda, Charlie confirmed that she was still studying Michael, still taking notes. He would need her thoughts on this interview later.

"Where is Amanda now?"

"She lives alone in an apartment. In NoHo."

"Why there?"

For the first time, Michael's peaceful façade slipped. "What?"

"Why does she live in a studio apartment in a dangerous neighborhood in NoHo? Where's all the money she inherited from your parents?"

"I—I hadn't really thought about it." Ruffled, Michael glanced at the metal tabletop as though the answer would be written there.

"You didn't think to ask her how she was living?"

"I told her to lay low after the publicity got to be bad. I didn't want her to be…tainted by my case."

Pausing at Michael's words, Charlie thought of his sister, how she'd believed she was tainted once, and so she'd run away to Los Angeles to protect Charlie. Charlie had tracked her down and saved her life. He knew something about how siblings could have misguided ideas about protecting one another.

Leaning forward in his seat, Charlie said, "She's been through a lot. I can understand that you want to protect her. Can you tell us more about the abuse she suffered?"

Michael stiffened at the question, but he didn't shy from answering. "Amanda kept it secret for years, even from me. I don't know how she did it. When I asked her why, she told me she felt ashamed. It's such a cliché, I know. I hate that she was afraid to tell me." Michael squeezed his hand into a fist. "But then she did, the summer before I left for college. Part of the problem was our mom— Amanda had told her years before." Pausing, Michael had to rein in his obvious anger. "Our mom did as much damage as our father. Our father abused her, but our mom shamed her, told her to keep the abuse a secret. So Amanda never told anyone." On his last words, he slammed his fist down on the metal table. He looked up at the ceiling.

"I'm sorry. You'd think I'd have gotten these emotions under control by now."

For the first time, Miranda spoke. "You don't have to apologize. Not to us."

Examining her, Michael tilted his head one way, and then the other. "I see it now. You're his sister."

Miranda smiled her close-lipped smile, the one she used either when she was about to cause trouble, or when she was impressed. "Correct."

"Amanda and I look alike too. People used to think we were twins." Michael looked back at Charlie. "I bet people say the same about you."

Charlie nodded. "They do."

"They won't say it to us anymore. Not if I'm in prison for the rest of my life."

"That's why we're here," Charlie said. "To make sure that doesn't happen. Tell us what happened next."

Michael Dunworth looked skeptical, but he continued. "The summer before I went back to college, I gave my parents an ultimatum. I said to my mom that she had to move out, and take my sister with her. My mom said she wouldn't do it, that she'd be broke because of the prenup." Michael sounded so betrayed when he described his mother's choice, money over her children. "So then I confronted my father. I told him to stop or I'd go to the cops. At first my father denied molesting Amanda. I was so angry that I was about to dial 911 right then. When he saw that I was serious, he stopped denying and agreed to stop. He was weeping in our living room, the coward." When talking about his father, there was no betrayal in Michael's voice, only scorn and anger.

"Tell us about that morning."

"I'd just gotten home from break. I go to school on the east coast."

"Where?" Miranda asked.

"Princeton."

Miranda's eyebrows raised slightly, and Charlie knew what she was thinking. Of all the top schools, Princeton was the toughest for a rich kid to con his way into. It's where Miranda herself would have gone if she hadn't sacrificed herself to stay home and take care of their mother, attending Cameron University instead.

Michael Dunworth was no rich kid who bought his way into college. No, this kid was smart. He'd had a promising future. And now he sat across from them in a jumpsuit.

"The night I got home, I could tell something was wrong with Amanda. I took her out to dinner at our favorite spot in Santa Monica. Finally, I asked her directly, and she told me dad hadn't stopped like he'd promised." Michael paused. "You have to understand, Amanda is so small." He gestured at himself. "I'm basically an elf. Amanda looks like a tween. It's what my dad likes, the pervert."

"Liked," Charlie said.

"Yeah." Michael agreed. "Liked."

Snorting a little, Miranda said, "An elf?"

Michael tried to fight a smile, and failed. "Sorry. It's the first word that came to mind."

Here was another good reason to bring Miranda along, Charlie thought. Even the darkest interviews didn't faze her. And the darkest interviews were the ones most in need of some levity—which he could count on Miranda to provide. The levity kept the interviews on track.

"What happened at breakfast?" Charlie asked.

"I confronted my parents about the abuse. I said, *You promised you would stop. I told you what would happen.* I held up my phone, ready to call the police. My dad said, *You think they'll believe you? Two children? Over me?* And I realized he was right. He's a retired state senator. A corporate attorney. A former judge. We were going to look like bratty kids. Our own mother supported his side of the story." Michael's sadness was evident in the way he yanked his hair. "I begged him to stop. He said, *Make me.* So I ran to his room, grabbed the gun he kept in his bedside table, ran back, and shot them both."

Charlie looked at Miranda, and this time she met his eyes, brows raised. She nodded.

They were going to win. This was an easy case. The theories were clear: Heat of passion. Imperfect defense of another. A simple plea to voluntary manslaughter, and the kid might never see the inside of a jail cell. If he did, he could serve on the weekends in Beverly Hills.

They only needed one thing.

"You didn't murder your parents, Michael," Charlie said, carefully.

"What do you mean?" Michael's tone revealed that he thought Charlie might be a little off his rocker.

"I mean, although what you did is a type of homicide, it is not legally murder. It's called a 'heat of passion' killing, which is, legally, a lesser crime than murder. It falls squarely into something called 'voluntary manslaughter.' You don't even need to go to trial. We will negotiate a plea with the prosecutor."

For the first time, Michael's expression changed from one of complacency to one of hope. "What do I have to do?"

"Nothing, really. We have your story. You'll need to tell it again to the prosecutor, on the record, just as you told it to us. And we'll need to interview your sister, and get her story on the record—"

"No." Michael's voice was emphatic.

"But we need her to corroborate—" Charlie said.

Michael cut him off. "Amanda is off-limits."

Putting her hand on Charlie's to silence him, Miranda spoke. "Tell us about your sister."

Michael took a deep breath. "I won't make her go through that again."

She spoke in a calming voice. "Tell us what she went through."

"We were all over the news when I killed my parents. It was bad enough, what I did. But someone at the police station leaked Amanda's interview with the cops, and the story of her abuse was everywhere."

"You don't want her to suffer anymore." Miranda spoke quietly, slowly.

"I couldn't protect her. For seven years, I couldn't protect her. Even after they were dead, I still couldn't protect her." He sounded close to tears. "I gave her my inheritance—all of it—I want her to have everything so she can protect herself."

Miranda said, "You're protecting her now."

Michael nodded.

Charlie felt the frustration building as he watched his sister converse with his client. The kid didn't know what he was talking about. How did he plan on protecting his sister while he was serving a life sentence? Amanda Dunworth might have money, but she was living alone in a neighborhood where she might end up mugged or worse while she walked to her damned car.

Michael was abandoning her, not protecting her.

Breaking into the conversation, Charlie said, "You're charged with first degree murder. *First degree.* Right now, the plea offer on the table is second degree—that's all the prosecution will let you plea to with the evidence we have. If we go to trial, based on what you've said, they will win if they charge you with second-degree murder. All of the evidence points to a rich kid killing his parents for money." Charlie let his words hang in the air. "Are you willing to risk that?"

"Yes."

Charlie slammed his hand on the table in frustration.

Miranda kicked his foot.

Charlie knew what to do in a situation like this. He was supposed to change the subject. Ask something innocuous. "How are you sleeping?"

"Pretty well, actually. I'm finally no longer worried about Amanda. Being here is better than being in their house ever was."

Hearing the peaceful tone of Michael's voice, the urgency Charlie felt surged even more strongly. Michael, who'd shot his own parents, was sleeping peacefully.

What had Lala said about Miranda yesterday? *Her conscience is clear.* And so was Michael Dunworth's.

Looking at Michael, at his calm face and his hands resting on the metal table, Charlie's memories ripped him from the interview room and into a different room, a large room with large windows, in his parents' home back in North Carolina. His mother stood before him, his sister beside him.

His sister, whom he couldn't protect, and his mother, whom he couldn't save.

He couldn't let Michael Dunworth be punished for a crime that wasn't a crime.

Pleading, Charlie said, "Let me save you."

"I don't need saving."

Charlie believed him.

"And if you talk to my sister," Michael said, "I'll fire you and plead guilty to murder."

Closing her laptop, Miranda stood. "We understand, Michael. We won't do anything without your permission."

"You're the older one." Michael smiled. "I couldn't tell at first. But it's clear now."

Miranda nodded. "You're correct." Turning to Charlie, she said, "Get the guard. It's time to go."

———

ONCE THEY WERE IN THE CAR, HEADING HOME, CHARLIE STARTED THE debriefing. "Was he telling the truth?"

"Yes," Miranda said.

"About which part?"

"All of it. Including the part where he said he'll fire us and plead guilty to murder if you go near Amanda."

Squeezing the steering wheel, Charlie said, "I can't let him go down for this. I just can't." The car felt small, suddenly, like the roof was pressing down on him, like there wasn't enough air.

"Little B." Miranda squeezed his forearm. "He's not you."

Charlie laughed, trying to fool her into thinking everything was okay, when everything was very much not okay. "I know that."

Miranda released his arm. "Then act like it."

Charlie shrugged. "It's hard, knowing that it could have been me in there."

Miranda scoffed. "That would never have been you."

"Only because of who we are, because of Dad."

"That's not why. The situation was entirely different. The truth is out now, Charlie. Even the prosecutor back home knows exactly what happened and agrees that what you did would never have even warranted an arrest."

Even as he heard her words, he couldn't make himself believe her.

"You know," Miranda said, "when you first came out to L.A., and you were obviously not okay, I was relieved. That meant I wasn't the only one messed up by that awful day. But then you got over it so quickly. I didn't question it—but maybe I should have. I don't know how you can put something like that behind you."

"I don't think I have. I think I pushed it really far down, and now it's back."

"I think you're right." Miranda sounded worried. That was a bad sign. "I think you should hand off this case to someone else."

"No. I can't do that. This one is too important."

"Charlie." She rested her hand on his forearm again. "That's why you have to hand it off."

"I can do it, Miranda." He glanced at her. "You can keep me on track, okay?"

Miranda sighed. "I can try."

Chapter Nine

Back at their apartment, Charlie and Miranda unpacked their things on the dining table like they had so many times before. Once they were ready, Charlie dialed the prosecutor handling Michael Dunworth's case, setting his phone on speaker.

The prosecutor answered, expecting their call.

"George," she said.

"I'm here too, Sunita," Miranda said.

"Ah. Hello, other George."

Charlie spoke. "We'll plead to voluntary man for Michael Dunworth."

There was a long pause on the other end of the line before Sunita spoke again. Meeting Miranda's eyes, Charlie hoped against all logic that Sunita would give them a lucky break.

"I don't like this case," Sunita finally said. "I never liked Gray Dunworth. When he was a judge, everyone knew he was dirty, and I don't just mean corrupt. I mean the young girls. I mean trafficking. They were building a federal case against him and his friends. It's an open secret." She paused. "But I don't have any evidence to hang voluntary manslaughter on."

"We'd have Dunworth's sworn statement."

"It's not enough. Give me something else."

"You have the witness statement from the sister at the time of arrest—which your office leaked, by the way."

Sunita paused. "That was not good."

"It wasn't," Charlie said. "It's hurting my case."

"If it's any consolation, we caught the guy who did it. Three months suspension without pay."

Miranda raised her brows. That was a really big suspension for leak. But the leak had jeopardized a high-profile murder case, so it made sense.

"Regardless," Sunita continued, "the witness statement is still not enough. I need more."

Miranda clamped her hand on his wrist and shook her head vigorously. *No*, she mouthed. *No.*

"What about a sworn statement from his sister, too? This is a straight-up heat of passion killing. An imperfect defense of another, too, protecting his minor sister from certain future harm. It couldn't be more clear cut."

"If I have them both, I can make it happen. I'd be happy to make it happen. The sister's sworn testimony, plus the case the FBI has built so far, will be enough."

"Thanks, Sunita."

"This is an ugly one, George. I'm glad he has you on his side. Like I said, I don't like this case at all."

Charlie smiled. "You know what, Sunita? You're all right when you're not trying to rip me apart."

Sunita laughed. "I don't think you have anything to worry about from me. Bye, Miranda."

"Bye, Sunita. Come over to my pool sometime. The retirees miss you."

"Sure thing. You have my number."

After hanging up the call, Charlie looked at his sister. "I have to interview Amanda."

"You do not have to interview Amanda. In fact, you must not interview Amanda." Miranda rested her palm on her forehead and shook her head. "When did I get so sensible?"

"I'll get Sunita to subpoena her."

"He'll plead guilty before Amanda ever answers that subpoena."

Frustration surged. "God damn it. There has to be something I can do."

"Give yourself some time to think on it," Miranda said. "You'll come up with some brilliant solution; you always do. Remember, you said you would listen to me on this one."

He gritted his teeth.

"Don't make me go behind your back."

"You'd rat me out to Birch?" he said, horrified.

"Of course not. I'd lie to a paralegal and say you thought the case would be better for a first-year associate and get it handed off."

Charlie felt desperation churning in his stomach. "Please don't do that to me. Give me a chance to win."

Miranda paused, looking him over. "Answer me this. Do you want to win it for him, or for you?"

Charlie knew the right answer. But he also knew that his sister would know that he was lying. "For me."

"Well, at least you're not deluding yourself. But please, don't be stupid."

"I won't." At least, he hoped so.

———

THAT EVENING, CHARLIE STOOD AT THE VERY END OF THE FARTHEST DOCK of Marina del Rey, a long, wooden arm reaching out into the Pacific. Behind him, yachts valued in the millions floated alongside ratty houseboats with paint peeling off the sides, different worlds brushing right up against one another. Light from the setting sun reflected off the tower where Miranda had bought her condo, where he lived with the sister whose life he'd saved with a gunshot.

Miranda, falling to the floor, eyes dull, half-open. Dying.

Charlie, gun in his hand.

His mother Sorcha, blood blooming on her chest.

To save his sister, he'd had to pull the trigger.

But no. That wasn't right. He couldn't lie to himself any longer.

He hadn't needed to fire the gun. He'd chosen to, in a moment of panic. And he'd chosen wrong.

His mother should still be alive.

After taking a sip of the beer in his hand, he looked down at his fingers. He remembered the pillow he'd yanked from the sofa and pressed to his mother's body, trying to stop the blood and keep her alive. He'd dialed 911 with one hand, screamed into the phone— Miranda dying next to him, his mother dying under his hand, *by his hand.*

He couldn't remember the words he'd said on the phone, not exactly, but he remembered the sound echoing off of the mullioned glass in the sunroom of his parents' old southern mansion. He remembered screaming. *Help.*

He chugged the last of the beer, then tossed the bottle into a large trash bucket on the dock. He picked up the second beer he'd set at his feet. The only way to manage the memories that the Dunworth case had dredged up was to drink them to death, it seemed. So that's what he planned to do. Watching the sun dip lower, he drank half of the second bottle.

Unbidden, Tory Murphy's face drifted into his mind. Not her gorgeous smile from Thursday night, but her look of betrayal from that morning—when he'd said so many hurtful things. He didn't talk like that about anyone, let alone someone he actually cared for. Maybe that was the problem—he'd never actually cared for anyone he'd slept with before. There'd been plenty of girls; he'd heard Miranda call him *slutty* that morning, and she wasn't wrong. But Tory —Tory was special. She'd always been special. *The one,* Miranda had called her.

That's why he'd held her at arm's length all this time.

And then, suddenly, this week of all weeks, he decided it would be a great time to get her in the sack?

He tossed the second bottle in the trash and picked up the third.

He was a complete ass, but he didn't know what to do about it. One thing was certain, he needed to keep his distance from Tory, at least in that way. He was liable to hurt her worse if he didn't.

He finished the third beer, then tossed it in the can with the others, the shattering glass causing a feeling of satisfaction.

He headed back down the dock, his gait unsteady, taking care not to trip on a rope and end up in the ocean. Miranda would never let him live that down.

When he was back on land, he tilted his head back, looking up at the building, at the very top, where his sister was waiting for him.

Where she would have questions about what he'd told her earlier about his nightmares, about the guilt he still felt over their mother's death. About his behavior earlier at the jail with Michael Dunworth. About Tory, even. He didn't want to answer those questions right now. Maybe not ever.

So he kept walking, heading to the Typhoon instead.

This wasn't his first drunken walk to the bar, not hardly. He could make his way there plastered, in the dark, and alone. No problem. But it was his first time making the walk with his guts ripped open.

When he stumbled in, Lala took one look at him and shook her head. "Don't you sit at my bar looking like that. You're bad for business."

He ambled over and winked. "How can you say no to this pretty face?"

Rolling her eyes, Lala pulled a bottle from the wall, mixing him a quick gin and tonic. "Here. Take your charming somewhere else."

"Someday you'll fall for me."

Lala pointed at an empty booth. "Sit before you fall over and I have to call the cops."

Charlie grinned at her, then took a seat at the booth. Once he was settled, he dropped his façade. Lala might grouch at him, but he knew she liked him a lot, him and Miranda both. But keeping up appearances was wearing him out.

The Dunworth kid. He couldn't stop thinking about him, about everything he and his case had brought to the surface of Charlie's mind. Charlie sucked down his G&T and signaled Lala for another.

She rolled her eyes and started to pour.

Moments later, a hand dropped his drink on the table. Before he could thank Lala for bringing his drink over, a voice he didn't recognize spoke. "Move over, big boy."

A woman he didn't know—skinny, blonde, stacked, everything he usually loved in a girl—dropped down next to him, setting her drink next to his.

"You look lonely," she said. "Let me help you with that."

Charlie gave her the half-smile that had girls dropping their drawers all over the southern United States of America. He asked, "What's your name, darlin'?"

"Goodness," she whispered. "Is that accent real?"

He chuckled. "Absolutely."

"I'm Regina," Her hazel eyes were half-lidded. Then she grabbed his shirt by the placket, yanked him to her, and kissed him hard.

Every thought fell out of his head.

At that moment, Charlie was willing to do just about anything to empty his brain of the things he didn't want to think about.

He wrapped his hands around Regina's tiny waist and stood her up on her platform heels. Taking her hand, he led her to the bathrooms in the back of the bar. He banged his fist on the door to the men's room, and when no one called out, he opened the door and looked around. Finding the stalls empty, he brought her in with him and locked the door behind them.

"Nice to meet you, Regina," he said. "I'm Charlie." Then they were kissing again, and he lifted her up and pressed her back against the door. She hooked her ankles behind his back, and within minutes she was screaming with pleasure. Those screams and his own raw need drove every awful memory from his head.

Afterward, she washed her hands in the sink while he leaned back against the door.

She glanced at him over her shoulder. "Damn, Charlie No-Last-Name, where have you been all my life?"

He gave her his winning smile again. "Here and there."

"If I give you my number, will you use it?" She leaned one hip against the sink and crossed her arms.

"Hard to say," he said. "But I'll take it."

Pulling a card from her purse, Regina pressed it into his palm. Then she reached around him and opened the door.

On the other side of the door stood Lala.

Regina gave him a little wave, then she drifted away to join the Friday night crowd that was growing on the patio outside.

Hands on her hips, Lala glared up at him. Somehow, even though he had more than a foot on her, she made him feel six inches tall.

"I make no judgments about how a woman chooses to get her rocks off," Lala said, gesturing at the crowd that had enveloped Regina. "But you, Charlie George, do not have permission to funk up my bar. You want to sleep with someone, you find a bed in a room with a door."

"There was no time," he said, rubbing the back of his head and giving her a grin.

"Are you serious? What is wrong with you?" Lala sounded really angry. Lala never got angry with him.

"I'm a little drunk I think."

"Not too drunk, though. The lady looked happy enough."

Running his hand down his face, he felt the frustration mounting. Every bit of oblivion that the drink and the sex had brought him was being washed away under the wave of Lala's scolding. "Get off my back, Lala."

"Get off your *back?* Oh no. You do not get to be rude to me." She pointed at the door. "It's time for you to leave."

"Come on, Lala. I just want to sit and have another drink."

"Not tonight. Get out."

"Jesus. You're acting like my mom." As soon as the words left his mouth, Charlie knew he'd screwed up. He pressed his lips together in a tight line, waiting for the storm he knew was coming.

Lala leaned forward, as angry as he'd ever seen her. "Go home, jackass, or I'm texting your sister."

"Fine. I'll go."

The last thing he needed was a furious Miranda showing up, standing shoulder-to-shoulder with Lala. Neither of them cared about the sex. But they cared about him disrespecting a woman in her place of business. He'd stepped wrong the moment he insulted Lala.

What was wrong with him? He adored Lala. He didn't want to treat her badly, but he'd done it anyway. He couldn't stop himself.

He was heading off the rails.

He didn't know what to do about it.

Chapter Ten

Monday morning, Tory rode in Daphne's car, drinking a hot cup of coffee that Daphne had brought for her. Daphne was scoping out locations for a film she was helping produce, and she'd brought Tory along to assist as an expert.

All morning, Daphne had led her from medical clinic to medical clinic, looking for the right spot for filming, for the something special that would catch Daphne's professional eye.

Tory's job, apparently, was to explain to the medical staff what was going on and to lend what credibility she could to the strange questions Daphne asked.

Mostly, though, Tory suspected Daphne had brought her because of what had happened on Friday with Charlie.

"I don't care about what Charlie said about me," Tory said. "Sure, it sucks to hear the awful things a guy says about you when he thinks you aren't there." Tory herself was guilty of saying some not-nice-things about guys after they'd left her apartment.

"Charlie should never have said those things," Daphne said. "He's supposed to be your friend."

"All friendship bets are off once you sleep together. Those are the rules." And she'd broken them. It was all her fault. "The worst part is I'm worried I've lost my friendship with Miranda. I said some horrible things to Charlie before I left, and she heard me. I wouldn't blame her for being mad at me about that."

"She might be more understanding than you think."

"But she's also super protective of Charlie. I would imagine that she's allowed to call him names, but not anyone else. I haven't heard from her since Friday, which is unusual because we usually talk every day." Sipping her coffee, she continued. "Before I met you guys, all I did was work all the time. I didn't really have friends." It was true. Tory had always had a hard time making close friends. Daphne had basically grabbed a hold of her and refused to let go.

Turning left, Daphne said, "I'm pretty sure Miranda would be pissed if you stopped hanging out with her because of her idiot brother. You're her best friend. She doesn't make friends easily, either."

Tory asked, "Should I just send her a text like nothing is wrong?"

"Nothing *is* wrong, you dodo." Daphne took a sip of her own coffee. She glanced at Tory, her eyes kind.

Tory had worried that Daphne was going to give her a hard time after what happened with Charlie. Daphne had warned her, after all. Instead, early that morning, Daphne had showed up with fresh coffee and dragged her out of the house, insisting that Tory help her. Tory enjoyed feeling useful, even if she wasn't making any money.

Worried about Miranda, Tory looked at her phone. Then she typed out a text: **Are we okay?**

Miranda wrote back immediately: **omg r u serious.**

Tory couldn't tell what that meant. **Yes?**

Miranda took a moment to reply. **will u go 2 the dance w me y/n?**

Tory smiled. Things were looking up. **Yes**.

Miranda: **ok we r going steady let's get margaritas 2nite.**

Tory leaned back in her seat. "OK, things are cool with Miranda."

"I told you."

A few minutes later, Daphne pulled into the lot of what her location scout had told her was a free women's clinic. Located just east of Santa Monica, the place looked faded and run down. There was no sign out front, just numbers indicating the address.

"This doesn't look like the right place," Daphne said. "Let me call Carrie."

To Tory, the building did look like the right place, based on what Daphne had told her about the clinic. Free clinics tended to look just like this—underfunded. And if they served women who might be in trouble, they might not have a sign.

But before she could explain any of her observations to Daphne, Daphne had dialed her almost-sister-in-law Carrie. Carrie was her fiancé Marlon's sister, as well as Daphne's location scout. "Carrie? It's Daph. I'm at the address you texted me. Yeah, that's the one. But it looks like a dump, and there's no sign. Oh yeah, there's a big metal door, security cams, the whole nine yards—Fort Knox for sure. OK, we'll head in. Thanks." Turning to Tory, she said, "Carrie says this is the place."

"Did she tell you that they keep a low profile because they serve a vulnerable patient population?"

Daphne's brows drew together. "Yes? How did you know?"

"You brought me along as a medical expert. I'm experting."

Daphne snorted, opening her door. "They're expecting us."

They climbed out of Daphne's car and headed to the entrance. As they stood on the cement step, a faded yellow awning shading them from the sun, Daphne pressed the buzzer. After a few moments, a woman's voice came over a speaker. "How can we help you?"

Daphne explained who they were and why they were there, and then the door unlocked.

A young Black woman in scrubs greeted them in the waiting room, her name tag reading only *Mary*. Tory glanced around. In the waiting room, there were two other women, one white, one Latina. The white woman was visibly pregnant and had a vivid black eye. Her gaze was fixed on the floor. The Latina woman had a baby in a carrier strapped to her chest, and she smiled at Tory.

Mary shook Daphne's hand, and then Tory's. "I'm Mary Jefferson, the office manager. I'm also a nurse. Everyone here does more than one thing."

"Daphne Saito," Daphne said, laying her hand on her chest. "Useless Hollywood leech. This is my friend, Dr. Tory Murphy, formerly of the Cedars-Sinai emergency department."

Turning to Tory, Mary raised her eyebrows. "Where do you work now?"

"I'm currently applying for new positions."

Gesturing for them to follow her through a door she opened with a keycard, Mary said, "Burnout?"

"No," Tory said. "Kind of the opposite, actually. I want more hands-on care with people. The ED is just so much triage, it felt like a never-ending stream of body parts after a while. Too impersonal."

"Wow," Mary said. "You want faces to go with your GSWs."

Tory laughed. "Yes, I guess you could put it that way."

"You'd fit right in here, then," Mary said. "Come on. Boss Lady Jean is right this way."

After leading them down a long hallway, Mary knocked on an open office door. "Hey Jean, your guests are here." Mary made introductions, indicating that the woman in the office was Dr. Jean Baker, the director of the clinic.

Jean Baker stood from behind her desk. She was a tall and lean white woman in her mid-fifties, with skin that had been abused by the elements and iron-gray hair cut short. On her desk and wall were photographs of a younger Jean in faraway places wearing shirts with the logo of Doctors Without Borders.

"Thank you, Mary," Jean said. "How's our nine o'clock doing?"

"I'm hoping we don't have to call an ambulance. She has two broken ribs. She should have come in sooner instead of waiting for her appointment."

"Make sure she knows we're staffed 24-hours before she leaves. And make sure she believes it."

"Sure thing." Mary left.

Closing the laptop on her desk, Jean folded her hands across the top. "So you're interested in shooting some scenes in my clinic."

"Yes ma'am," Daphne said. "But, to be honest, I didn't realize the clinic was so secret. Maybe using it as a set is a bad idea. I don't want to put your patients at risk."

"Your scout—Carrie? She mentioned you would only shoot in the interior of the building."

Daphne nodded. "That's correct. The exterior is a different building whose interior isn't the right fit."

"Then I don't mind. No one will be able to identify us if you don't shoot the exterior." She sighed. "And the money your company offered to donate in exchange for using our space is half of our operating budget for an entire year. I can't say no to that."

Tory's eyes widened. She didn't realize there would be such a significant financial transaction.

Daphne nodded. "Show us around, then. I'll see what I can do to make sure your clinic is the one we choose."

Jean smiled. "I'd appreciate that." Standing, Jean led them out the door and down the hallway. Gesturing to her right, she said, "These are the admin offices. Through this door are the exam rooms." She opened the door on her left with a keycard. "We keep tight security here. Our patients are exclusively women and women-identifying people who are at risk: domestic abuse and sexual violence victims, addicts, sex workers, and undocumented women who don't feel safe going to a hospital. Our security is strong, but just in case, we keep every section of the building locked. If abusers get in, they can't get far."

Daphne nodded, looking around, taking in things that Tory imagined were different than the things she herself noticed. Tory noted the old, but clean, linoleum tiles in a dark beige. The beige walls with a wooden hand rail like you'd see on a labor and delivery floor. The drop ceiling with clean white tiles. The exam room doors painted a bright, cheery yellow. To Tory's trained medical eye, it seemed that the clinic didn't have much, but that they made the most of what they had.

Inside the exam room Jean showed them, the exam table was upholstered in a bright yellow vinyl to match the doors. The countertop was a yellow laminate, and the cabinet doors were also yellow.

Everything was tidy, ready for patient care.

Daphne looked at Jean. "This is actually perfect. I won't have to convince anyone. What made you all decide on the bright color scheme?"

"Honestly," Jean said, "the yellow exam tables were deeply discounted. Those are the most expensive items in our office. But then Mary said something like, *There's enough darkness in the world,* and so we painted everything yellow to match, and here we are."

Tory spoke without thinking. "Mary's right."

Jean gave her an assessing look.

Tory smiled. She'd told the truth. She'd seen a lot of dark in her old job.

Daphne gave Jean a few more details, and told her that she'd follow up to finalize things.

Then, as they were leaving, Tory pulled Jean aside for a moment. "Can I ask you a quick question?"

Jean nodded, a concerned look on her face. "Do we need to go to my office?"

Shaking her head, Tory said, "Oh, no. This isn't private. I was just wondering, if I gave you my resume, whether you would consider me the next time you were hiring."

"Didn't Mary say you used to work in emergency at Cedars?"

"That's right."

"But you quit."

"Correct."

"Why?"

Tory tried to think of a reason Jean would believe, but decided to go with the truth instead. "Because I was looking for a place like this."

Jean nodded. "Send over your resume. I'll let you know if something opens up."

Tory felt a prickle of disappointment that Jean wasn't a little more positive, but she hid the emotion. "Wonderful. I'll send it as soon as I get home."

Back in the car, Tory tapped her finger against her chin, thinking about Jean's words about darkness in the world, and her thoughts drifted back to Charlie George.

Daphne started the car, her dark hair in a long ponytail over one shoulder.

"Hey Daph. Can I tell you secret?"

Daphne met her eyes, concerned. "Of course."

"I'm serious. You are the worst gossip. You have to keep this a secret."

"Fine, yes." Daphne pursed her lips at Tory's words, but she didn't try to defend herself. She looked over her shoulder to back out of the parking space. "Hey, are we going back to your house?"

"I don't care. Listen. When I stayed over at Charlie's, after we, you know. He fell asleep before me."

Daphne snorted. "Of course he did. He's a dude."

"Stop interrupting. After he fell asleep, he had the most horrible nightmare. He kept saying 'no' and talking to his mom—she's dead, right? And something about killing Miranda. And a gun." Tory paused, remembering how upsetting that night had been. "There's more, but just trust me. Something was wrong with him."

Daphne paused, and finally said, "What do you mean?"

"I mean, I worked in a hospital with lots of traumatized patients. What I saw Thursday night wasn't an ordinary nightmare. It was a PTSD flashback."

Silently, Daphne drove through West L.A. toward Tory's house. Tory kept waiting for Daphne to say something, anything, in response to what Tory told her. But she was silent and grim-faced.

"Well?" Tory said. "I can tell you're thinking about something."

"I am. But I don't know what I should tell you."

Frustrated, Tory snapped, "You had plenty to say about Charlie the other night."

Stopping at a red light, Daphne turned to face her. "He's not a puppy you can adopt like Daisy. He's a grown man, and he hurt you."

"I don't want to adopt him. But I think he might be in trouble. Did you know that on Wednesday, he came home from work early because he punched a coworker?"

Daphne's eyes widened in surprise.

"I couldn't believe it either."

In obvious frustration, Daphne tugged on her ponytail. "I can tell you this much. Charlie and Miranda watched their mother die. It was very traumatic for both of them, but they don't like to talk about it."

Shocked by the news, Tory said, "Why has Miranda never told me this before?"

"She's put it behind her. She's healed, I think. She's at peace. But Charlie, I don't think he ever had a chance to deal with it." Daphne rolled her eyes. "He's not good at dealing with stuff, period."

Annoyed with Daphne's harsh judgment of Charlie manifesting yet again, Tory said, "What is going on, Daphne? Charlie isn't so terrible. I mean, he was an asshole to me on Friday, but you've known him for years. You spend lots of time with him."

Daphne's ordinarily serene face clouded over. "I realize how I must sound to you. Like a backstabber or something. But Charlie is a womanizer. He's a shark lawyer. He's a rich playboy. I literally can't think of a good reason why you would want anything to do with him."

"Because he's a supersized version of Brad Pitt?"

Daphne groaned. "Be serious."

"Why? You're not. I tell you that your good friend's brother is in trouble, and you insult him."

"He slept with you and then said horrible things about you!"

"That's true." Tory considered the situation. "But Ms. Honey said something to me that is starting to make sense the more I think about it." *Something has changed recently to make him act out. You wouldn't have gone home with a boy you thought was bad for you.*

"Well?" Daphne said, impatient.

"When was the last time Charlie punched someone at work?"

Frowning, Daphne said, "Never."

"He's never done anything remotely like that because he's always calm, always under control. That's his thing. He might be a womanizer, but no woman would ever say that Charlie was an asshole to her. They always come back for more."

Daphne nodded in agreement. "They do. It's incredibly irritating."

"So what's changed?"

"No," Daphne said. "Stop it."

"No? No what?"

Parking in front of Tory's house, Daphne turned and took Tory's hand in both of hers. "Don't try to fix him."

"Why not? It sounds like he needs someone to help him. It might as well be me—especially since his other friends don't want to." Tory couldn't keep the frustration out of her voice.

Daphne dropped her eyes.

"How about we make a deal," Tory said. "I promise to be careful with Charlie. And you promise to let go of some of these prejudices you've developed. Try to see why he might act in ways you don't admire, especially when you also see him act in ways you do." Tory pulled her hand from Daphne's. "I know you have. Don't deny it."

Daphne nodded. "No, you're right."

"Sometimes people push other people away for a reason—remember Miranda?" Tory opened the car door. "Deal?"

"Yeah. Deal."

As Daphne drove off, Tory felt relieved to have won Daphne over to her point of view. But she wasn't sure she actually wanted to have anything to do with saving Charlie George, despite how much she jumped to his defense in Daphne's car. Sure, there was a part of her that wanted to solve the puzzle of his illness—she had few doubts about her diagnosis—but another part of her knew that getting close to him again might leave her open to being skewered once more, and she might not come through okay a second time.

Chapter Eleven

Around noon on Monday, Charlie hauled himself from bed. His pounding head reminded him how late he'd been drinking the night before. After forgiving him for being an ass on Friday night, Lala had allowed him back into the Typhoon, and he'd spent the weekend drinking himself into a fugue state. At least he'd tried to. No matter how blasted he got, he couldn't stop seeing his mother's face right before he pulled the trigger.

Over and over and over and over.

And over.

He stumbled into the shower. Once there, he leaned against the cold tiles. Turning on the water, he washed off the stink of liquor and sweat. He couldn't go on like this, but he didn't know what else to do.

Only one possibility kept creeping into his head.

He had to save Michael Dunworth.

He had to set one thing right.

Don't be stupid, Miranda had begged him. But saving Michael wasn't stupid. It was the only sane path that seemed open to him.

Amanda Dunworth was the key to saving her brother. Charlie knew one thing—he couldn't go alone to the home of a traumatized teenaged girl. He needed someone with experience with girls like Amanda. And there was no way Miranda was going with him, not after Miranda expressly forbade him from going. He could probably sneak around Miranda, he thought, but who could he get to go with him? Someone else at his firm?—No, Miranda would find out.

Inspiration struck: *Tory*. He needed Tory. Before she quit her job at Cedars, she worked with traumatized women every day. Tory would know just what to say to put Amanda Dunworth at ease.

Just as fast as the inspiration arrived, regret punched him in the gut. Friday morning, he'd said the most awful things to her. Jesus. He'd spoken every word he could think of to push her away, knowing it would hurt her, all because he'd been terrified of what she'd seen.

And the hell of it was, Miranda was right. Tory was the one. The only one who'd ever mattered. That's why he'd kept his distance for years. But now that his barriers had broken down, he'd headed straight for her.

But he didn't deserve someone as good as Tory Murphy. Not when he literally had blood on his hands.

Climbing out of the shower, he looked at himself in the mirror. He had three days' worth of beard. Dark eye circles. Overgrown hair in need of a trim. He didn't recognize himself, not the Charlie George who could get anything he wanted with either a wink or an imperious glare, depending on what the situation required. The Charlie George who was always impeccably in control.

No, the man in the mirror was a wreck.

He pulled on a pair of boxers and sat on the edge of his bed. Picking up his phone, he dialed Tory. He wasn't surprised when the call went to voicemail.

"Tory, it's Charlie. I realize I was a complete asshole when you were here Friday morning, and I'm sorry. I can't explain how sorry I am. I don't deserve to have you speak to me ever again, and I certainly don't deserve to have you help me with what I'm about to ask you to help me with." He took a deep breath. "There's this witness in an important case. She's an abuse victim, and I need you. I can't talk to her alone, and you—you're just the right person to go with me. I'll explain more if you call me back. Just—I'm sorry. I'm so sorry."

Hanging up the phone, he dropped his head in his hands.

Two minutes later his phone rang. It was her.

"Tory." He held his breath.

"I wanted to talk to you, too," she said.

"Really? To rake me over hot coals?"

She paused. "No, actually. But I can do that, if it would make you feel better."

"You know, it might." It would assuage his guilt a little.

"I thought so. Let's talk in person."

"Where?" Charlie couldn't believe she wanted to even look him in the face.

"I don't want to come there. You can come here."

"You'd let me into your home?"

"Of course not. But you can come into my yard."

Feeling like he'd been given a reprieve from the guillotine, Charlie got dressed—dressed to visit a witness, in a suit, hoping against hope —and drove over to Tory's.

Knocking on the garden gate, he was greeted by a dog's barking— the dog she'd adopted, whom he hadn't yet met.

"It's okay, Daisy," Tory crooned from the other side of the gate, and the barking stopped immediately.

The gate opened, and Tory stood before him in tiny running shorts and a tank top. For a moment, Charlie was speechless, staring at her perfectly toned legs—not skinny like Regina's, like those of every L.A. girl who threw herself at him when he took clients out on the town.

No, Tory had glorious curves and trim muscles and, as his hands recalled, the firmest ass he'd ever felt. More than that, she looked at him with a warmth that told him she could see him for what he really was, and, incredibly, she liked what she saw.

Once again, regret coursed through him.

"Are you finished?" Tory asked cheerfully, knocking him out of his reverie.

Not nearly, he thought.

"This way." She turned, and he was treated to a view of that perfect ass, one he'd never get to touch again, and it was his own stupid fault.

She led him to a pair of Adirondack chairs in the garden. She didn't seem to care that he was wearing Armani when she gestured for him to sit on the chipped wooden surface. He lowered himself into the chair. She dropped into the other one, the dog flopping down in the grass next to her.

"Is that Daisy?" he asked.

Tory nodded. "I've had her two months now, but it feels like two years." She sounded like she was in love, and Charlie felt an uncomfortable pang. "Do you like dogs?"

"I do, actually," he said.

"Miranda loves them! I was so shocked when she met Daisy and she basically turned into an entirely different person, rolling around in the grass." Tory laughed. "Miranda and nature are not things that go together."

Charlie nodded. "We weren't allowed to have pets."

"She told me. I wasn't either. And then with med school, and residency, it was too much time away from home."

Charlie understood. With the hours he billed at his firm, there was no way he could take care of a dog or even a hermit crab. He reached out and Daisy bounded over to him, shoving her head under his hand. He could do with some unconditional love right about now, he thought, looking into the dog's eyes, one blue, and one brown.

Staring into Daisy's open expression, Charlie realized this was a moment for truth. He inhaled deeply, exhaled slowly. "Do you remember when you were talking about how you quit your job? On my balcony last week? You said you had someone waiting at home for you."

Tory laughed. "I remember."

Charlie was not one to go for broke—it was too risky. But he was going to do it anyway. He had to make Tory understand that he felt something for her that was special. That he'd been afraid on Friday morning, and how sorry he was. She didn't have to forgive him, but he had to say the words.

"I was so..." He laughed at himself, remembering the moment. "Jealous. I couldn't figure out when you would have met someone, and fallen in love, and gotten so serious that you were living together. How could that have happened under my nose? I think that's when I knew for sure—when I thought that I'd lost you to someone else." Running his hand through his hair, he fumbled for the words. "You're so open and honest. But also so strong and fearless—and I've known these things for years. But thinking I'd blown my chance with you brought it all into focus." He paused again, thinking of some pretty words and then casting them aside. He'd go with simple, instead. "I'm so sorry I hurt you."

Tory was quiet. Too quiet. "I don't think we should talk about this."

"Will you please let me explain the rest?"

She paused. Took a breath as though to speak, then paused again. "Maybe later."

Charlie nodded. He would accept a *maybe*. It was more than he deserved. "I understand. I'm sorry I brought it up."

"Thanks." She looked down at her hands, where her fingers were interlocked.

He felt like an ass. Again.

"So," he said, changing the subject. "You said you wanted to talk to me about something?"

"No." Tory pointed at him. "You go first. You said you needed my help with a witness?"

He took a deep breath. "I want to hire you to help me interview a witness. She's an abuse victim, and I think you'd be helpful to have along, given your experience."

Tory looked interested. "I don't work for you, though."

"I have a consultant agreement in the car." He'd printed it out before he'd left home, just in case she said yes.

Tory laughed. "Of course you do."

Worried by her laugh, that she might be taking his request lightly, Charlie said, "The firm can pay you." The firm could pay her a lot, actually. They paid medical consultants hundreds per hour, and he could make sure she made top dollar.

Tory shook her head, frowning slightly. "Since I'm unemployed, I'll take the money. But I want something else from you, too. A favor."

Charlie wasn't a fan of open-ended balances owed. "Do you know what you might want?"

"I have an idea." Her face gave nothing away.

"Any chance you'll give me a hint?" He gave her his most charming half-smile.

She shook her head. "I'll tell you later, once we're done."

"All right. I agree."

Tory stood. "Come here, Daisy." Tory pointed to the far corner of the yard, where mulch surrounded a tree. Daisy trotted over and started sniffing around. To Charlie, Tory said, "Daisy needs to do some business, and then I need to clean myself up and get dressed." Tory pulled a green baggie from the pocket of her shorts.

Charlie reached for the bag. "Here, let me do that. You go get ready."

"Really? Charlie George scoops poop?"

Charlie laughed, mostly at himself. "I'm not above taking care of a good dog."

"All right," she said. "Tell me where we're heading."

"North Hollywood. Not the nice part."

"Yikes."

"Yeah." It wasn't a place where one wanted to stick out.

Tory pointed. "The trash bin is around the side of the house. Wait here, and I'll be out in a few minutes." She entered her apartment.

After Tory was out of sight, Charlie tilted his head back, staring at the cloudless sky, feeling the first glimmer of hope in days.

———

As she stepped outside and locked her apartment door, Tory took in Charlie, seated in the Adirondack chair with Daisy's head resting in his lap, completely disregarding how his bazillion dollar suit was getting more disheveled. Tied in a knot, the poop bag sat on the ground near his foot.

I think that's when I knew for sure—when I thought that I'd lost you to someone else.

What did he mean? Knew *what* for sure?

But thinking I'd blown my chance with you brought it all into focus.

Brought *what* into focus?

Did Charlie George *like* her?

No way. Not after all of these years, and not after last week. She must be hallucinating.

But she wasn't hallucinating the bag of scooped poop and the love he was showering on Daisy. It was enough to make her forget all of the horrible things he'd said. Almost.

She wanted to hear his explanation, first.

"I'm ready," she said.

He looked up when he heard her voice. "Hey—I just need to drop this in the trash."

"I can do it later."

"Naw. It's all right." When his deeper southern accent poked through his poshness, Tory always melted a little. Sometimes he did it on purpose. But right now, he was just regular Charlie. The guy she'd known for years. Flawless. Perfect. Who apparently scooped poop.

Focus, Tory Murphy.

In Charlie's car, Tory read and signed the contractor agreement of Charlie's law firm, ensuring her confidentiality during her employment on work-related matters, and her pay rate. She understood most of what the agreement said—she'd seen contracts like it before when her parents had been asked to be expert witnesses for medical malpractice cases. After she signed, Charlie filled her in on the case. Michael Dunworth, who'd killed his parents to protect his little sister from sexual abuse, would go to prison for life if his sister didn't testify to what she'd witnessed that morning—and to the abuse she'd suffered for years at the hands of her father.

After hearing the Dunworth name, Tory remembered when the case had hit the headlines months before. The sister had been trashed by the media. The brother had been painted as a killer after their parents' fortune. What an awful case for Charlie to handle alone. No wonder he'd asked her to come along. But something didn't sit right.

"I have a question," she said. "Michael *did* kill his parents. How isn't that murder?"

"Murder is a technical term. It refers to something premeditated," Charlie said. "Think of the words *cold blood* and you get the picture. Michael didn't plan to kill his parents—it was done in what we lawyers call the *heat of passion*, which makes him less culpable. He was also defending his sister from harm—and although the harm wasn't imminent, we can argue that it was ongoing and likely to occur again, given what his father said."

"So it's not murder because he was wound up and protecting his sister? That sounds like semantics. Words don't matter to the dead person." Tory paused to think. "I can understand these arguments about him killing his father, I suppose—but his mom? She wasn't abusing his sister. She might not have been perfect, but she wasn't the monster their father was."

Charlie went silent—so silent that Tory turned and looked at him. If he weren't driving on the freeway, his hands making subtle movements on the steering wheel, he would be a statue.

It seemed like an eternity before he spoke again. "You have to understand what *heat of passion* means. It means that you are provoked beyond your ability to think clearly." He paused again, seeming to consider his words. "In this case, Michael was provoked because his parents, *both* of his parents, taunted him with their refusal to stop the horrific abuse of his sister." He paused again. "And it was horrific."

Tory considered his words, trying to find the truth behind the legal jargon. She thought of the domestic violence victims who'd come to her emergency department over the years. She remembered the few she'd known who'd ended up killing their abusers. There weren't many, but there were a few. Some ended up in jail, but some didn't.

She knew from the stories she'd read that some of the women had planned the killings: purchasing guns, hiding them, waiting for the right moment. One had hidden in a closet until her boyfriend came home from his nightly visit to the bar, surprising him when he was too drunk to defend himself. Another one put poison in her husband's morning coffee. The murders she knew about had been carefully planned, not *heat of passion*. No—in the heat of passion, if these women tried to fight back, they would have been overpowered or even killed.

One thing was certain: never again would these women come into the emergency department with broken orbital bones or shattered eardrums, snapped ulnas or dislocated shoulders. Did they deserve to go to jail for stopping abuse they'd suffered for months or years?

What would it feel like to be so trapped? To see only one way out?

Tory asked, "Amanda's testimony is all you need for the prosecutor to agree to the plea deal?" Tory asked.

"Correct." His voice was still cold. "The prosecutor and I reached that agreement right after I spoke with Michael Dunworth."

After Charlie crossed the hills on the 405, he headed east. Finally, he exited, driving north into NoHo. They passed through the up-and-coming neighborhoods and eventually pulled into the parking lot of a two-story apartment building. Amanda Dunworth's building was far from the new brewpubs and tapas restaurants that were springing up in the central part of North Hollywood. No, this was a building that gentrification forgot. The chipped, pink stucco exterior spoke of decades of neglect, and most of the metal grates over the windows looked like they'd been bent by crowbars during burglary attempts.

"She's in apartment 201," Charlie said, leading the way up the rickety wooden stairs.

Avoiding the grimy railing, Tory followed.

Charlie knocked. After a few moments, a girl opened the door. "Yes?"

She even sounded young. She looked no more than fourteen—but her eyes were much older. Charlie had told Tory that Amanda Dunworth was eighteen years old, but she was so tiny and so frail. Her thin, dark hair was dirty, and her large, hazel eyes seemed to take up half of her face.

"Amanda Dunworth?" Charlie asked, his voice gentle.

"Yes?" Amanda did not sound happy that someone knew her name.

"I'm Charlie George. I'm your brother's lawyer." Charlie handed Amanda his business card. She took it, but she didn't look at it. "This is Dr. Tory Murphy, my associate. Can we speak with you for a moment?"

"Sure." Although she sounded uncertain, Amanda let them into her small studio apartment.

Despite the sunny day, the apartment was dark—Amanda had all of the shades drawn tight. She looked pale, as though she rarely ventured out, and her coffee table—her only table—was littered with take-out boxes.

"I'm—I'm sorry. Let me clean up the mess." She scooped up some of the containers and carried them to the kitchen area. She dropped them on the counter, which was already covered in detritus. From what Tory could see, Amanda hadn't cleaned her apartment in weeks, if not months.

"Can we sit, Amanda?" Charlie asked.

"Oh, yes. Of course." Amanda wrung her hands, nervous and uncertain, finally sitting in the one armchair.

Charlie and Tory sat side-by-side on the love seat, with Charlie closest to Amanda. He said, "You understand that your brother has been charged with first-degree murder in the killing of your parents, yes?"

Amanda sucked in a breath and nodded.

"You've been speaking to him while he's been in jail?"

She nodded again. "He told me about you."

"Good. I'm glad you're staying in touch. That's important." Charlie glanced around the apartment. "How are you doing?"

"I'm fine."

"Can I ask—why are you living here? In this neighborhood? It's not very safe for a single woman. You can afford better."

She shook her head vigorously. "I don't want to spend any more of their money than I have to."

Tory understood. The girl's parents had been wealthy, but she'd suffered so much at their hands. To her, that money would forever be tainted. She'd rather live in desperate poverty than spend the money of the man who'd raped her since she was a child.

Nodding as though he also understood, Charlie spoke. "Let's talk about your brother, then."

"Okay."

Tory's heart clenched. Amanda's voice sounded so small. Amanda could heal, but not for a while, and not without support. But she was all alone as far as Tory could tell. Who would be there for her? Who could help her?

Charlie spoke slowly, keeping eye contact with Amanda. "There's an excellent chance that I can get him released with time served, or with a very light prison sentence."

Amanda's eyes widened. "How?"

"Legally, what he did wasn't murder, but something called voluntary manslaughter."

"Not murder?"

"No," Charlie said, speaking faster now, enough that Tory noticed, enough to concern her. He sounded jittery, like he'd had too much caffeine. "Your brother isn't a murderer. He was defending you."

Amanda nodded, but her expression was uncertain.

Charlie continued, giving Amanda no time to ask questions. "All I would need is to collect a statement from you today to share with the prosecutor, and then for you to come in and give the same statement under oath."

Amanda looked to the side, her nervousness evident to Tory. "What statement?"

Instead of pausing in the face of Amanda's obvious fear, Charlie pressed harder, his voice a runaway train. "You would have to testify about the events of the morning your parents died."

Tory wanted to put her hand on his sleeve and warn him to slow down. There was danger ahead. Why couldn't he see it?

Charlie said, "And about your abuse at the hands of your father."

"No." Jumping to her feet, Amanda backed away from them, shaking her head. "You have to leave. When I spoke to him, Michael swore you wouldn't do this to me." She backed into the far corner of the kitchen, pressing against the cabinets and dirty countertop.

Tory watched the tragedy unfolding before her, shocked. This is why Charlie brought her along. He'd known how Amanda would react—that she'd be traumatized. But this girl wasn't merely traumatized. She was so insensible with pain and grief that she couldn't care for herself—bathing, feeding, cleaning—let alone make good decisions about something so complex as her brother's legal case. And for some reason, Charlie George, who could usually read people so well, was screwing up this entire visit.

Why?

Charlie stood, holding out his hands like he was calming a wild animal, but his words pressed on, out of control. "It's not that big of a deal. You don't have to testify in court. Just tell me what happened, and I'll record it on tape. And then—"

"No!" Amanda screamed. "No!" Covering her ears, she closed her eyes, fell to her knees, and started sobbing.

"Amanda, please." Charlie started pleading. Tory had never heard him sound so desperate. Something was wrong, something beyond this case.

Standing, Tory grabbed his arm and dragged him toward the apartment door. "Charlie, stop it," she hissed. Opening the door, she shoved him through. "Wait here," she told Charlie and closed the door in his face.

Tory approached Amanda. "Amanda—I'm Dr. Murphy, and you can call me Tory."

"Stay away." Amanda held up her hands in front of her as though to ward off an enemy, tears streaming down her face.

"Okay. I'll stay here." Tory remained by the door. "But I'm not a lawyer. I'm a doctor. I just want to make sure you're safe." Extracting her old business card from her purse, Tory set it on the coffee table. "I don't work at the hospital on this card anymore, but the mobile number still works. If you need anything, please call me. If you come see me as a patient, everything you tell me is confidential."

Amanda stared at Tory but said nothing, arms wrapped protectively over her chest.

Tory spoke in soothing tones. "I'm leaving now. Please call me if you need anything."

No response.

"I will help you. No matter what you decide to do about the case." With those words, Tory left.

Joining Charlie on the porch, Tory looked him over. His hands were shaking, his eyes bloodshot as though he'd been rubbing them. Something was seriously wrong, far beyond the desperate case he was working. She tried to balance her anger at him over how he'd treated Amanda with his obvious suffering now.

He dropped his head into his hands. "Tory, I don't know how to explain, but I really need her to testify."

"I can see that. Let's go home, and you can tell me all about it."

Charlie nodded, leading the way to his car.

She climbed into the passenger seat. "I haven't seen a lot of witness interviews—okay, I've seen zero—but I don't think they normally go like that."

He shook his head as he buckled his seatbelt. In silence, he started the car, then headed south toward the freeway.

"You don't have anything else to add? Because what you did was wrong. That poor girl was a wreck before we ever walked through her door, and you made everything worse."

"Making things worse is a theme for me lately."

"Lately? Since when?"

He clammed up, shifting gears as he pulled onto the 101.

Aggravated, she said, "Since when, Charlie? Before you dropped a stink bomb on me Friday morning? Or before you punched a guy at work?"

He rolled his eyes, refusing to rise to the bait.

She wanted to scream at him to tell her what was going on.

After a while of riding in silence, she tried a different approach. "What's going to happen to your case without her testimony?"

He shook his head again.

Aggravated, Tory reached for the radio control and turned to a station she liked, cranking it loud enough to mask the fact that Charlie refused to talk to her.

No problem. If Charlie wouldn't talk to her, his sister would.

Chapter Twelve

Around five o'clock Monday evening, as his car neared the exit that would take them to Venice Beach, Charlie turned off his radio. He knew why Tory had turned it on. He knew that she should be angry with him—he was angry at himself. He was angry that he'd even imagined going to Amanda Dunworth's apartment was a good idea. He was angry that he'd dragged Tory along. He was angry that Tory had seen him at his worst, again.

He was angry. So angry. And helpless. And afraid—for Michael Dunworth, that Charlie might not be able to protect him from a long prison sentence. For himself, that he'll never be able to sleep again, or even be alone again without hating himself.

Tory shifted in her seat, and even knowing she was so near made his eyes sting. His entire life, he'd been the luckiest guy on planet Earth. Blessed. He knew it now. Now, when it was all he could do not to fall apart. He took a deep breath, blinking a few times. Called on all of his reserves. Acted like everything was normal.

He could do this.

Glancing at Tory, he said, "I'll drop you at home. Thanks for going with me on this goose chase, even though it was much worse than I expected."

Tory's voice was an ice-cold drink on an August afternoon. "Take me to your house. I want to see Miranda."

Charlie also needed to talk to Miranda. What he'd just done, going against their client's direct request, most likely required a contingency plan or three. "I need to talk to Miranda about work stuff."

"That's fine," Tory said, stiffly. "I'll wait on the balcony with the door shut."

He'd never heard Tory use such a firm tone of voice. Not with him, anyway. And the last thing he wanted was for Tory to be there when he begged Miranda to save him from his terrible mistake. "I really need to talk to Miranda about this case."

Tory snorted. "I bet you do. But you also owe me an explanation, and you refuse to talk to me. In fact, after what you pulled today— and last week—you owe me a lot more than just an explanation." She sounded really angry. "I'm not going anywhere but to Miranda's apartment."

"Fine," he snapped. He turned toward home, his thoughts in a jumble. He needed Miranda. She would help him clarify what he needed to do. She would help him see through the murk that had become his life, help him make a plan.

He parked in the garage under his building, and Tory followed him to the elevator. They rode up in silence. He wished he knew what he could say to make her understand how everything he'd ever counted on had suddenly been jerked away. He couldn't trust his instincts. He couldn't even trust his hearing, his eyesight. He kept seeing things that weren't there. In one moment, he'd be in the present. The next moment, he'd be in the past.

His mom, lying on the floor, eyes staring at the ceiling, blood on her chest, soaking the pillow, his hands, his arms.

How could he explain to Tory when even he didn't understand what was happening? All he could feel was the panic pressing on the back of his neck whenever he thought of Michael Dunworth going to prison for murder. If Michael Dunworth deserved to suffer, then didn't Charlie? Even Tory said it in the car—how different was he from Michael, in the end?

Charlie had barely touched his key to the lock when Miranda flung the door open, her eyes on fire. "What the hell did you do?" she said to him.

Charlie shut his eyes. *Disaster. His fault. Again.*

When Miranda saw Tory standing behind him, her tone changed.

"I'm sorry, Tory, but I have to speak with my brother about something private."

Tory gave Miranda a wry smile. "Can I wait on the balcony?"

"Yeah, that's fine."

Tory slid open the glass door to the balcony and made her way outside, closing the door behind her. Watching her lean forward on the railing, Charlie felt overwhelmed with regret. Had things been different, he could have been out there with her, tucking a loose strand of hair behind her ear, holding her close.

Miranda looked fit to be tied. She dragged him into his bedroom and closed the door, giving them more privacy. "Charlie—where were you just now?"

Leaning back against his dresser, he sighed. "You already know, I can tell. We went to interview Amanda Dunworth."

Exhaling, Miranda shook her head. "Why? Why would you do something so stupid?"

He tried to defend himself. "I brought Tory with me to help. You know, she takes care of people like Amanda."

"That's fine, Charlie. But your client told you specifically not to interview his sister."

"Something's happened. Tell me what happened." He could tell from the tightness around her eyes.

"Birch called," she said. "He tried to reach you, apparently, but you didn't answer the phone."

Charlie remembered the loud music in the car. He wouldn't have heard his phone ringing. "Shit."

"Yeah, shit. The Dunworth kid fired the firm."

Looking heavenward, Charlie felt like he might cry in desperation. He never cried, not even at his mother's funeral. The last time he cried was the day his mother died. The time before that he couldn't remember. And now, twice in one day he'd nearly come to tears. "What else? I know there's more."

"Dunworth agreed to the prosecutor's plea. Second-degree murder." Miranda shoved him with one hand, frustration evident in her every muscle. "Nice job, Charlie."

He'd never heard Miranda so angry at him before. In the past, she'd gotten upset with him, but his mistakes were made out of love, and she'd always known that. This time was different. She sounded scornful. Disappointed.

She sounded like she was done with him.

But she wasn't done. "First you deliberately hurt Tory. Then you insult Lala—I still don't know why she forgave you for that. And now you deliberately tank a client's case, sending him to jail for the rest of his life! And what about Chalk? Before, that was an outlier. Now? You look like you're the problem, not him." She ran her hand through her hair. "Charlie, I know you're struggling, but you need to get your shit together. There are consequences that even I can't protect you from."

She was right. Miranda had spent her whole life protecting him. Miranda had nearly died protecting him. He couldn't ask her to do that anymore. It wasn't fair. She needed to be able to move on with her life.

"You're right," he said. "I should go." Reaching into his closet, he pulled out the black leather duffle bag he used for overnight trips.

"Wait, what? What are you doing?" Miranda watched him, hands on her hips.

He packed essentials, and then some clothes he could wear for a few days. He would have to come back for suits to wear to work—but he could get those later. For now, he needed to find a place to stay.

"This is your home, Miranda. You don't need me weighing you down."

"You know that wasn't what I meant, jerkface."

"I know. But I think this is the right thing. Who lives with her brother after she turns thirty? It's time for John to move in." He needed to keep the conversation light. He needed her to believe that he was making the choice because he wanted to, not because he felt he had to.

Miranda rolled her eyes. "That loser?"

"Yeah. That loser. The loser you're madly in love with, who probably already has a ring for you in his sock drawer."

Miranda made gagging sounds. So mature, his sister. God, he loved her. She was the only family he had, and he'd disappointed her completely.

He gestured around the room. "I'll come back for the rest of my crap when I figure out where I'm staying."

"Which you will tell me, immediately."

Charlie smiled, feeling his gut crunch. He had no idea where he would stay. For the first time in his life, his future was clouded, and he couldn't see a way through it.

He pulled her to him. "I love you."

She hugged him back, then shoved him off of her. "I can't believe this is happening."

He gave her his most winning grin, but inside, he felt himself withering. *Me neither*, he thought.

———

WHEN SHE HEARD THE BALCONY DOOR SLIDING OPEN, TORY TURNED around and leaned against the railing, the evening sun warming her back. Charlie stood in the doorway, a duffle bag over his shoulder.

"I'm leaving. I wanted to say bye."

Something about how he said the word *leaving* caught Tory's attention. "What's in the bag?"

"I'm moving out. It's time."

Wildly surprised by this turn of events, Tory asked, "Did Miranda kick you out?" It seemed impossible that anything could come between the George siblings.

He shook his head. "She's mad at me, but not mad enough to make me homeless." Looking off to the side, he seemed nervous—and younger, less polished.

Before she could speak, Charlie's phone rang. "One sec," he said to her, and he answered it. "Hey, Birch." He stepped inside to take the call. A cool expression lowered over his face like a dark curtain. Nodding, he listened to the person on the other end of the line. "I understand…Yes." A long pause. "I'll come by and pick up my things from the front desk and turn in my phone…Yes, sir."

Hanging up, Charlie rejoined her on the balcony. He glanced past her at the water. "I just got fired." His voice was strangely calm, like the voice of a patient who'd walked into the emergency department with a massive stab wound, related the incident to the check-in nurse, and then collapsed on the floor.

"Because of Amanda Dunworth?"

"Yeah. Her brother fired our firm."

"Did you know going to see her would destroy the case?"

His face looked so pained she wondered if he was physically hurting. "I just wanted to save Michael. I didn't mean to hurt her, and it would be so easy—just, one hour of testimony, and he's free." He looked down at his feet, exhaling.

From the way he said the words, Tory suddenly knew that the case was about so much more than Michael Dunworth, and she wanted to know why.

"You screwed up."

"I really did."

"But you meant well."

He looked up at her. "Yeah, I did."

"Charlie," she asked, studying him closely, the red eyes, the unkempt hair. "Are you okay?"

He shrugged.

"If you leave here, where are you going to stay?"

He shrugged again. "The Ritz?" he said, noncommittally.

The Ritz-Carleton was just around the corner. Tory triaged quickly: Charlie was unemployed, and the Ritz was extravagant, even for a kid with a monster trust fund. Staying there could cost easily twenty thousand a month. Plus, he was obviously in a dark place, and at the hotel, he would be alone. Under these circumstances, the Ritz sounded like a terrible idea.

Pushing back against his choice, she said, "Can you afford to stay there without your job?"

Again he shrugged. "I have alternate sources of income."

At his shrug, she gritted her teeth. "I know you do. But is it enough to live at the Ritz?"

Pausing, Charlie seemed to be doing math in his head. "Most likely, yes."

"Most likely? You're making major life decisions based on likelihoods?"

"You have a better idea?" He gave her the beginning of his charming half-smile, but she could tell that the smile was fragile—it didn't have the strength that he usually put behind it.

The infallible Charlie George had lost his charm, even. He was in the direst of straits.

"Stay at my place tonight," she said. "By tomorrow you'll come up with a better plan than a thousand-dollar-a-night hotel room."

Shaking his head, Charlie looked past her at the horizon. "Why are you being so nice to me? I was horrible to you last week. I was completely out of line at Amanda's this afternoon. My own sister has had it with me." He ran his hand down his face, finally meeting her eyes. "But you're completely unfazed."

She wasn't unfazed. She just knew he needed more than an empty, overpriced hotel room. He needed his family and friends, even as he pushed them away.

"Twenty-three," she said.

Charlie lowered his eyebrows in confusion. "Twenty-three what?"

"That's my record. The highest number of gunshot victims I've treated in one shift. Twenty-three."

His brows shot up. "Holy crap. That's a lot."

"Indeed it is. You, Charlie George, don't even raise my stress-o-meter." She could handle Charlie George and whatever mess he was in. She had a strong guess about what was ailing him because she'd seen it before, many times, far more than she'd seen GSWs.

Charlie met her eyes again, and this time the smile he gave her was real. "All right, Ms. Twenty-Three. I'll come stay with you."

Chapter Thirteen

Tory rode with Charlie to her house, worried now that she was making a terrible decision. Not for him, but for herself. When she'd seen him with the bag over his shoulder, she'd made a snap decision and invited him home. Now that she'd had time to think about it, she was having regrets. This wasn't the first time she'd taken in a wounded stray. But this time was different, she told herself. Charlie was her friend, first and foremost.

This time was different.

Charlie parked on the street out front, then followed her to the fence gate. She appreciated how he waited a few steps back to give her privacy while she punched in the gate code.

She led the way to the green door that was the entrance to her ground-floor apartment. Above, Ms. Honey sat on her deck facing west, sunning herself and keeping cool with a painted bamboo fan strapped to her wrist.

Ms. Honey glanced down as they approached. "Well, hello there."

"Is that—" Charlie began, whispering to Tory.

"Yes," Tory whispered back. To Ms. Honey, she said, "This is Charlie, a friend of mine. Charlie, this is my landlady and my friend, Ms. Honey."

Charlie stepped forward, smiling up at Ms. Honey. "Pleased to meet you, ma'am."

"*Mon dieu*. That accent is a delight to my ears. Where are you from?"

"North Carolina, ma'am."

"And manners, too. Tory, this one is far superior to the one who had you all upset last Friday."

Tory felt herself blush.

Charlie cleared his throat.

"Ah. I see." Ms. Honey laughed. "I hope you made him apologize. A bunch." She propped her feet up on the railing. "I let Daisy come up here with me, in case you're looking for her."

"All right," Tory said. "I'll come get her later."

"I don't mind keeping her tonight." Ms. Honey winked.

Rolling her eyes even while she blushed again, Tory unlocked her door and led Charlie into her apartment.

Tory knew her place was small, especially compared to Miranda's palatial condo. Ms. Honey's house had a square footprint. The garage took up part of the ground floor, and the remainder was Tory's apartment: an L-shaped space with a bedroom on the short side and a long, open living and kitchen area divided by a countertop bar. There were lots of windows, which kept the apartment bright, and the ceilings were high. She'd covered the tile floor with a bright green shag rug and she'd brought her own bed. The rest of the furniture had come from Ms. Honey—the leather sofa and chair, the glass coffee table, the bar stools.

"This is my place," Tory said. "Not quite what you're used to."

Stepping in, Charlie set his bag on the armchair. "It's cool. Cozy but also hip. This furniture looks like it came off of a movie set."

"It's Ms. Honey's. It might actually have come off of a movie set."

"Why do you call her that? Isn't her name Honoria Thibault?"

"Everyone in the neighborhood calls her Ms. Honey. I don't know why. I never asked." She glanced at him. "Sometimes people want to start over, I guess."

"But anyone who sees her will know who she is. Hers isn't an easy face to forget if you ever watch reruns on television."

"Maybe, but after a while, even those reruns will stop running. The kids around here, the teenagers, they don't know her as anything other than Ms. Honey. That's all she'll ever be to them."

Charlie looked unconvinced, but he didn't try to argue.

Tory said, "Everything fades eventually, doesn't it?"

Charlie laughed a painful sounding laugh. "Not in my experience, no."

At that moment, Tory's phone rang. She fished it out of her purse and answered. "This is Tory Murphy."

"Dr. Murphy, this is Dr. Jean Baker."

Mouthing *I'm sorry* to Charlie, Tory dashed into her bedroom and shut the door quietly behind her. "Hi, Dr. Baker. How can I help you?" She hoped she didn't sound breathless.

"I'm looking at your resume here."

Tory had emailed her resume over to the clinic after Daphne had dropped her off at home that morning. She certainly didn't expect to hear from Dr. Baker so quickly.

"Your qualifications are impressive." Dr. Baker didn't sound like she was giving Tory a compliment so much as stating a fact.

"Thank you."

"I've already called your references."

"You…have?"

"Yes. Everyone speaks highly of you. I didn't expect that. I figured you must have left Cedars under a cloud, actually."

Taken aback by the negative words, Tory asked, "Why is that?"

"You had an excellent job, and you left. For no apparent reason. And then you applied to work here. None of that makes any sense." Before Tory could explain her decisions, Dr. Baker continued. "Mary told me some story about how you wanted more personal interaction with your patients, but I don't believe her."

Again, Tory was taken aback by Dr. Baker's direct speech. "You don't? Why not?"

"Because of who your parents are."

Tory fell back against the wall, the strength leaving her body. *Of course.* She felt the job slipping through her fingers.

Dr. Baker continued. "I went to medical school with your mother. I recognized your face immediately because you resemble her so much. I couldn't believe that the daughter of Caroline and Francis Murphy would want to work in a free clinic for sex workers, drug addicts, and abuse victims." Dr. Baker maintained her tone of detached observation, which made her words seem even colder.

Feeling a rush of anger at Dr. Baker's statement, Tory spoke before she could stop herself. "You don't think your patients deserve excellent doctors?"

Dr. Baker chuckled quietly. "Well." She paused, taking a breath. "I was hoping you would say that. Indeed, I believe our patients deserve only the best doctors." She paused, and Tory could hear her typing. Then she spoke again. "Can you start Wednesday?"

Tory stood up straight, shocked. "Are you serious? That was a test?" In her swirl of emotions, Tory found space to realize that Jean Baker just called her *one of the best doctors.*

"Not really." Dr. Baker sighed. "Maybe a little. Call me Jean."

Tory inhaled deeply and expelled whatever annoyance she felt. She took a few steps and dropped to her full-size bed, the largest that would fit in her small bedroom. She kicked off the flats she'd worn to visit Amanda Dunworth, and lay on her back.

She put herself in Jean's position, trying to figure out who to hire: what it must be like to see resumes, looking for people who were good enough, but who would also see the patients as real people and who would stay for the long run. Tory couldn't fault Jean for making sure Tory wasn't just looking for a way-station on her road to better things.

"Wednesday would be great," Tory said. "Thank you for the opportunity."

"I'm glad to hear it. Come by tomorrow morning to fill out the paperwork and jump through the administrative hoops. Mary will get you set up with the schedule and everything else you need."

After a few more pleasantries, Jean signed off.

Tory was thrilled. Then she remembered Charlie in the other room, who'd just been fired.

Tory stepped out into her living room to find Charlie on her couch with a beer in his hand and another at his feet, unopened.

Tory picked up the second beer and dropped onto the couch next to him. "Why go to Amanda Dunworth's when you knew it was wrong?"

Examining his beer's label, Charlie picked at it with his thumb. "It was the only way I could think of to save her brother."

Tory paused, making the connections hidden behind his words. "Is it your job to save him?"

Charlie didn't answer right away. Finally, he said, "I need to save him. He can't go to jail for protecting his sister from abuse like that. It's not right."

"I don't know much about being a lawyer, but it seems like you've let this one get too personal."

Charlie huffed a laugh. "Yeah, you think?"

He looked at her then, meeting her eyes for the first time since she'd sat next to him. She was struck, once again, by how magnetic he was, even now, when he looked so beaten down.

"Are you hungry?" she asked. "I don't cook, but I have frozen pizza."

Charlie nodded. "Frozen pizza sounds perfect."

In the kitchen, Tory pulled a pizza from the freezer and turned on the oven.

Charlie followed her over and sat at the bar. "Who called you when we came in?"

Tory deliberated about what to tell him, worried about poking the recent wound about his lost job. "It was nothing."

Charlie raised a brow. "Nothing, huh? What's his name?"

A laugh burst from her. After a moment, she said, "Jean."

"Jean." Charlie turned the name over in his mouth like the word tasted badly. "Is he French? You don't want to date a French guy. Ask Miranda. They're really domineering with their girlfriends."

"Charlie, are you jealous? Seriously? After the way you acted Friday?"

Charlie looked at her so deeply that she wanted to take a step back. "I'm so sorry, Tory. Friday morning is inexcusable. But I can tell you why. My feelings for you terrified me, especially after you saw me at my absolute worst, so I acted like an asshole to push you away." He swallowed the last of his beer, then grabbed her half-finished bottle. "I like you, Tory. So yeah, I'm jealous." He took a sip from the bottle he stole.

Tory hadn't wanted to hear his apology earlier in the day when they'd sat in the sun, Daisy romping around them. She hadn't wanted to hear his explanation about why he'd done what he'd done.

Charlie George cared for her. He *liked* her. The same way she liked him. He scooped her dog's poop. He didn't hang out with her because she was his sister's friend; he wanted to hang out with *her*.

But for three years, he'd held back. Now, when he felt most vulnerable, he was reaching out for her. She knew what that meant. It meant his feelings were real, but it also meant he had a hole he wanted to fill with her.

She knew something about filling holes. She did it all the time, but she didn't do it with people she cared about. Frustration welled inside her. His feelings were real, she did believe that, but they were mixed up with his pain. She couldn't be with him when he was like this.

"Tell me about this Jean." He pressed her.

"Jean's a doctor." Tory slid the pizza into the oven.

"A doctor? Fancy. What's his specialty?"

"I can't believe Charlie George is jealous. You could have anyone." Yeah, sure, she was fishing. She wasn't too proud to admit it to herself.

He nodded. "Probably. But I don't want just anyone."

Teasing him was wrong when she had no intention of following through, not until she knew for sure he had bested whatever demons he was wrestling with. But Charlie George wanted *her*—that much was true After all of these years, she'd discovered she hadn't been imagining the zing she felt when she was near him, when their hands touched by accident. No. It had all been real.

She tapped her chin. "Jean's specialty is internal medicine, I think."

"You think? You haven't been seeing each other long?"

"It's early in our relationship."

Nodding, Charlie took another sip. "What does he think about me?"

"You're not really a topic of conversation, to be honest."

Charlie frowned. "I'm hurt."

"You are not." Tory pulled another beer from the fridge and popped the lid.

Charlie rested his elbows on the bar, leaning toward her, his brown eyes bottomless. "I'm really sorry for how I treated you Friday morning."

Tory's heart beat sideways. This wasn't the apology of a man desperate for her help with a legal case, or one trying to get her naked.

She stepped back from him, leaning against the fridge. "You don't need to keep apologizing."

"Nevertheless. I will until you believe me."

Tory nodded. "You know, you didn't have to be embarrassed that I saw your nightmare. I'd never think badly about a person for something like that."

"I know." His voice slipped into a deeper southern accent. "This has been the second-worst week of my life."

Tory figured the worst week had been when his mother died, and she wanted to know more.

"I keep making the wrong decisions, and one of them was you. I'm sorry."

Turning away from him to hide her expression, Tory said, "What exactly are you sorry for?"

"What do you mean?"

"Are you sorry we slept together?" She glanced back at him.

Raising his brows, eyes wide, he said, "Good Lord in heaven, no."

Tory smiled, "Me neither. Just don't be such a dick next time."

As soon as she said the words, she wanted to take them back. *Next time?* Why did she say that? Charlie George made her lose her mind.

But instead of making a flirty joke or something else equally predictable, Charlie lifted up his beer in a toast. "Agreed."

She clinked her bottle against his, and the deal was struck.

———

After dinner, Tory brought Charlie bedding for the couch. "This is nowhere near as comfortable as your bed, but at least you're not sleeping on a park bench."

"I do have a super comfortable bed."

Tory agreed. "You really do."

"What will Jean think about you talking about my bed with me?"

Tory helped him tuck a sheet over the couch. "Charlie, Jean Baker is a woman, and she just hired me to work at a medical clinic. I got a new job, but I didn't want to tell you because you just got fired."

Charlie dropped the pillow at one end of the couch. "I see. Well, at least I don't have to be jealous of some handsome French guy stealing my girl."

Tory blushed at *my girl*, wishing the lights were off so he wouldn't see.

Charlie reached out and touched her cheek. "I have always loved how you turn pink."

She felt herself turn even pinker. "It's just my fair coloring, which makes it easier to see the vasodilation from an adrenaline rush."

"Ah. But what's causing the adrenaline rush?" He stepped closer to her, cupping her cheek in his hand.

Looking up at him, she wanted to lean into him, to press her body against his, to say *yes*.

But she knew that collapsing into Charlie's arms right now was the worst thing she could do. Charlie wasn't making good decisions—Amanda Dunworth was a perfect example. His desire for her was all mixed up with his hurting.

Taking a deep breath, she put her hands on his chest and pushed. "Back off, dude."

He knees collided with the back of the couch, and he flopped down, defeated. "What? Why?"

"I'm not a beer for you to drown your sorrows in. Besides, I have to stop by my new job in the morning, and I don't want bed head."

"Cold, Dr. Murphy."

"You'll survive. The remote control is on the table there. I go to sleep early because I get up to run. I'll try not to wake you."

"I can go with you. I packed sneakers."

"Really? You want to come running with me?"

"Yeah, I do." The way he said the words, though, made it sound like he wanted to do everything with her, not just running. "Why wouldn't I? It's something you love."

She needed out of there, and fast. She was losing her resolve. "Good night."

"Sweet dreams." He gave her his half-smile, and she opened her bedroom door. But at the last minute, she glanced back at him.

She was struck by what she saw. He stared at the wall in front of him, his body rigid. He looked like he was steeling himself for something hard, like a difficult trial. Or a fight. Part of her wanted to ask him what was wrong. Or to invite him into her room, to hold him —he looked like he needed it.

Instead, she stepped into her room and closed the door. Tomorrow, she told herself, she would ask him more questions. Find out why this was the second-worst week of his life.

She washed her face, read twenty pages of a romance novel, and was asleep by nine o'clock.

Chapter Fourteen

Around two a.m., Tory bolted from bed, awoken by screaming and a loud crash.

Someone was breaking into her apartment. But Daisy wasn't barking—no, Daisy was staying with Ms. Honey tonight. For a moment, she felt terror.

But then she remembered. *Charlie.*

She dashed into the living room. Her lamp had toppled from the side table. Yelling in his sleep, Charlie lay on his back, half off the couch, trapped in a flashback again. Tory ran around the coffee table and sat next to him.

"Charlie. It's Tory."

He opened his eyes, but he still didn't see her. "Don't let her die. You have to save her."

"You're safe, Charlie. You're in my apartment."

"I shot her. You have to save her."

"Miranda's safe, Charlie."

"My mom. She's dying."

His mom?

He fell back onto the couch, eyes closed, then slowly opened them again. "Tory? Wait. Where am I?" He sat up, the blanket falling to his waist. For a moment, Tory averted her eyes from his bare chest, his toned stomach. She hoped for both their sakes he had on something beneath the blanket.

Meeting his eyes, she said, "You were having another…nightmare. I woke you."

He put his feet on the floor and rested his face in his hands. "It's so awful. I haven't slept in a week, except…" As trailed off, he looked up at her with bottomless eyes.

Except that night with you. She sighed, remembering the night and the morning after. She knew she could bring him into her room right now, and he could spoon her from behind and sleep peacefully. She could do that for him. But she also knew that if she invited him into her bed, they wouldn't stop with spooning.

She wouldn't be able to help herself.

When Tory was in the fourth grade, she brought home a baby bird with a broken leg. She made a nest for it in a shoebox, and kept it in her bedroom. She researched how to feed it and make it better, and for a week she did everything she could to nurse it back to health. Every morning, she opened the shoebox, and the bird's bright black eyes looked at her, only her, and it chirped, and she knew that she was the center of the bird's universe.

Downstairs, somewhere, her parents were locked in their office together, finishing a paper on some groundbreaking research, unaware of the bird she'd saved. Unaware of her.

Every day, she rushed home from school and opened the box. The bird would hop on its unbroken leg, thrilled to see her. She fed it with an eyedropper and hoped for the day when she would be able to set it free. But part of her didn't want to. Part of her wanted to keep it so that its bright black eyes would always be waiting for her.

On the seventh day, she awoke, opened the shoebox, and the bird was dead.

Her parents didn't notice her sobbing as she carried the box into their small back yard. They didn't notice her dirty hands when she came back in after she buried the tiny body in a hole she dug with a trowel. After she buried the bird, she put the shoebox in the recycle bin, made her breakfast, and walked to school.

She was a sucker for bright eyes that looked at her for fixing.

In high school, there was the soccer star with the torn ACL. In college, there was the graduate student who'd been in a car wreck and broken three ribs and torn his rotator cuff. She moved in with him and helped him finish his master's thesis. He thought it was love, but she knew better.

All along, she'd known what she was doing, but she couldn't stop herself. The alternative, of course, was a string of meaningless nights with nice guys whom she cared little about, so that's what she'd chosen to do. For years, those guys had been satisfying enough—until three years ago when she met Charlie George. But he was out of reach. No matter how much she might have wanted him, he gave her no clue that he felt the same way about her. Not until this week.

The second-worst week of his life.

She wanted so badly to break her bad habit of needy boy codependency. So she'd adopted Daisy as practice. When she found Daisy at the shelter, the dog was emaciated. She had ear infections and roundworms. She needed extra care at home, follow-up medical appointments, a special diet for the first months, and medication three times a day. Tory hired an experienced dog sitter to help when she was on a long shift, and Ms. Honey helped too.

Now, Daisy was healed. Tory could sit in the yard while Daisy romped in the shrubbery and trotted around the fence. Every few moments, though, Daisy glanced back at Tory, making sure she was still there. With every glance, Tory felt what she'd hoped she'd feel for Daisy. Love that extended past need.

Daisy had been good practice. Like climbing a small hill.

Charlie George was Everest.

Sitting next to Charlie on the couch, she rested her hand on his shoulder. "It's time for me to call in my favor," she said, referring to the deal they'd struck when she agreed to help him interview Amanda Dunworth.

He smiled weakly. "Really? Now? I'm hardly in any condition to fulfill an agreement."

"Tell me why the Dunworth case has thrown you for such a loop. And don't leave anything out. How do you lawyers put it? I want the whole truth—no omissions. Start with why you punched that guy at work."

Charlie stood, unfolding his tall body from the couch—the bottom half clad in boxer briefs—and pulled a t-shirt over his head. "Don't you have work in the morning? If you want the answer to this question, we're going to be up all night."

"You have to tell someone. It might as well be me." She leaned back against the arm of the couch, tucking her feet underneath her.

"I might need another beer."

Tory cocked her head, noticing for the first time all of the beer bottles on the floor—Charlie had consumed at least six beers after she'd gone to bed. "You're drinking to stop the nightmares."

Charlie flopped down at the other end of the couch, his legs bent in front of him, his feet nearly touching her.

"I punched Chalk because he brought me the Dunworth case and kept needling me about it. I think he pulled my mother's autopsy report—it's sealed, but in the end, it's still public record." Charlie paused. "I shot her. That's how she died." Tory could tell he was watching her closely, as though looking for a reaction.

Tory kept her face neutral—she had plenty of practice in her line of work. But inside, her head was spinning. Charlie and Miranda had a massive secret. And Charlie—he was carrying a massive burden.

Tory nodded.

He continued. "That's why I chased you out Friday morning. More than you seeing my nightmares, I didn't want you to find out about what I did. I saw the way you reacted to Michael Dunworth's case. I know what you must think of me. But you asked for the truth, and there it is."

Tory remembered her words in the car. She argued about murder and the legalities. She said that what Michael had done was wrong. And the whole time, Charlie must have heard her talking about him.

"I'm sorry I said those things. If I'd had any idea about you—"

"You would have said something different, but felt the same way." Charlie George, as usual, pulled no punches.

"You're probably right. But your explanation made sense, Charlie. Michael was defending his sister. I saw her—if I hadn't seen her, I might not have believed it. But I saw her." Charlie remained silent, so she pushed on. "Will you tell me what happened?"

Charlie took a deep breath and nodded. "Sorcha—that's my mom —she tried to kill Miranda."

"Oh." Tory exhaled. The Dunworth case seemed to cut closer and closer to the bone.

"She held us at gunpoint, forcing Miranda to poison herself. When my mom lost her focus for a moment, I got the gun away from her, and I shot her." Charlie scrubbed at his face. "Sorcha wasn't well. She had a mental illness that was usually under control well enough."

"Not that day, though."

"No. That day she was out of her mind. She thought she was protecting us from something, and we couldn't reason with her. In her mind, the only way to save us was to kill us."

Tory thought back to the stories she'd heard—never witnessed, thank the Lord—of parents who'd killed their children to protect them in moments of psychosis. She knew what Charlie was describing. What she couldn't believe was how *normal* Charlie and Miranda were after going through something like that.

"She held you at gunpoint? Made Miranda eat poison? Based on what you told me in the car, what you did sounds like self-defense."

"Legally, it was. They might have charged me with manslaughter, and we would have argued self-defense, and we would have won. My parents' firm—well, my dad's firm now—is the best defense firm in the south. One of the best in the country. But my dad didn't want our family name to go through the mud, so he made the whole thing go away. Before I took the bar, though, he set things straight. It wasn't easy, but he did it."

"And you think your coworker suspected, and that's why he brought you the Dunworth case."

Charlie nodded. "The week my mom died was the worst week of my life. Miranda almost died, my mom did die, and I'm the one who killed her. And then Chalk brings me this case, and now the case is bringing all these memories back. I can't sleep, I can't think straight, and I feel this unstoppable…I don't know…*need* to get the Dunworth kid off the hook for what he did."

The similarities between the two cases crashed together in Tory's mind. A brother, killing his parents, to protect his sister. "What about your dad? Didn't he try to protect you?"

"My dad only wanted to protect himself. Miranda and I are in L.A. to get away from him and everyone who knows him. We're not here because we love the Hollywood life." He laughed. "Miranda hates it, as you know. That's why we live in the Marina."

"I thought you two liked hanging out with the AARP crowd."

He smiled. "They're pretty great actually."

She thought of something he mentioned earlier. "Wait. Why is your co-worker named Chalk? That's a stupid name."

Charlie hooted with laughter, and Tory was so glad to see the dark expression leave his face. "His real name is actually Chalkley. Apparently that's Old English or something. I gave him a hard time about it. I bought a case of chalk and kept leaving boxes of it around the office." Charlie paused. "He's a terrible person. I don't pick on people who don't deserve it."

Charlie struck her as someone who'd be popular and charismatic —sure—but who would never in a million years punch down. She wouldn't have fallen for him otherwise. "I believe you. I think you put up a tough façade, but you have a gigantic heart."

Charlie took a breath, smiling at her like she was the sun warming his face. "Do you really believe that?"

"I've always believed that, from the first time I saw you, wearing your heart on your sleeve for your big sister. You didn't bust into a movie star's house for no reason. You came to save Miranda." She grinned at him. "You're a hero, you just don't want to admit it."

He scrubbed his face. "Some hero. I can't believe you think that after what I just told you."

"What you told me doesn't change who you are."

He looked at her, brows pulled together. "Miranda laid into me after you left Friday morning."

Tory laughed. "I can imagine." She was startled to find that the pain of that morning was nearly gone. So much had changed in three days.

"She said something that was so obvious, something I'd been denying for I don't know how long." He shut his eyes, as though reliving the memory.

"Are you going to tell me, big boy?"

"I'm deciding. I thought I was gonna, but now I find myself feeling shy about it. It's very unlike myself." He stifled a grin.

"You're lying. You're not the slightest bit shy." She had no idea where he was going with this.

"I'm not lying to you. I'm nervous as a long-tailed cat in a room full of rocking chairs."

"A what?" Sometimes Charlie seemed cosmopolitan, and sometimes he seemed like he came from some town with one stoplight.

"She said—talking about you, mind—" His accent was getting even deeper; he must actually be nervous. *"She's the one, and you know it."*

Tory blinked at him.

"If you don't believe me, you can ask her yourself. I felt like someone slammed my head in a door."

"I think I know what you mean. I'm feeling similarly. I've had a crush on you for years, but never thought anything would come of it. But then, bam. It's like everything became clear on Thursday night."

"It's wild, don't you think, that we're just figuring this out now?" He gestured around them at the tossed-about room, the lamp on the floor, the empty bottles, the darkness through the windows. "I had to fall into this pit for me to figure out that you're the best thing in my life?" He shook his head. "I guess sometimes losing everything makes you realize the good thing you're already holding in your hands."

Tory swallowed. "Charlie—we can't. Not right now."

"Can't what?"

She didn't even know if he was proposing anything or just spilling his guts, but she had to draw a line. "We can't do anything about what we're talking about. Our feelings."

"You mean, that I think you're the best thing since sliced bread?"

She rolled her eyes. "Yes, those feelings."

"And by *do anything*, you mean things like Thursday night? Those things?"

The way he said the word *things* made her shiver. She tried to hide it, but she failed.

He grinned at her, eyes twinkling.

"I'm serious, Charlie. Like you said, you're in a pit. I don't want to be someone you're reaching for to make yourself feel better."

He looked offended. "Weren't you listening? None of what I'm feeling for you is new."

She steeled herself. "Same here. So that means what we feel will last through tough times, right? We can wait?"

He leaned further back against the arm of the couch, looking displeased. "I suppose. But I don't have to like it."

"If it makes you feel better, I don't like it either."

He smiled. "That does make me feel better." He looked at her, his gaze hot. "What about after these," he waved his hand in the air, "tough times. What then?"

She thought back to Thursday night. Of having as many Thursday nights as she might want. She felt dizzy even considering it. "I'll make a deal with you."

"Another one?"

"I'll wait if you will. I'll be here for you. You make it through this rough patch—"

"More like a crater, but okay."

"You make it through your crater, and I'll be there. I'll wait for you, however long it takes. That's the deal."

For a while he was so quiet that Tory began to feel stupid. She'd just offered to stay monogamous for Charlie George, who could barely keep it in his pants, ever. What if he didn't want the same? Why would he? All he'd done was say a few nice words to her. Oh no, she could feel the blush coming on. Why wasn't the couch swallowing her? *If he doesn't talk in the next two seconds, I'm running into my bedroom.*

"Deal," he said.

Tory's heart kicked.

They sat in silence for a while, but Tory didn't want to leave, not yet. She wanted to be near him, to revel in this whatever-it-was they'd created for a few more minutes. To study his features in the shadows through the windows, how the moonlight cast his face in silhouette. To imagine touching him again.

She asked, "Does anyone else know about your mom?"

"I told John and Sandy a long time ago, back when Miranda was in trouble. I told Daphne then, too, and she told Marlon, probably. I don't know about Greta and Timmy. Maybe them. Maybe not. Daphne tells Greta everything though, so probably them, too."

"I'm the only one of our friends who doesn't know about what happened to you?" Tory was taken aback. Everyone had kept the Georges' secret, even from her. Did she feel hurt? No—because they'd been protecting their friends.

He dropped his head back and stared at the ceiling. "This is the worst part. The part I can't get over. And no one else knows this but Miranda." He took a deep breath, released it. "I didn't have to shoot her. After I got the gun, I just panicked. Miranda was dying on the floor…" Another deep breath. "God. I can barely talk about it. When my mom was on the ground, I tried to save her. I held a pillow on the wound to stop the blood, but it was everywhere. All over my hands, my wrists." Charlie wrapped his hand around his wrist, around a watch he wore, sliding the watch back and forth. "In my dream, Miranda is on the ground, dying, and I'm holding that bloody pillow, trying to save my mom, and there's nothing I can do. I'm trapped in that room. I can never escape. Just—"

"Stop." Leaning forward, Tory wrapped her hand around his ankle. "Don't relive it again. It'll only make it worse."

"OK." He dropped his face in his hand. "I realize that the event itself was totally screwed up, but why am I having nightmares like a baby? Miranda doesn't. She's had her own problems, but hers aren't like this at all. She's not…cursed."

Tory knew that Charlie had PTSD and that he was having flashbacks. He was never going to get better if she didn't tell him. She figured he wouldn't react well, so she braced herself. "Do you know what post-traumatic stress disorder is?"

He scoffed. "I'm not an idiot."

"That's why you're having nightmares. It's why you're jittery and having trouble making good decisions. And you've been lashing out at people you care about. Like Miranda." She paused. "And me." She waited, hoping he'd listen to her, but figuring he would not.

Shaking his head, Charlie started thrumming his fingers on the back of the couch. "I realize you're a doctor, so it's easier to think in terms of diagnoses, but I don't have a disorder. I'm not the victim here. I killed someone."

He was wrong. Killing other people gave soldiers PTSD all the time. "I'm sorry, Charlie. I'm sorry about what happened to you. But I'm right."

"I didn't have to kill her," he said, his brown eyes pouring all of his misery into hers. "But I did it anyway. I didn't know what else to do."

"I don't know what happened that day. But maybe you should talk to Miranda about this. I know you should talk to someone. You've pushed everyone away—"

"Everyone but you."

She nodded. "Everyone but me. I'm right about the PTSD. At least consider what I'm saying. I can help you with your pit or crater or whatever. You don't have to stay there. I can refer you to someone—"

"No." His voice was firm.

"But you're not sleeping, and you're making bad decisions. You just said that you can't seem to stop."

"I'll figure it out. I did before."

"What do you mean, before?"

"Before, when I first moved here. The nightmares went away. They came back with the Dunworth case."

Tory considered his words. Sure, certain events could trigger a re-onset of PTSD, but she suspected the real problem was that Charlie had never dealt with the tragedy he'd lived through. And until he did so, he'd never be free of it.

She stood. "I care so much for you Charlie. You wouldn't be here if I didn't. I want what's best for you. I want you to get your career back. I want you to sleep, damn it."

He reached for her hand.

She held his for a moment, then let go. "Charlie, no. We can't."

He nodded. "I get it."

But she didn't think he did.

Running her hands through his dark golden hair, wishing everything were different, if only for a little while, she said, "Good night."

Chapter Fifteen

Tuesday morning, Tory stumbled out of her bedroom at eight o'clock, far later than she usually slept. There would be no going for a run this morning. She and Charlie stayed up talking till nearly four a.m. The only thing she minded about the experience was that he refused to even consider getting help for PTSD.

She passed a sleeping Charlie on her way to the coffee pot, then headed back into her bedroom to shower. By the time she came out to make a travel mug to take with her to the clinic, Charlie was up drinking a cup of coffee—black, she noted—and sitting on one of the kitchen stools. He looked terrible, like he never fell asleep after she'd left him.

"Are you going to your new job now?" he asked.

"Just for a little while. I have to fill out the paperwork and get my pass and stuff. Shouldn't take longer than an hour."

"I—do you mind if I come with you?" He didn't meet her eyes when he asked, almost like he was embarrassed. Her heart ached for him.

"I don't mind, but it's a women-only clinic. I'll have to ask if men are even allowed in the building."

He laughed at that. "Imagine if you told them I killed my mom."

Tory's heart stopped. "That's not funny."

"It is to me." Setting his mug on the counter, he grabbed his bag and strode into her bedroom to get dressed.

———

Charlie offered to drive Tory to her new job. He felt like he owed Tory—for her help with Amanda Dunworth, for giving him a place to stay, for listening to him the night before—and for doing all of those things after he'd been such a royal ass on Friday. Plus, if he were being honest, after sharing his story with her, he was feeling raw. The thought of sitting alone in a strange apartment didn't appeal to him very much. Almost as much as her idea of waiting till he was somehow healed before they could touch each other again. They'd already admitted their feelings for one another—unless Tory was lying because she felt sorry for him.

What a humiliating thought.

"I spoke to my boss," she said, cutting into his thoughts. "She said that men are only allowed through the staff entrance in the back, and only with an employee escort. They're not allowed anywhere patients go, only in the staff offices or by the emergency exit." She explained that some of the men who came to the clinic delivered supplies. Some were EMTs who came with ambulances to take emergency cases to the hospital.

As Tory directed him to the staff parking lot in the back of the building, Charlie noted its location east of Venice, across the street from a payday lender, and only a few blocks over from the local police station. It was part of Charlie's job to know where all of the police stations were.

Part of his *former* job.

He shook the thoughts from his head and focused on Tory. Glancing around, he realized that her new clinic was in a terrible part of town. Charlie was immediately worried.

"Why is your job here? This neighborhood is a disaster."

Tory didn't answer. She was dialing a number and pointing at the gated entrance to the lot. He pulled up to the gate and waited.

"Hi Mary, it's Tory. We're outside. Yeah, the black BMW. No, it's not mine." She laughed. "See you in a minute."

The tall, metal gate clanked open, and Charlie pulled in, wondering if his wheels would still be on his car when they came back out again.

He met her on her side of the car, taking in the low, concrete-colored building. "This place is a dump."

"Then why don't you donate a million dollars so they can fix it up?" she snapped and headed for the door.

Well, he'd definitely said the wrong thing. But he wasn't incorrect. The place really was a dump. At the back door, Tory pressed a buzzer, smiling at the security camera. Then she grabbed his arm, dragging him in front of the camera as well. A moment later, the door unlocked. Before she could reach for it, Charlie opened the door for her.

He heard her mutter "Whatever, dude" under her breath as she stormed past him.

Following her into the building, Charlie took one last look at his car before closing the door tightly behind him. The interior of the building was hardly more enticing than the exterior. The hallways were grim and dull. The offices small, cramped, and dark. There were no windows in most, and those windows he could see were barred so tightly that hardly any light crept through.

Tory waited in the hall. Stepping up next to her, Charlie asked, "What kind of women's clinic is this?"

"A free clinic for at-risk women."

"At-risk?"

"Sex workers. Addicts. DV victims. Undocumented women. Anyone who doesn't feel safe going to the hospital, or who can't afford it."

Charlie rocked back on his heels. Tory chose to work here? No wonder she and Miranda were such good friends. They were both unrelenting do-gooders.

"Why didn't you stay in the emergency room if you wanted all this awfulness?"

Tory wouldn't meet his eye. When she finally spoke, her tone was ice cold. "It's called the emergency *department*." Speaking to him like he was an idiot, she put emphasis on the second word.

After a few moments, a new woman joined them, and Tory

seemed surprised to see her. "Dr. Baker," Tory said. "I was expecting Mary."

"Mary's with a patient. And I told you to call me Jean." Dr. Baker eyed Charlie from head to toe. "Who's this character?"

Tory glanced at him. "He's my friend's little brother. He's hanging out with me today."

Crossing her arms, Jean tapped her finger against her elbow. "Did you feel unsafe coming here alone?" She didn't sound concerned— she sounded annoyed.

Tory snorted, laughing. "Oh, no. Sorry, I don't mean to laugh. I feel fine coming here alone." Glancing at Charlie with narrowed eyes, Tory added, "We're just hanging out today, that's all."

Charlie got the feeling that Tory nearly said she was keeping him company because he didn't want to be alone—which was accurate, but hard to swallow. He thought back to last week, to Miranda's party, how Tory had looked at him with such admiration. But now— was that a trace of pity in her voice? The balance in their relationship had shifted, and they weren't on even footing anymore. It felt like she was babysitting him, and he didn't like that feeling at all.

After directing Tory—and Charlie by association—to an empty office, Dr. Baker gave Tory some paperwork to fill out and notes about scrub color and other details for working at the clinic. The place was called Infinity Women's Health, but from where he was sitting, things looked very finite.

After twenty minutes of watching Tory fill out paperwork, Charlie got a text from Miranda: **r u moving back home or what?**

He considered his answer, thinking about the look of aggravation on his big sister's face when he'd blown things with the Dunworth case, the look of pity on Tory's. He didn't want to be anyone's burden. **No. Signed a lease on a new place.**

Miranda: **last chance. J is gonna to move in if u dont.**

Him: **Excellent. Tell the loser I said hi.**

Her: **im serious last chance.**

Him: **ill have you over for little sandwiches once I have a table.**

"I'm almost done," Tory said, glancing up at him.

"Seriously," he said, running his hand across the scuffed surface of the table. "Why do you want to work here?" He held up his hand when she narrowed her eyes. "I'm just trying to understand. You could have such a better job."

Tory squeezed her hand into a fist on the table. "Why is it so hard for you to understand the desire to help people who need your help the most?"

He stared at her blankly.

She poked him in the forehead. "Think! Why are you so upset by the Dunworth case? Why are you so eager to champion a kid who shot his parents? You're a smart man, Charlie, but sometimes you're a dumbass."

Charlie leaned back, the air leaving his lungs. "Yeah, okay."

Maybe, just maybe, he and Tory weren't so different after all. And thinking about his glossy office back in Century City, that very idea threw him for a loop.

As they left Infinity, Tory let Charlie hold the door for her again. She was still hurt by his obvious scorn for the place, but during their last conversation he seemed to understand, at least a little bit, why her work was important to her.

"I'm sorry I snapped at you," she said, leaning against his parked car. The sky was the crisp blue of morning, its brightness making the run-down buildings seem even more derelict.

"I'm sorry I was a dickhead. Honestly, my first instinct was to worry about you coming to this neighborhood alone."

"People—women—come here all the time."

"I know that." He chuckled. "I'm trying to imagine saying these same words to Miranda, and the story in my head ends very badly."

Tory snorted.

But now that Tory wasn't angry anymore, a familiar guilt had set in. She rarely got angry. A cool head was required in the ED. Plus, there hadn't been much anger in her home growing up. Not many strong emotions at all, actually. When she had gotten angry, even as a child, afterward, all she'd felt was guilt like she was feeling now.

When she was eleven, starting middle school, her father had promised her a ride on the first day of school. She waited for him by the front door and watched the school bus pass her house. When her father finally emerged from her parents' home office, she felt the familiar pain—he'd forgotten about her, again.

"Dad?" she said. "I'm going to be late." She was so angry. She'd dressed up special for the first day. She wanted to make a good first impression on her teachers.

"Late for what?"

"You were supposed to drive me."

"Don't you ride your bike to swim practice?"

He'd not only forgotten to drive her, he'd forgotten that school was starting at all. Tory rarely got upset at her parents because she accepted that her parents' work was important. But then she thought of being late on the first day of school, and how all of the students would stare at her and she'd turn beet red. She'd have to apologize to her teacher, and it wasn't even her fault. She wanted to scream.

"How could you?" she said. "You promised me!"

Her father's face froze. "I don't have time to waste on a temper tantrum. When you have your emotions under control, I'll be waiting in my office."

"I'm sorry, Dad," she said immediately, not wanting to be any later than she already was. "I understand that mistakes happen."

He stood up straighter and sniffed. "I'll get my keys. If we hurry, perhaps you won't be tardy."

She'd learned, long before the sixth grade, that the best way to handle her parents was with humor and patience. The few times she slipped, they made her feel terrible afterward, as though her anger were uncivilized. Somehow, she ended up feeling like she didn't have a right to express her emotions because her parents hadn't done anything wrong. Just innocent mistakes.

She felt that same guilt now. Charlie hadn't deserved her lashing out. He hadn't really done anything wrong. He wasn't incorrect in his assessment of Infinity. The place was indeed run down. A person might truly be confused about why she wanted to work there. Even Jean Baker had grilled her about it. His tone could have been more respectful, sure, but his questions were legitimate.

She shouldn't have lashed out at him. She almost apologized again, but he spoke before she could.

He took her hand in his. "I shouldn't have criticized the clinic."

Caught by surprise, she tried to make excuses. "I know what this place looks like." She gestured around her. "I know what the neighborhood looks like. Yeah, your words were direct, but they're not inaccurate. My parents would say the same thing." And they would, soon, when they found out where she was working. Tory was already coming up with defenses. "It's just—so many people need my help, and this is where I want to help them."

"Why'd you leave the emergency *department*? Weren't you helping people there?" He emphasized the proper word as she'd done inside.

She blushed at the reminder of her anger. "It's hard to explain. It has to do with why I chose to work there in the first place." She looked away from him, at the payday lender sign across the street, its flashing neon catching her eye. "I'm trying to change."

He tugged her fingers. "Change what?"

"I was second in my medical school class. I could have picked any residency in any specialty. Everyone—meaning my parents—was shocked when I picked emergency medicine instead of surgery or literally anything else. But I just did what I always did. Tumbled into the next thing that felt right."

"Emergency medicine felt right? Why?"

"The patients moved fast. I fixed them up, and sent them along. I didn't get to know them. No long-term care, no relationships with patients or their families. Not until Daphne came in after that awful car accident and adopted me like a puppy." Tory smiled at the memory.

Although Daphne had been her patient first, afterward, she'd become Tory's close friend—the first of Tory's entire life. Sure, Tory had lots of acquaintances, but no one she was close to. She hadn't realized that until Daphne.

Daphne hadn't given Tory a choice. She'd kept coming back, dropping by the hospital to see Tory, sometimes dragging her to dinner because she knew Tory rarely carved out enough time to eat. And Miranda, once she'd gotten to know Tory, had been even worse. Miranda called her all the time, making sure Tory showed up for things. Pestering her when she didn't. They'd overwhelmed Tory with affection, and with predictability. They were always *there*.

Tory crossed her arms over her chest. "Between Daphne and your sister, one day I realized I wasn't alone. And that's when I realized how alone I'd been before. I'd chosen the ED. because it felt normal and right. I didn't want to do long-term patient care. I didn't want to get to know my patients, or even my co-workers." She gazed past him, eyes lost in the distance. "I didn't know how to, really. I sound so pathetic. I didn't know how to have friends."

Charlie pulled her to him, wrapping her in a hug she hadn't realized she needed. "But you seem to get along so well with people," he said, his voice low near her ear.

"When I know I don't have to see them again, sure." She rested her head on his shoulder. "I hate to complain about my parents when you..." She hesitated, not knowing what to say.

He chuckled, and she could feel the rumbling throughout her body. "When mine are dead and sadistic?"

"Right." She sighed. Taking a deep breath, she let his scent fill her lungs. Her body relaxed, and he held her tighter.

"I wasn't abused or anything, not at all," she said. "My parents are nice people. They didn't yell at me or hit me or lock me in the closet. It's just that I was alone a lot." She felt Charlie tense, but he didn't say anything, giving her space to talk. "They were really busy with work. So I had to do my own thing. Get ready for school by myself, and make my own dinner. You know."

"Not really. Miranda and I had housekeepers who cooked for us." He made a chef's kiss.

"Oh my God." She snorted, grateful that Charlie was keeping the mood light, even as she spoke of hard things. "I think, maybe, I didn't learn very well how to make friends because I wasn't around other people much. I don't know. I hate to blame everything on my parents. That seems like a cop-out."

Charlie was quiet for a while, and she wished she could see his face better. Finally, he said, "You don't seem like a person who cops out very frequently."

She shook her head, rubbing her cheek against his shirt. "I don't want to be."

Charlie stepped back from her, keeping his hands on her shoulders. "You were second in your medical school class? Slacker."

Tory nearly growled. She would never forget that day, missing first by a few hundredths of a point. The guy who beat her out—Justin Peebles—had been so smug when he came to congratulate her.

"Say it." Charlie gave her a look out of the corner of his eye. "I would never judge."

"Say what?" she said, confused.

"What you're thinking about the person who came in first."

The familiar aggravation filled her. "He was such a jackass!"

Charlie laughed, taking her hand and squeezing. "My God, you are adorable. Tell me more."

"Whenever he got a higher grade than me on an exam, he acted like grades didn't matter. When I got the higher grade, he freaked out and complained about the test being unfair. He did everything he could to game our professors. And he tried to game me, too. He'd show up where I was studying and make that place his new favorite study location so I would have to move. There's so much more; I could go on."

"Where did he end up?"

"Some surgical residency back east. I lost track of him after that. Deliberately." Remembering his smug look on graduation day, she muttered, "Wanker."

"Wanker?" Charlie laughed.

"My parents had a British junior researcher in their lab. She babysat me a lot." Tory headed toward the car. She was itching for the run she'd missed that morning.

Glancing back at Charlie, she noticed he was giving her an assessing look. "Your parents weren't around very much?"

"Don't pity me. I learned to be resilient."

"It's one thing to have parents who work a lot, but who are totally there for you when they're around. My mom was like that, when she wasn't sick. Litigators work crazy hours. But I knew, without a doubt, that Miranda and I meant everything to her." He pressed the button on his key and unlocked the car.

Listening to Charlie talk about his mom, Tory felt two emotions at the same time: immense sadness for him, knowing what had happened the day his mother died. And jealousy of his mother's love for him. She hated herself for feeling jealous.

"What do you normally do in the afternoon?" Charlie asked her as he opened her door.

"Go running with Daisy if I didn't in the morning." She eyed him as she sat down. "How about you?"

"Hang out at the Typhoon like an old sailor."

Tory snorted.

He climbed in the car next to her, started the engine, and headed back toward Venice.

At the first stoplight, he glanced at her. "Why do you run? I get it that some people jog for exercise, but you take it a little more seriously than that. With the marathoning and everything."

"Have you ever wondered how much you could endure?" she asked him.

He laughed, the familiar half-smile tugging at his lips. "No."

"I do. That's what running is all about. Well, it is now. At first, I did it for bad reasons."

"Look, running is basically terrible anyways, so I'm really wanting to hear about these bad reasons."

Tory laughed again. "Enduring the pain makes me feel alive, *real*," she said. "But at first, running for fun wasn't enough."

"Running's fun?"

She elbowed him. "So that's why I started running road races, and that's why I ran the marathon. There's nothing like feeling as though your body's falling apart to make you feel real. But I won't do another marathon—I know what I was trying to fix by pushing too hard, and it didn't work. I was basically invisible to my parents, and I thought I was okay with being invisible." She chewed her lip. "Turns out I wasn't okay with it."

Pulling to a stop in front of her house, Charlie turned to her, his eyes on fire. "I see you just fine."

Tory felt the pull of Charlie, the pull she'd felt for years. How could one person be so magnetic? She wanted to touch him so badly.

The half-smile returned. And that's when she realized that he knew just what she was thinking.

He leaned toward her, wrapped his hand around her cheek, and kissed her. This wasn't the jolly, tipsy Charlie from the week before. This Charlie kissed her with intent.

She was a goner.

He pulled back, tugging on her ponytail. "I've always loved your hair."

But the pain he'd been in the night before was still there, under the crystalline surface he'd covered himself in now. He could shatter again at any moment. This was the same person who, only yesterday, had driven to the home of an abused girl in a desperate move to save her brother—and himself.

Tory realized something when he wrapped his arms around her outside the clinic and listened to her talk about her secret pain. She could, very easily, fall in love with Charlie George. She was already halfway there.

"No, Charlie." She pulled back from him. "We can't do this. Not yet."

"Not yet." His voice was smoke. It was heat, and she almost lost her resolve. What was it about the Georges and their animal magnetism? Did they receive special training when they were young? Miranda George hadn't paid for a drink since arriving in Los Angeles, and she'd be the first to tell you that she didn't look anything like a typical Hollywood starlet.

Instead of kissing him again, she opened her door. "I'm happy to have you stay with me until you find a place. But we stick to our bargain."

Charlie nodded, and if she hadn't been watching him closely, she would have missed the expression that briefly crossed his face. It was one of sadness, and guilt, and dejection. She'd hurt him, and he didn't want her to know.

Then the smile was back, firmly in place. "I appreciate you letting me stay. Do you want to take Daisy for a jog together? I'll try to keep up."

"You just said you hate running."

"For you, I'd learn to like it."

Chapter Sixteen

On Sunday afternoon, Charlie held Daisy's leash as he walked her down the side streets of Venice. In his Guns-N-Roses t-shirt, worn jeans and leather flip-flops, hair in disarray and face unshaven for over a week, he fit right in with the rest of the inhabitants of Venice Beach. But he'd never felt less like himself.

But he wasn't just falling apart on the outside. He knew he was barely together mentally. Tory had worked all day Wednesday, Thursday, and Friday at Infinity, each day coming home happier than the day before, more satisfied with her switch in careers. He was happy for her—how could he not be, when all he wanted was to see her happy?

But he hadn't told her that every day when she left early, he'd slept past noon, trying to recover the sleep the nightmares stole. Then he spent hours trying to recover from the hangovers that railroaded him due to the booze he drank trying to keep the nightmares away. He'd hidden a stash of scotch behind her couch so she wouldn't know how much he was drinking, only pulling the bottles out after she fell asleep. Each night, he drank nearly half a bottle in an attempt to put the nightmares down. It didn't work.

Each day after he showered, he ate as much as he could stand without puking, and then he took Daisy for a walk to clear his head. On these walks, he looked at the houses around him, some old and run down, some old and fixed up nice like Ms. Honey's place, and some new, built where the old houses had been torn down. He looked at the blue sky, at the ocean, at the gorgeous and quirky world around him. Most of all, he tried to convince himself that he wasn't going crazy.

Around six o'clock each day, Tory got home from work. She'd come in, and he'd be on the couch, reading the news on his laptop, acting like he cared about what was happening in the world. Each day she gave him a giant smile as though she were so happy he was there. All he could think about when he saw that smile was that moment in his car, when they'd kissed and then she'd pulled away, and how her pulling away from him had hurt far more than he'd thought possible.

How she'd said *not yet*, and he'd agreed. In that moment, he'd believed that *not yet* meant *soon*.

But now, even under the bright Venice sunlight, with a happy dog trotting at his side, he knew he was spiraling down, and he knew that Tory's *not yet* was looking a lot more like *never*. Tory might not know it, but he did. He knew he wasn't thinking straight. He was sleep deprived. He couldn't stop seeing his sister's glassy eyes as her body hit the floor and his mother's face as he pulled the trigger of the handgun, blowing a bloody hole in her body.

The blood pumping from the wound in his mother's chest.

The blood-soaked pillow.

The thoughts came more and more frequently, and more and more vividly. He was getting worse. And Tory was slipping away from him.

Two days ago, on Friday, Tory came home from work a little early. He'd just come in from his afternoon walk with Daisy when she opened the door.

"Hey," she said, her face breaking into the smile she always gave him, the one with heat in her eyes that held such promise, a promise that destroyed him because he knew it was a promise she wouldn't be able to keep. "I'm going out of town for the weekend, to my grandparents' house in Santa Barbara. Do you want to come?"

Of course he wanted to come—he wanted to be near Tory all the time. But he couldn't go as her charity case. He didn't want to meet her family as her friend; he wanted to meet them as her *man*. The shame that filled him nearly sucked the oxygen from his lungs. "I can't," he managed to say. "I have a thing with Miranda." A blatant lie, one that she would be able to figure out if she called his sister.

"You do? That's great! I'm so glad you two are talking again."

"Yeah. It's about time right?" In fact, he hadn't spoken to Miranda since the day he'd left her condo. The last time he'd answered her texts was the day he'd told her he wasn't moving back in. He'd ignored her ever since.

"Well, if you're not coming," she chewed her lip, "I have a favor to ask. Would you take care of Daisy? I usually hire a pet sitter, but she's really taken to you." Her voice trailed off.

Would he? Of course. After letting him stay in her apartment all week, pet sitting for her was the least he could do. "I don't mind at all. Besides, it's not like my calendar is full."

"Charlie." She took his hand. "Resting isn't nothing. As little as you're sleeping, it's obvious that you need it." She hesitated before speaking again. "I just wish you'd see a doctor about the flashbacks."

Taking his hand back, he felt anger rise. He was tired of her treating him like he was broken. She wouldn't touch him, or let him touch her, because she wouldn't let go of this idea that he needed to see a doctor. All he needed was sleep, some goddamned peace. "Just stop, Tory. Let it go." His voice was sharp, and he immediately regretted it.

"Fine," she snapped back. "I'm going to pack. I'll be back Sunday night."

And then she left, and he was all alone with his nightmares and his scotch.

Now it was Sunday, and after two days alone, he'd begun to hate himself. With Tory gone from the house, he realized something true: as much as he wanted her, he was never going to rise to her standards.

What he felt for Tory—it was hopeless.

He and Daisy arrived back at Ms. Honey's house, and he dropped the poop bag in the outdoor trash. After turning Daisy loose in the yard, he headed back out again to the Typhoon.

When he sat at the far end of the bar, Lala's back was to him. He leaned his head against the worn, dark wood of the wall. For a few minutes, Lala didn't even notice him sitting there. Strangely, the invisibility felt comforting. He shut his eyes, taking it in. For so many years, he'd stood out—his height, his good looks, his family name—all so damn visible. Now, he was just another derelict, inside and out.

"Charlie George, what on earth?" His eyes snapped open.

Lala was eyeing him like he was a dirty dish someone forgot to wash.

"Hey, Lala."

"Haven't seen you in a while."

"Been getting my beverages elsewhere lately."

At this, she merely tilted her head and waited for further explanation.

"Can I have a scotch, please?"

"Your regular brand?"

He nodded, resting his face in his hand, suddenly exhausted. He hadn't realized how tiring his own company had been over the past few days.

A voice spoke from his left. "I was hoping I'd see you here again."

Hiking herself up onto the barstool was…what was her name? Had he ever known it? He remembered her though—the woman from the bathroom, the night Lala had thrown him out of the bar.

"It's Regina," she said. "And you're Charlie." Regina waved down Lala and held up two fingers.

Lala shrugged and poured two tumblers of scotch, setting them down in front of Charlie. "Don't make a mess in my bar again," she said to him as she stalked away.

Regina held up her glass. "Cheers."

"What are we toasting?"

"Old friends?"

Charlie laughed despite himself. "All right." He clinked his glass with hers.

She sipped the scotch and didn't cough or choke like he expected her to. Caught by surprise, he asked, "What do you do around here?"

"I'm an ICU nurse. Twelve-hour shifts. Three days on, four days off."

The first time Charlie had met Tory, when he'd learned she

worked in the hospital, he'd deliberately asked if Tory were a nurse. He'd said it to piss off his sister—knowing she'd flip out that he thought any woman working in a hospital had to be a nurse, not a doctor. He'd been such an ass—insulting Tory and insulting nurses all at once.

Tory was smart to push him away. And now things would stay that way. Even as he made his decision to let Tory go, it felt like his chest was being ripped open. He knew, right then, that Tory might mean everything to him. But it didn't matter.

Not yet. Not ever.

He'd held her outside of Infinity on Tuesday, and she'd told him about how her parents had ignored her as a child. *They were really busy with work,* she'd said. *I had to do my own thing.* Even as she defended them, Charlie heard what she hadn't said. That she wished they'd paid more attention to her and taught her how to let other people care for her. Remembering how she felt in his arms, his throat closed.

He threw back the last of his scotch and clacked his glass on the bar. Lala gave him a stinkeye, but she refilled it. He threw the second glass back too.

Not ever.

Focusing on Regina and blocking out everything else, he said, "You're off now, I'm guessing, if you're day-drinking with me."

Regina laughed. "When you work like I do, there's not much difference between day and night."

Charlie conjured up one of his most charming smiles. He was surprised he still had it in him. "In that case, isn't it getting late?" He faked a yawn. "I really could hit the hay, you know?"

Regina tossed back the last of her drink, setting her empty glass on the bar next to Charlie's. She leveled her big green eyes on him. "Then let's beat it."

Back at Tory's apartment, they were dropping their clothes as soon as the door shut. Charlie might not have remembered Regina's name, but he remembered her long legs and tiny waist. But even as he lowered himself to the shag rug in Tory's living room, pulling Regina on top of him, burying his face in her honey-scented neck, he wished her legs were more muscular, her bottom more round, her hips wider. Her hair darker and her face sprinkled with freckles.

He squeezed his eyes shut to force what he could never have from his mind. And as he did so, he heard the terrible sound of the apartment door unlocking.

He looked over Regina's bare shoulder and saw Tory's face.

He heard Tory's gasp of shock. Before Tory could see any more, he snatched the blanket from the couch and covered himself and Regina.

Tory's hand covered her mouth. And her eyes—they filled with tears. She ran into her bedroom and shut the door.

"What the hell, Charlie?" Regina said. "You have a girlfriend?" She was furious. Naked, she stood, snatching her clothes from the floor.

"No—she's not. I'm couch surfing." He sat up, the blanket on his lap.

"That's not what it looks like from here." Regina grabbed her shorts and tank and pulled them on. "Get your shit together, dude." Carrying her shoes, she slammed the door behind her.

Sitting on the floor naked, half-covered with a blanket, he dropped his head into his hands, and wondered how much worse his life could get.

———

Tory stood in the middle of her bedroom taking deep breaths to slow her heart rate, to stop her hands from shaking, to stop the tears from stinging her eyes.

She'd cried in front of Charlie George, over Charlie George.

She'd told him she was falling for him, that she would wait for him, damn it, and he'd said he'd do the same. But as soon as she left town, he brought a beautiful woman to Tory's home, a woman Tory could never be. It was as clear a rejection as Charlie could deliver. Tory wasn't what he wanted, and she could never be what he wanted. He had a type, and Tory wasn't it. He didn't even respect Tory enough to sleep with a woman somewhere else.

The worst part was, even after finding him with the other woman,

Tory still ached for him. As much as she hated herself for it, she couldn't stop herself from feeling what she felt.

She felt like a damned doormat.

She sat on her bed. Her breathing had returned to normal, and her hands had stopped shaking. Her tears had dried, even. But the pain, that knifing ache between her ribs—she didn't know what to do about that.

There was a knock at her bedroom door.

She took a deep breath.

The knock sounded again. "Tory," he said. "Please talk to me."

Talk about what? she wondered. How could she explain her reaction? Her humiliating tears? She wanted to lock her door and never emerge. But she wasn't one to hide from things that scared her.

She opened the door six inches.

"I'm so sorry," he said. He'd pulled on his clothes, but he still looked rumpled.

"What for?" She was proud that her voice didn't shake.

He sounded sorry, he really did. But she had to know, for her own sake, what he was apologizing for.

He paused, surprise on his face. "What do you mean?"

"What are you sorry for, exactly?"

He rubbed a hand over his overgrown stubble. "You shouldn't have had to walk in on that. Not in your own home. It was disrespectful."

She nodded. "That's true. Anything else?"

He paused. He had no idea that he was breaking her heart. He had no idea that, for her, this was the most important question.

"I—I don't know."

"Okay," she said, shutting the door in his face. She stripped off her clothes, climbed in the shower, and cried.

———

CHARLIE SAW THE PAIN STREAK ACROSS TORY'S FACE JUST BEFORE SHE closed and locked her bedroom door. He knew he'd hurt her— bringing Regina here had been reckless, even if Tory had come home hours early. But more importantly, Tory had still believed they had a chance together. Before she walked through the door, she was still holding onto a fantasy in which the two of them made it through this dark tunnel to the other side.

He'd taken that fantasy, and he'd broken it forever. Thinking back to earlier that afternoon, when he'd invited Regina home with him, he wondered: had he planned on getting caught all along?

Yes, of course he had. He was a yellow-bellied coward for using Regina to destroy what he might have had with Tory.

And Regina knew she'd been used. He was an asshole all around. In a very short amount of time, he'd traumatized an already-traumatized teenaged girl, caused a young man to be sentenced to life in prison who didn't deserve to be, gotten fired from his job, lost his home, alienated his sister, and emotionally destroyed the only woman he'd ever truly cared about in his life.

When people talk about rock-bottom, he supposed, this was the kind of situation they were referring to.

In the living room, he scooped Tory's blanket from the floor and folded it. He stripped the sheets from the sofa and brought them over to her washing machine, starting a load. Then he packed his belongings into his duffle bag. Reaching behind her couch, he pulled out all of his bottles of scotch, both empty and full. He put the empty ones in the recycling, and then, after some thought, left the full ones on the counter.

He looked around her apartment one last time, at the long couch where he'd shared the worst about himself with Tory, and she'd never balked, never judged. She'd done the opposite—she'd opened her heart and told him she'd wait for him. He wanted to break down her bedroom door and fall to his knees, apologizing, begging, anything that would make her let him stay and earn back her trust, even if all he could have was her friendship.

But he would never do that to her—to anyone. If Miranda had taught him anything, it was to respect a woman's boundaries.

He'd forgotten about that at Amanda Dunworth's. He knew he should never have imposed on her the way he had. He had pushed her too far, trying to bend her to his will with no regard for what she needed.

He would not make that same mistake with Tory.

———

As the sun set that evening, Charlie lay back on a grassy knoll in front of the beachfront homes in Venice, some ramshackle, some majestic. Above him, palm trees swayed in the ocean breeze, the cloudless blue sky deepening as the light faded. He faced the ocean and the sunset, his head resting on his bag. He'd layered his clothing so he wouldn't get cold—he hoped—wearing two long-sleeved t-shirts and two pairs of socks. As he let his mind drift toward sleep, he joined the many other homeless people preparing to spend the night under the sky. Sure, he could afford a hotel room. He just didn't think he deserved a warm bed that night. After what he'd done to Tory, to everyone who mattered to him, the cold ground was all he was worthy of.

Tomorrow, he would figure out another way forward, one that didn't burden his sister, or Tory, or anyone who'd ever cared for him. He'd always been able to figure out a way through even the worst situations. It was what Georges did. They picked up the pieces, and kept going.

Somehow.

Chapter Seventeen

round eight o'clock Monday morning, Miranda held open her door so John could carry in yet another computer monitor the size of a Great Plains state.

"Surely that's the last of them," she said. "Otherwise I'll have to move out and let you live here alone with your electronic gak."

"My equipment is not gak." He set the monitor on the dining table, grabbed her around the waist and kissed her. "I can't believe this is really happening."

Miranda shoved him away. "Gross. You're covering me with sweat."

"You're deflecting."

She rolled her eyes. "You're used to it."

"What I'm not used to is living in a retirement home. I must really love you."

Miranda tapped her lip. "You do love me, it's true. But you shouldn't bag on retirement life. It's pretty great."

"Marina del Rey is the most uncool part of Los Angeles. And yet you live here on purpose."

"Obviously I don't care about being cool."

"You have never cared about what others think of you."

Miranda thought about her mother, and her father, and the life she'd left behind. "I'm not sure that's true. But I do know it's a luxury not to worry about what others think. It's very freeing."

John pulled her to him. "You're worried about something right now, though. I can tell. Is it Charlie?"

She nodded. He'd been avoiding her calls and texts for nearly a week—the longest they'd ever gone without talking to one another except when she'd been comatose or suicidal. But she didn't voice her concerns. "He'll be fine." She wanted to believe it. Kissing John, she said, "I'm glad you're here."

He gave her a warm smile. "I'll go grab another box."

He left, closing the door behind him. Miranda sat on one of her kitchen stools, taking in the mess her condo had become. Charlie still hadn't come to get his stuff from his old bedroom, which meant John couldn't set up his office in there like they'd planned. Miranda was annoyed, since Charlie had told her he'd signed a lease nearly a week ago. What surface was he sleeping on if his bed was here instead of at his new place? Honestly, she didn't want to know. When it came to Charlie, the answer probably involved women. Plural.

For now, she let John set up in the spare bedroom she used as her office. She could make room. There was plenty. He used to live in a studio apartment whose entire footprint was smaller than her office. Despite how much gak he owned, John knew how to keep his stuff organized.

Miranda hadn't thought she'd ever feel what she was feeling right now: cracking her space, and her heart, wide open to let someone else in—and liking it.

Her phone rang—it was Tory. Stepping out onto the balcony, she answered. "What's happening, hottie?"

"Is Charlie there?" Tory sounded out of breath.

Miranda's senses went on alert. "No. Why would he be here? He told me he had gotten his own place."

"He did?" Tory paused. "Then he lied to you. He was staying here at my place all week, until yesterday. And then…" Tory's voice trailed off.

"Tell me what happened. Details."

"I walked in on him." Tory's voice sounded hurt.

"Having sex with someone. In your apartment."

"Yes." Tory's voice was a whisper now.

"Then what?"

"He apologized, and then I took a shower. When I came out, he was gone. I thought he went home to your place. He hasn't been answering my calls or texts."

Miranda paused, considering. "He didn't come here. It's likely he went to a hotel."

Tory was silent for a moment. "Miranda? Please don't get mad."

Curious, Miranda said, "Why would I get mad?"

"You sound strange. You sound, I don't know, cold."

Behind her, the door opened. John stepped in with a box in his arms, setting it on the floor against the wall. When he saw her, he came quickly onto the balcony, a concerned look on his face.

Miranda said to Tory, "Can you hold for a moment?" To John, she said, "What is it?"

"You tell me." He sounded worried.

"What do you mean?"

"You look like something's happened."

Miranda took the phone from her ear and handed it to John. "Talk."

She sat at the dining table, pulling a legal pad to her and uncapping a pen. She made a list.

The Ritz.

Lala.

Birch.

She paused, considering, then she wrote: *Sandy.*

After a few minutes, John came in from the balcony and sat next to her at the table. "Tory told me what happened. Are you really worried about where he went? He has a no-limit credit card."

"I'm not worried."

"Well," John said, "you seem worried."

"I can find him. There are ways. If he signed a lease. Or changed his car registration or driver license address—any of those things would pop."

"Jesus, Miranda." John gestured at all of his computer equipment. "I can find him, too. That wasn't what I was asking." He rubbed his hand down her back. "What has you so worried?"

Miranda felt her rigidity start to give way. For a moment, she was afraid. Without the impenetrable barrier between her and the world that had sustained her for most of her life, how could she save Charlie now that he needed saving again?

Then she glanced to the side, where John sat, his hand on her back, his warm eyes full of concern and yes, unconditional love for her. She remembered, then, that she didn't have to battle the world alone ever again.

She crumpled into him and began to cry. "I'm so worried, John. I should never have let him move out. I knew something was wrong. How could I let him leave?"

A few minutes later, Tory arrived wearing bright pink scrubs. Miranda was still working on her plan to locate her brother—adding more items to her list and expanding on the items already there.

As soon as Miranda opened the door to let Tory in, Tory started talking. "John invited me over to tell you what I learned about Charlie while he stayed with me last week."

"He did?" Miranda looked behind her to the shared office, where John was still setting up his gear.

John stepped out. "I did."

"I only have a few minutes before I have to leave for work," Tory said. "But I wanted to help."

Miranda took one look at Tory, and so much became immediately plain. Tory had fallen for her brother. Miranda wondered if Tory even knew. Love. It made everything so much more complicated.

The three of them sat around the dining table. Miranda glanced at Tory, waiting for her to speak. When she didn't, Miranda asked, "Why were you worried when you couldn't find him?"

"Do you know about his nightmares?"

Miranda nodded. "They've come back. He had one the night you stayed over. The day after he was assigned the Dunworth case."

"He told you?"

"Yeah. That's why he was such a dick in the morning."

Tory cleared her throat, turning pink. "So, let's think about what's happened. He got in a fist fight at work. Then he screwed up the case by going to the client's sister's house." Tory paused, looking in John's direction. "Is it okay that we're talking about this in front of John?" Tory gestured at him. "Isn't there client confidentiality?"

Sure, talking in front of John was technically a breach. But at that moment, Miranda wasn't worried about it. "Keep going."

"And then he got fired—"

"What did you say?" Miranda was shocked. Surely Charlie would have told her something so momentous.

"When I was here, after you guys fought about him going to Amanda Dunworth's house, someone from his work called and fired him."

"He didn't tell me," Miranda whispered.

Tory nodded. "And then he said he was going to go stay at the Ritz, and I said that was stupid and he should stay with me."

Also pretty stupid, Miranda thought, given the obvious love in Tory's eyes, but she kept that opinion to herself. After all, she was grateful that Tory had taken care of Charlie.

"Then, that first night at my house, he was on the couch, but I could hear him screaming. So I went out, and woke him up, and he told me everything." She looked at John, eyebrows raised.

John smiled. "Yeah, I know everything."

"Okay. So I joined this little screwed-up club—we should have a secret handshake by the way—and by then I was certain that he has PTSD, and I told him that."

Miranda pictured Tory and Charlie, sitting on a couch together in the middle of the night, and Tory diagnosing him with a mental health disorder while he was likely thinking about how to get into her underpants.

He would not have been receptive to her words.

"So after he laughed off PTSD, what happened?"

Tory narrowed her eyes at Miranda. "I let him stay with me for the rest of the week. I started work at my new job on Wednesday—hey, I got a new job."

"Congrats."

"And then I went out of town on Friday, and he stayed behind to dog-sit for me. And when I came back, I walked in on him screwing another woman on the living room floor." Her voice hitched as she finished.

One thing was certain. Tory had it bad for Charlie. Just as bad, Miranda knew, as Charlie had it for Tory. For Charlie to have screwed around in Tory's own house was another bad sign. He deliberately torpedoed any good thing he could have had with Tory.

It wasn't so long ago that Miranda had been on a similar path, wrecking everything with the people who cared most about her—like John—because she knew that her road was going to end in an untimely fashion.

"After he left, he stopped answering my calls. What can we do?" Tory said. "Just sit around and wait for something awful to happen?"

John spoke up. "Something awful already has happened. He lost his home, his temporary home, his friends, and his job. What else is there?"

"John," Miranda said sharply. "There's always more to lose." She stood. "All I've done is look out for him to make sure he never had to worry. I'm not going to stop now just because he's being an idiot."

Tory piped up. "He told me he drinks every night at some bar in Venice."

"It's The Typhoon's Widow, our regular place." Heart squeezing, she looked at John, pleading, hoping, he'd be okay with what she was asking.

Standing, he took her hand. "We'll just continue what we were planning today. You and I will share your office. We'll share your bedroom. There's plenty of room in this place for all three of us."

She threw her arms around him. Whispering in his ear, she said, "I love you so much."

He whispered back. "I know."

She grabbed her cell phone, dashing off a text to Charlie: **Write me back asshole. I know u don't have a lease. I know u don't have a job.**

He didn't reply.

Her heart raced.

After a few minutes, she texted Lala: **Is he there?**

Lala: **Not right now. But he will be.**

Miranda: **Let me know when he comes in?**

Lala: **Thought u would never ask.**

———

AT TWO O'CLOCK MONDAY AFTERNOON, LALA TEXTED MIRANDA: **HE JUST walked in**.

Miranda and John had just finished setting up the office that they would share. John's L-shaped desk nearly touched hers, taking up half of one wall and half of another, his monitors and his computer towers whirring softly, the humming sound a familiar comfort to Miranda after all of their years together.

Looking up from her phone, Miranda said, "Charlie is at the Typhoon. I need to go get him."

John finished attaching a cable and turned to her. "I'll go with you."

"No," she said. "He and I are probably going to argue, and then he'll attack you just to piss me off."

"But I find it so charming now that I know that it's just a defensive tactic."

Miranda smiled despite her worry, feeling warm toward John for his patience with her little brother despite how rude Charlie could be. When they first met, Charlie had treated him really badly, calling him meaningless, just another guy that Miranda would chew up.

Charlie had been wrong.

"Stay here, and if I need you, I'll call. I promise."

"All right." John hugged her and let her go.

Miranda walked to the Typhoon because she knew parking would be impossible. It was afternoon at the beach, and the tourists would be out, even on a Monday. Plus, she knew that Charlie wouldn't leave quickly after arriving, so she had time. The ten-minute walk went quickly, and just before she walked in, she paused on the sidewalk and texted Lala: **he still there?**

Lala replied: **At the end of the bar surrounded by a gaggle.**

Strolling through the open door, Miranda looked to her right. There was a group of young women in college T-shirts. Looking a little closer, she could read *Oregon* beneath their sorority letters. Charlie was going for easy targets today—out-of-towners.

Miranda stuffed her hands in the back pockets of her jeans and stepped up behind one of the college students, a white woman whose brown ponytail hung to the middle of her back.

Charlie didn't notice Miranda, and so she eavesdropped on their conversation.

"Naw," Charlie said, "I didn't move here for the movies. I'm a lawyer." He turned to one of the young women. "But you look like you could be in pictures."

Miranda rolled her eyes. Her brother had amped up the accent. He might not be in the movies, but he sure could play an act.

"Oh my goodness, you are so sweet," the young woman said, placing her hand on his knee.

Miranda examined her brother, taking in his T-shirt and shorts that clearly hadn't been laundered lately, his hair that hadn't been cut, washed, or brushed, and his face that hadn't been shaved, and she wondered how these college women were still taken in by him. He looked like every other hobo wandering around Venice Beach. He didn't look like her brother at all. And yet, when he opened his mouth, when he smiled his Charlie smile, even though she could tell he hadn't brushed his teeth in twenty-four hours at least, the charm rolled off him in waves.

At least he has that going for him, Miranda thought, *even if he has nothing else.*

When one of the college women invited Charlie to leave the Typhoon to go back to their hotel, Miranda decided it was time to step in.

"I'm sorry ladies, but he can't go with you today."

As a group, the four college students turned and looked at Miranda.

The one with the long brown ponytail spoke first. "Oh crap. Are you his girlfriend? We are so sorry."

Miranda smiled slightly. "No, I'm not his girlfriend."

The one closest to Charlie, who'd put her hand on his leg, looked at Miranda and then back at Charlie. "No you guys, look! She's his twin sister. You can tell."

As one, the four young women looked at Charlie and then at Miranda, nodding in agreement.

Charlie had turned away to face the bar, and he was throwing back what looked like scotch on the rocks. From the empty glasses lined up next to him, this one was his third.

"Charlie," Miranda said. "I need to talk to you."

"That's fine," he said, losing all but the real part of his southern accent. "But I have nothing to say to you."

"Why are you angry at me?" she asked, genuinely confused.

"I'm not."

Oh no, she realized. He was angry at himself. Dealing with him was going to be more difficult than she'd first thought.

The college women still waited, unsure what to do. Miranda spoke to them. "I can tell you all are smart. You go to a good school, and you're here on vacation right?"

The four of them nodded.

"All right. This guy is indeed my brother. And he and I need to have a serious talk. And so, unfortunately, I have to take him off your hands. Maybe in a few days, if you're still around, you might be able to find him here again. So check back then. Does that sound fair?"

The one with the long brown ponytail said, "Sure thing," and she led the others outside to the patio.

Miranda took the seat next to Charlie, nodding at the three empty glasses. "Scotch is hardly a liquor for day drinking. Gin and tonic is our drink for that."

"Since when did Lala become such a rat?"

Miranda stifled her anger at Charlie's words. He was trying to get a rise out of her, and she wouldn't let him. "Lala is worried about you."

"Is that why you're here?"

"Our mother was many things, including an alcoholic. I can't watch you do this to yourself."

"Then don't watch." He held up his hand to flag down Lala. Lala shook her head and turned away from him.

"Seriously? You cock-blocked an entire sorority, and now your booze-blocking me too?"

"Tory told me you got fired."

"So Tory's also a rat."

Forcing herself to ignore the insults Charlie was hurling at the women he cared about most, Miranda reminded herself that he'd regret his words later. There was no need for her to rub them in his face now. "Tory also told me she walked in on you with another woman in her apartment. That's tacky, even for you."

Charlie grinned like he was picturing a fond memory. "Ah, yes. Regina. She's amazing. She hates me, too. Add her name to the list."

"No one hates you, Charlie."

"Oh no. Regina definitely hates me." He stared into the bottom of his empty glass.

Miranda took a deep breath. "I want you to move back in with me."

Charlie looked at her sideways. "What about John?"

"We're sharing my office. Your bedroom is still yours."

Charlie cracked up. "You want me to live with you and the loser?"

Miranda rolled her eyes. "Please be more creative with your insults. You sound like a frat brat."

"No."

"Really, I can help you. I have a great insult vocabulary."

"I'm not moving in with you and John."

"Where did you sleep last night?" Miranda scoffed. "In a doorway?"

Charlie stared at the wall behind the bar.

Miranda drew in a breath. "You slept outside? Why? Why not get a hotel room?"

"Why won't you leave me alone, Miranda?"

"Because you're my Little B. It's my job to stay on your case."

"No, it isn't. Not anymore." He stood, towering over her. "I'm all grown up."

She stood to face him. "Then act like it."

He picked up his duffle bag and tried to shoulder past her toward the door. She grabbed his arm. "Charlie, wait."

He turned to face her, suddenly angry. "Get out of my face, Miranda," he said, his nose to hers, his face so close she could smell the booze on his breath. He put a hand on her shoulder and pushed her away from him.

Miranda's jaw dropped. He'd never touched her in anger in his life. Captivated by her brother's anger, Miranda barely heard Lala's whistle.

Suddenly, two bouncers appeared, one on either side of Charlie, looping their arms through his elbows. Charlie, furious, tried to pull free. Miranda, horrified to see Charlie fallen so far from the brother she loved, stepped closer to him.

How could she help? What could she do?

Charlie yanked his arm loose from one bouncer's grasp and his closed fist flew.

Miranda's face exploded. She fell back against the barstools, crashing to the floor.

Gasping in pain, she curled into a ball just in case the fight wasn't over. It wasn't the first time in her life she'd been hit, but it was the first time lately. She'd forgotten how much it hurt.

Moments later, Lala was there, helping her up and holding a damp towel filled with ice to the side of her face.

"Damn, chica," Lala said. "You're going to have a massive black eye."

"Shit," Miranda said. "Ouch." She steadied herself against the bar. "I'm still dizzy."

"Well, your brother is a giant. Of course it hurt."

Miranda growled. "Where is he?"

"Probably out in the street."

Miranda took a step toward the door, but Lala stepped in front of her. "Where are you going? You want to get punched again?"

"He hit me by accident. Besides, I might get a little guilt leverage out of this."

Lala looked concerned, but let Miranda pass. "Let me know how it goes."

Outside, Miranda found her brother sitting on the curb, his bag between his legs. She stood in front of him holding the ice pack to her face. He glanced up at her, then looked at his feet.

"Where will you go now that you've lost your favorite place to get wasted?"

"I'm so sorry."

She reached for familiar words, their usual banter. "You should be sorry, asshole." She took the ice pack from her face. "Look at this." She actually had no idea what her face looked like, but from Charlie's reaction, she could tell it was bad.

"I don't know what's happening to me," he whispered.

"I do," she said. "You're diving head first into a sinkhole. Stop doing that." She nudged his toe. "Come home with me."

"No."

"No?"

"I don't want to live with you anymore."

"I'm good enough to punch, but not good enough to live with?"

Charlie stood, picking up his bag. "That's not what I meant."

"Then what did you mean?" She felt herself getting frustrated, and her face was really starting to hurt.

"I don't want to be what any of you want me to be, so stop trying to fix me."

"I'm not trying to fix you. I just want you to come home and talk."

"You are! You, Lala, Tory—you think I'm broken. I'm just pissed off and need a break."

"Then take a break at our place, Little B. We'll order pizza. I'll tell John to stay in the office, and you can pretend he's not there."

Charlie shook his head. "I'm not your Little B anymore."

Taking her heart with him, Charlie walked toward the busy boardwalk and disappeared from view.

———

MIRANDA OPENED HER CONDO DOOR QUIETLY. SHE WANTED TO GET MORE ice on her face before John saw it and worried about her more than he should. She could feel it swelling.

Pulling open the freezer, she yanked out a bag of frozen peas. At the same moment, John stepped out of the office.

"Any luck?" he said.

She turned to face him, the pack of frozen peas over half her face. "No."

"What happened?" He came closer to her, his hand reaching for her face.

She stepped back, not wanting him to see what was beneath the bag of peas. "It was an accident. There was a tussle with some bouncers."

"You tussled with bouncers?"

"They were holding Charlie back, and when he fought free, his fist found my face."

John reached forward and gently took the peas away. From the way his brows drew together, she could tell that he was upset.

"Where is he now?"

She looked at the floor, the pain she felt unrelated to the throbbing of her eye. "I don't know."

"He wouldn't come home?"

"He was a mess, John." She dropped down onto the couch, leaning her head back, covering one eye with the peas.

Rage she didn't know she'd been feeling surged up. She couldn't believe Charlie was throwing everything away. She was only finishing law school now, in her thirties. He had his law degree in his mid-twenties, and a perfect job before he'd even graduated. And now?

She stood and hurled the peas across the room. She felt disappointment that the bag didn't explode when it hit the wall. "I'm so angry with him. All of the things I did—all of the abuse I took, the sacrifices. He's throwing it in the trash. *I just need a break*, he said." She scoffed. "He needs to be hosed down like the stray dog he's starting to look like."

John tugged her arm until she sat down again, wrapping his arms around her and pulling her close. "You shielded him from your mother's moods and alcohol abuse, and from your father's abusive neglect." He kissed the top of her head. "You're amazing."

She scoffed again.

"But you couldn't protect him from that one awful thing. He killed his mother, Miranda. I know you both loved her. But I don't know what it takes for a person to come back from that. He's not throwing his life away, and you know it. He's hanging onto it for dear life."

Thinking about John's words, Miranda remembered what she could of that awful afternoon. She remembered falling to the floor and watching the world go black, hearing her brother's roar. She hadn't heard the gunshot because she'd already been gone. Charlie had been all alone for Sorcha's death.

Charlie's hurt had lingered so deep that even Charlie hadn't known, not until the Dunworth case ripped him open and the pain shot back to the surface.

John spoke. "I've been thinking about Charlie this past week, since you told me he punched that guy at work."

"Yeah. Chalk."

"I still can't believe that's a person's name."

Miranda laughed, meeting John's eye. "He's as awful as he sounds. He tried to ask me out once, calling me a *hot babe* to my face."

John raised his brows. "Really?"

"I told him to eat shit, obviously." She sighed, shaking her head. "What were you going to say about Charlie?"

"When did your brother mourn? He killed your mom, and then you were in a coma. And then there was the funeral, and then you took off on, let's face it, a suicide mission. So he comes out here to save you, and right after that, he dives into his new job and life here with you."

Miranda rolled her eyes. "I think I know where this is going. Why are you always so sensible?"

"He never took time for himself. Right now, everything that he buried those years ago is finally coming to light. That doesn't have to be a bad thing."

Miranda touched her face, pressing lightly on the bruise she knew was forming. "It feels like a bad thing." She turned to face him, placing her hand on his cheek.

"You love me because I'm sensible," he said, kissing her palm.

Pushing him away from her, Miranda made a gagging noise. "I may seem normal on the outside, but I'm still damaged. Watch it with the mush."

Laughing, John pulled her close again. "He'll be all right. I promise."

Feeling a stab of fear, Miranda said, "How do you know?"

"I just know."

Chapter Eighteen

On Tuesday morning, Charlie woke up on the beach again, and again with a pounding hangover. He remembered stumbling out of some bar at closing time, wandering near the water for a couple of hours, and then passing out when he couldn't stay on his feet anymore. He felt for his wallet and phone—they were still in his pockets—but his duffel bag was gone. He had no idea if he'd left it at one of the bars or if it had been stolen in the night.

He looked down at his rumpled clothes. His mouth felt like the inside of a shoe. And he smelled terrible. He counted back the days to his last night of sleep indoors—Saturday, at Tory's house, before Sunday, when she'd found him with Regina.

The look on Tory's face. The devastation.

He sat facing the ocean, his hands on his knees.

Tory said he had PTSD. His sister told him he was in trouble and begged him to come back home. He'd walked away from both of them when they'd tried to help him. Maybe he needed to stop doing that.

Tory told him that she'd wait for him, and he'd believed her. He remembered Regina's words. *You have a girlfriend?* she'd said. And when he'd denied it, she'd said, *That's not what it looks like from here.* Because he and Tory had indeed made promises to each other. He'd promised to wait, too, and she'd believed him.

He looked down at his dirty shirt. He was unemployed, homeless, and alone. He was haunted by memories and nightmares, and he drank too much to keep them at bay.

He was heading off of a cliff's edge, and he knew it.

Charlie George might be many things, but he wasn't stupid. He was going to call Tory, and hope that maybe, despite everything, she would still be willing to help him.

Pulling his phone from his pocket, he dialed, waiting until voicemail picked up. "Tory. This is Charlie." He paused, considering what to say. "I realize you don't owe me anything, and you probably hate me. But I need your help…" he laughed sadly, "again. I don't know who else to turn to—I'm not asking you to let me back in your home or even your life. I need—I need your doctor skills. I believe you now. About me." He signed off, and hung up.

He stood, preparing to spend another entire day alone.

Before he could return his phone to his pocket, it rang. Tory. "Hi," he said, hope in his voice.

"Meet me at the emergency department at Cedars," she said, her voice cold.

"I thought you quit Cedars."

"I maintained my privileges there so I can treat emergency cases from the clinic. And the occasional man." The way she said *man* she could have been saying *slug*.

"If you're mad at me, you don't have to help me. I could go there and see someone else."

"I'm very pissed at you, actually. But I'm also a doctor, and I'm not going to turn my back on a patient."

Charlie paused, wondering how to say the next part. "So, um, as I recall, my car is still at your place." He'd left his keys inside her apartment and his car parked out front.

Snorting, Tory said, "Yeah, it's here. I thought about driving it around as a way to collect back rent."

"Why didn't you?"

"I'll leave the keys in my mailbox and meet you at the hospital at one o'clock."

For the first time since the Dunworth case landed on his desk, Charlie felt hope.

———

CHARLIE SAT IN THE WAITING ROOM IN THE EMERGENCY ROOM—NO, emergency *department,* as Tory had corrected him—and watched the humanity around him.

He'd never entered an emergency department in his life. The day he killed his mother and Miranda nearly died, the police took him from the house for questioning.

While he rode to downtown Winston-Salem in the back of a police car, his sister and mother rode in ambulances to Wake Forest Baptist Hospital. The only thing he hated about being in the police station was that he wasn't able to be by his sister's side.

By the time he was released and reached the hospital, Miranda had been admitted and transferred to the intensive care unit, comatose. She stayed like that for months.

His mother had been transferred to the morgue for autopsy, required whenever there was a suspicious death, such as a homicide.

Homicide.

To his left, a few seats down, a young white couple sat close together, the man holding a small child on his lap, a young boy of maybe three years of age. His cheeks were red, and his cough sounded like the bark of a dog.

To his right, an older Black man rested his hand on an oxygen tank strapped to a pull cart, a clear tube running from the tank to a strap around his nose. His breathing was labored. He seemed to be counting to himself. But no, he wasn't counting. He was singing, quietly, as best he could with the air he could draw into his lungs.

Suddenly, a white woman with blond hair the same color as Miranda's crashed through the doors, alone, her huge pregnant belly preceding her, outshone only by her angry expression. She stomp-wobbled to the check-in station. Only then did Charlie notice that the legs of her yoga pants were wet.

"Hello," the check-in nurse said in a mild tone. She was an older white woman with steel-gray hair cropped short. "How can I help you?"

"I'm in labor," growled the woman. She did not sound happy about her situation.

"How far apart are your contractions?"

"Honestly, I lost count between changing maxi-pads."

Raising her eyebrows, the nurse stood. A puddle had formed around the pregnant woman's feet. "I see. Where is your driver?"

"Driver? Do I look like I can afford a chauffeur?"

Suppressing a smile, the nurse said, "I meant your spouse or partner."

"He's at work. I didn't want to bother him, so I drove myself."

Somehow, the nurse's eyebrows rose higher. "You drove yourself? And you're here alone?"

"I need to get out of these pants." The woman glanced down, noticing the puddle. "Oh, gross! Can't I get a room, please? The doctor on the phone said I should come in and be admitted."

The nurse was already signaling to an orderly to bring a wheelchair around. When the orderly, a young white man with acne still staining his cheeks, approached the pregnant woman with the wheelchair, she stepped back. "I'm not getting in a wheelchair. No way. Can't you just tell me where to go? I can walk, obviously." Even as she spoke, she bent over, a contraction pulling her forward. After a few moments, she stood again, shaking off the pain.

The nurse came around from behind the counter. She approached the pregnant woman, and the woman stepped back, her spine somehow stiffening even more. Then the nurse stepped forward again, and she wrapped her hand around the woman's arm. "It's going to be all right."

The pregnant woman tensed like a white-tailed deer about to bolt.

The nurse spoke again, in a calm, low voice. "Take a seat, and we'll take care of you."

Suddenly, the woman's iron spine relaxed. She dropped her forehead against the nurse's shoulder and sobbed. Then she sat in the wheelchair, and the orderly pushed her through the metal doors.

Charlie thought of Miranda, what she'd be like pregnant, scared but afraid to show it, needing help but afraid to ask for it. He promised himself, right then, that he'd be there for her when that day came. He'd be there for her, for her and John, because obviously she was going to be with John. And he knew, in order to be there for

Miranda, he needed to shake loose of whatever it was that was holding him down now.

AFTER HIS NAME WAS CALLED, A NURSE LED HIM BACK TO A ROOM sectioned off with a curtain. She took his vitals and then told him to sit on the exam table and wait for the doctor.

A few minutes later, Tory entered, dressed in blue scrubs and a white coat with her name embroidered on the front. She carried a clipboard and a pen and took a seat on the stool next to a counter. Resting her elbow on the counter, she looked at Charlie.

He knew what he looked like. Unshaven. Dirty. He probably smelled like week-old socks. But she said nothing, just taking him in.

"Are you ready to listen to me now?" she asked.

He thought back to that night in her apartment, when he told her the story about shooting his mom, and she told him about PTSD. He'd blown off her words, just like he'd blown off everything, and everyone, in his life.

That night they'd also promised to wait for each other. Looking at Tory's beautiful face was causing him physical pain.

"Yes."

"I'm going to ask you a series of questions. You're going to answer them honestly. And then I'm going to make a medical referral. What you choose to do after that is out of my hands."

"Thank you for this, Tory, I know I don't deserve…"

She held up a hand to stop him. "I'm not doing this for you. I'm doing it for Miranda."

He nodded. "That's fair."

She began her questions. Some of the questions were easy to answer. Questions about sleep, about memories, about intrusive thoughts. About traumatic experiences. About how all of these things were harming his livelihood and relationships.

"Can I ask you another question?" Tory said.

"Isn't that what we're doing here?"

"This one draws on my knowledge about your sister and your

family beyond what you've told me here. It might be—across the line."

"Yes. Sure."

"Tell me about your mother."

"Sorcha?" Charlie sucked in a breath. "What about her?"

"What did she look like? What did she sound like?"

Charlie thought back to his mother, how she'd been in the years before she died. "Sorcha, to me, was beautiful. She looked a lot like Miranda, actually. Just smaller, more frail. She wasn't frail, exactly— she seemed fragile, though. Maybe that's just my memory."

Was Sorcha fragile? She couldn't have been. She'd been a ferocious litigator. More ferocious than Charles Senior. The most ferocious in the firm. Around George Law she was still spoken about with reverence. But that was his memory nonetheless.

"She had dark blond hair like mine. She was about five-five. I think." He shook his head. "I hate that my memory of her is already fading. I hate that I can't call my father on the phone and talk about her."

"Why can't you?" Tory asked.

"Surely you know."

"Tell me."

"Miranda and I don't talk to our father. We have an uneasy truce. He sends us money, and we toe a line."

Tory raised her brows.

"I've fallen off that line a bit. Yeah. But he doesn't care enough to bother with me. He never has. As long as I don't do anything too embarrassing."

Even when Charlie had been arrested in high school, Charles Senior had sent his assistant to handle the problem. When Miranda had been arrested in Las Vegas, Charles Senior had sent local counsel.

He didn't bother with his children.

Miranda and Charlie didn't mind, not at all.

"My mother was beautiful, smart, funny, and ill. Then she died." He shook his head. "Then I killed her." He looked at his hands. "And now I'm here."

Tory squeezed his hand. "Thank you," she said. "My diagnosis remains the same. You have PTSD."

He nodded.

"I used to see these same symptoms a lot with homeless veterans and gang members who'd come in here. I see them now with the women I treat at the clinic, who've been abused by their husbands or pimps. PTSD is not common, but when you have it, it's terrible." She met his eyes, and he saw sympathy there. "I don't want to see you suffer, Charlie."

He looked down at his father's watch, remembering his mother's watch that he'd put in his dresser drawer at Miranda's apartment. Thinking about all of the time he'd spent destroying his life over the past couple of weeks, he felt tears prick his eyes. He was. He was suffering.

"What do I do?" he asked.

"You see a psychiatrist. And you take these." She handed him two prescriptions. "You should follow up with your psychiatrist about this medicine," she tapped one of the pieces of paper, "as soon as possible. It might not work right away, or it might not be the right medicine. Sometimes it takes a couple of tries to get it right." Then she gestured at him. "And you need to go home. Get some sleep. Get cleaned up. And please, stop torturing yourself. You know what you look like, and it's making you feel even worse than you already do."

He took the prescriptions from her, folded them carefully, and tucked them in his wallet. "I can do those things."

"And call your sister. She's worried about you."

Charlie shook his head. "I don't want to bother her. I want her to put herself first for once in her life."

Tory bopped him on the head with her clipboard.

For a moment, Charlie could only look at her in shock.

In an exasperated tone, she said, "She can't put herself first if she's spending all of her time worried about you." Under her breath she muttered, "Dumbass."

Charlie smiled. He loved Tory. He could admit that to himself. Despite her effort to keep things professional, her honesty and impatience shone as much as her beauty.

At that moment, the horrible image of her face when she'd walked into her apartment while he was on the floor, Regina naked on top of him, flashed before his eyes.

The pain on Tory's face. The horror and grief.

He'd done something unforgivable. But maybe he was redeemable. Maybe she could trust him again, enough to be his friend.

He stood up, keeping his distance from her, in part out of respect, and in part because he smelled so badly. "I'm sorry, Tory." He saw the mistrust in her eyes, but kept going. "I know I blew any chance I had with you as a man." The mistrust remained. "But I would like to earn a place as your friend. I'm going to do my best."

He turned, parted the curtains, and left.

———

In the parking lot, he texted Miranda: **Hey Big Sis.**

It took a while, but she replied: **Little B?**

Charlie: **Yeah, it's me.**

Miranda: **You OK?**

Charlie: **Getting there.**

Miranda: **Coming home?**

Charlie: **Naw. Getting a hotel. I'll text you where later today.**

Another long pause, then she wrote: **Promise?**

Charlie: **Promise.**

Miranda: **OK asshat cause if u don't I'll let John hack your location and I will bring my bat.**

Charlie: **Fair.**

Later that afternoon, Charlie checked into a room at a mid-range hotel a half-mile from the beach, a place he'd never ordinarily stay in. But if he was going to make changes, he was going to make changes everywhere. No more five stars. No more room service.

He did need clothes, though, so after he checked in, he texted his sister to bring him a suitcase full of stuff. Then he showered, wrapped himself in a towel, and waited.

When Miranda knocked on the door and entered, she raised an eyebrow, but she didn't say a word about his accommodations. "Why are you wearing a towel?" she said.

"My other clothes are in the trash."

"Should I ask?"

"No you should not."

Then she threw herself at him, hugging him like she hadn't seen him in six months, and he hugged her back, because honestly, he felt the same way.

"I've got some things I need to do," he said. "I'll be here. I'm not going anywhere, I promise."

"All right."

That afternoon, he filled the prescriptions. When he got home, he made an appointment with the doctor Tory recommended. That night, with the medicine Tory had prescribed for sleep, he fell asleep and stayed asleep because the nightmares didn't come. Because he was able to sleep, and because he knew it was the right thing to do, he stopped drinking. After a few days of sleeping and not drinking, of bathing and shaving, he felt better—about himself, and about where he was with his life.

After a week of good sleep and long walks on the beach, of brunches with his sister and apologies to Lala and John, Charlie started to feel more like himself again. No, better than himself. More focused. More clear about who he was and what his family meant to him. What it meant to be Charlie George, and to be a George at all. He wanted to live up to his mother's dreams for him, and he finally, after so many years, had figured out what that meant.

One afternoon, he drove over to the neighborhood where he'd dropped Tory at work, near the police precinct. He parked his car in a strip mall lot and spent the morning walking around, taking down phone numbers of buildings for lease and for sale. He looked for ones that held promise: room to grow was one requirement. Clients' safety was another—he remembered how safety was paramount at Tory's clinic. After three days of looking, he found the perfect building for lease. It was two stories tall and needed a paint job badly. There was plenty of parking, and a broken down fence with a gate, all of which could be repaired. Inside, he let his vision run free: old carpet replaced with Pergo; a waiting area in warm tones designed for comfort rather than intimidation or impressing clients. Plenty of rooms for offices for attorneys (two, at the moment, him and Miranda), and paralegals once they were off the ground. His vision grew and grew, and he'd never felt more *right*.

The next day, he filed paperwork with the state bar and the California Secretary of State, and he created a new bank account.

For three weeks, he worked on his new project. He saw his doctor, and he met Miranda for brunch whenever she asked. But he kept the project secret from everyone, even Miranda. He didn't want to get anyone's hopes up, especially hers. And, if he thought about it, his own.

Chapter Nineteen

Tory hadn't seen Charlie George in weeks, not since he was a complete wreck in the emergency department at Cedars. But now, as he stood outside the gate of the Infinity Women's Health parking lot, he appeared to be back in fine form.

He wore faded jeans that made her want to rub her hands down his thighs to verify if the fabric was as soft as it looked. And his legs, had they always been so long? And his shoulders, were they always so broad? Especially in that navy blue Indigo Girls concert t-shirt that was maybe a size too small, or maybe just right.

He smiled a half smile that suggested he knew exactly what she was thinking.

Damn it, she thought. *Someday he won't turn off my higher brain function. Not today, though.*

Over the past few weeks, Miranda had kept her apprised of Charlie's recovery. Charlie had followed Tory's instructions to the letter, and Miranda never stopped telling Tory how grateful she was that Tory had taken care of Charlie even though he'd treated Tory like, in Miranda's words, *a shithead's asshat*, and basically wasn't worthy to tie Tory's shoes.

When Tory had protested—*he's your brother!*—Miranda had said, *Then I should know.*

Now Tory was headed to her car after work, and he was standing just outside the gate with a small cooler at his feet. She walked his way, stopping with the tall bars between them.

"Hey," he said, opening the cooler lid. "I thought you might need a snack after a long day of work." Pulling out two pints of ice cream, he held them up. One was vanilla, and one was chocolate chip, her favorite.

"How did you know that was my favorite flavor?" she said, nodding at the chocolate chip.

"I asked Miranda and Daphne. Between the two of them I can find out just about anything."

"Daphne swore she wouldn't tell you anything ever again."

"Daphne always says stuff like that. It never lasts."

"Where's your car?"

"I was feeling hopeful, so I took a cab."

Sighing, Tory entered the code to let Charlie into the lot. "Did you know today's my birthday?"

Charlie dropped the ice cream back into the cooler, then followed her to her car. "I didn't." He sounded genuinely surprised.

Tory shrugged. "I guess they don't tell you everything."

Muttering under his breath, Charlie said, "Those stinkers."

Tory smiled, but inside, she felt a mix of regret and something else she didn't want to identify yet.

After a moment, Tory and Charlie were in her Toyota, and she could sense his body's heat next to hers. That's when the memory crashed into her of that horrible Sunday, Charlie with the beautiful other woman. She remembered how she'd been ripped open, and she never wanted to feel that way again.

She gripped the steering wheel and nearly told him to get out of the car. Nearly.

She glanced down at her phone where it sat in the cupholder. She was expecting a phone call that would make things awkward, but Charlie deserved it.

She took a deep breath as she put her key in the ignition. "Thanks for the ice cream. I think I'll take both pints, actually."

With surprise in his voice, Charlie said, "You don't want to share?"

"Not really." Part of her really did want to share. Part of her, the part of herself she hated, was overjoyed to see Charlie. She ignored that part, and listened to the sensible part of herself instead. "I think you meant this as some sort of peace offering?"

"Yeah. I did."

She pulled out of the lot and turned toward home. "In that case, I accept. She glanced at him. "Peace, Charlie."

He reached over and squeezed her hand where it rested on the steering wheel. "Peace, Tory."

At that moment, her phone rang. She glanced at the screen. This was the call she'd been expecting, the one that might get under Charlie's skin. If she were a better person, she'd ignore it. But all she could think about was Charlie on her living room floor, and the other woman, and the pain that hadn't gone away.

She answered the phone. Quentin spoke. "Happy birthday, babe."

Quentin had Mondays off from his job at Rivet, and they'd made plans for that night.

"Thank you." She shot a glance at Charlie, who was watching her carefully and probably trying to listen in on the call.

"How was work?" he asked.

"Nothing unusual."

"You sound disappointed."

She laughed. "Maybe a little."

"Do you know where your parents are taking you to dinner yet?"

"My mom's favorite vegan restaurant, just south of campus. It's where we always go for family things."

"But you're not vegan. Are your parents vegan?"

"No. They like it because the restaurant has free parking."

"They didn't ask where you want to go?"

"It's fine."

Quentin grumbled, not pleased by what he was hearing. "Eat light. I'm taking you someplace better afterward."

Quentin, she noticed, didn't ask her where she wanted to go, either. But he meant well. He always meant well. She'd been seeing him for two weeks now, a couple of nights a week, trying to make something out of it. He seemed eager to spend more time with her, and she was eager to try to spend more time with him, if only to see if she could have something like a normal relationship.

She said, "I'll call you when things are winding down."

"I'll be waiting."

They signed off, and she dropped her phone back in the cupholder.

Charlie said, "Quentin, huh?"

She nodded. "He and I are dating."

He paused for so long that she glanced at him. He was staring out the windshield, a thoughtful look on his face. "He seems solid."

She nodded again. *Solid* was a good word for Quentin. So was *smoker* though, and she didn't know how she was going to get over that character flaw. She didn't tell Charlie about the smoking. The last thing he needed was a way to wriggle past her defenses.

She thought back to the promise he'd made to her in the hospital all those weeks ago, the last time she'd seen him.

I know I blew any chance I had with you as a man.

Had he?

But I would like to earn a place as your friend.

Is that really what she wanted? For Charlie George to be her friend?

No. Despite what he'd done, despite everything, she knew how she really felt about Charlie. And it hadn't changed one bit since the day she'd first met him, despite how he'd treated her, despite the woman on the floor, despite her new relationship with Quentin.

Not even that awful Sunday could ruin how she felt. The week she'd spent with him, that night when he'd told her his secret, his apology in the hospital, how he'd listened to everything she'd said, and followed through—it had all made her love him more.

At a stop sign, she dropped her head to her steering wheel.

She was screwed.

"What is it?" he asked, concern in his voice. "Are you feeling okay?"

No, she was not okay. But she needed a quick lie to feed him. She could never tell him the truth—that he made her absolutely stupid.

A half-lie would do. "I don't want to go to dinner with my parents tonight. We have dinner on my birthday every year." She sighed. "It's not terrible, just awkward. Like, they always have to ask how old I am because they don't remember."

"Weren't they there when you were born?"

She shrugged. "I'm resigned to it. I don't see them often, thank God, and there's no point trying to change them now."

"Is that why you're letting them take you to a restaurant you hate?"

"I don't hate it. It's just not what I would have chosen. But what I want doesn't matter to them, and it never has. I've accepted that it never will."

"Then why do you go?" he said. "You're a grown woman, a freaking superhero. You get to decide what you want to do and what you don't."

She felt a twinge in her chest that felt a lot like love. "A superhero? Perhaps that's an exaggeration."

"No it is not. You pulled my ass out of the gutter." He snorted. "You're either a superhero or the Second Coming."

"Thank you for the compliment, but I think you're missing the point. Sometimes a detail like a restaurant doesn't seem important."

"Details are *always* important," he said. "And I think you know that."

She did. Details were what made the difference between a great doctor and a good one, and a good one and a bad one.

"Do you want me to go to dinner with you?" he said.

Shocked, Tory slowed. She pulled over to the side of the road, parking in front of a home on one of the neighborhood streets. "What are you saying?"

"Bring me along. It'll be more fun if I'm there."

"Birthday dinner with my parents isn't supposed to be fun."

He quirked his head at her. "When I was younger, and my mom was around and feeling all right, my birthday dinners were always fun. And my family home could be described as, at best, *fucked up*."

Tory looked at him, really looked at him, for the first time since he'd appeared outside of the gate of Infinity. His hair was neatly trimmed, his face cleanly shaved. His eyes had regained their familiar twinkle. He laughed easily. His confidence, while not the familiar cockiness she'd known for three years—was sound, and even more appealing than before.

"You want to come to dinner with me and my parents?"

He nodded. "I have a nice sweater in my bag."

"And then I'm going to take you back home and go out to a real dinner with my boyfriend Quentin?"

He nodded again, this time with a tightness around his eyes that revealed that he was not happy about her and Quentin, not at all.

She liked the idea of Charlie George being upset that she was seeing someone else. He was her friend, but she was not, it turned out, a doormat.

CHARLIE FOLLOWED TORY THROUGH THE GATE AT HER HOUSE, CARRYING the cooler of ice cream—and Moët, but he hadn't shown that to Tory. Charlie had known it was her birthday, actually, but she didn't need to know that, either. He had a few more surprises to share with her, and he'd wanted to do it with Champagne.

He'd wanted to share his news with her, and toast it with her in her yard with Daisy running around like a happy idiot. He wanted her, he realized, to be proud of him.

But she had a date with another guy.

He sighed. He was definitely not over Tory Murphy. He wondered if he ever would be.

She wore light pink scrubs and hot pink sneakers, hardly the most flattering clothes, but even still, he couldn't keep his eyes off of her. When Daisy came running up to her after she opened her apartment door, she knelt down to give the dog a hug. A yearning hit Charlie in the gut—even though he'd sworn he wasn't here to seduce, or even to charm.

Take your charming somewhere else, Lala had told him. He'd been so angry at Lala that night. He'd been angry at everyone for so long, mostly at himself.

For years, he'd been relying on his charm to get him by, and he hadn't even realized why. When they were children, Miranda had shielded him from the worst of his family situation, but he couldn't even use Miranda's sacrifice as an excuse—he'd learned years ago what she'd been doing. And if he really thought about it, he knew that he'd spent his whole life deflecting any close inspection of himself with his charming façade—Charlie George, always down for a good time, everyone's buddy, but no one's friend. He surrounded himself with shallow douchebags who didn't care about anything but cars and beer and girls, and the only person he ever trusted was his sister.

No one ever saw the real Charlie until Tory. He needed to apologize and to be her friend again if she'd have him. To wish her happy birthday. He'd checked in advance that none of their friends had made plans to surprise her that night. No—her birthday party would be on Friday at Rivet. He was grateful to be invited to that, too. This week, he'd finally told everyone what he'd been up to these past few weeks: the building he'd leased, the paperwork he'd filed. Miranda was proud of him. Daphne, grudgingly, had accepted that he wasn't a total waste of space.

He hadn't counted on Tory having dinner plans with her parents. Or dinner with another guy she'd been seeing. No one seemed to know about Tory and Quentin—he was certain they would have told him if they had. Even Daphne, if only to rub it in.

He set the cooler on Tory's kitchen counter. He unpacked the ice cream into the freezer, and snuck the two Champagne bottles into the fridge. He swallowed, hard. She could enjoy it all later that night with Quentin. He could be okay with that. He tried to picture her on her couch, later that night, drinking the Moët with another man.

He was not, at all, okay with that.

Tory emerged, dressed in tight jeans and a black sweater. As she prepared to leave, he tried to keep his eyes off of her, but he failed. Maintaining any sort of normalcy tonight was going to take a Herculean effort on his part. But she deserved it.

After the twenty minute drive to the restaurant, he followed Tory inside. The host informed them that her parents were already seated, and Tory looked concerned.

She whispered to him, "They never arrive early. I wonder what's going on."

As they approached the table, the attractive couple stood. Tory's mom had brown hair cut boyishly short. She was Tory's height, and looked to have a similar build. He wondered if she worked out as much as Tory did. Her dad was only slightly taller, and he had her coloring—the dark brown hair, the freckles, and the fair skin.

Charlie took the lead. "I'm Charlie George, a friend of Tory's." He reached out his hand to her father.

"Oh, hello." The man looked surprised to be meeting a friend of Tory's. "We didn't expect to have anyone join us."

Charlie smiled the smile he reserved for parents. "I apologize for crashing Tory's birthday shindig. She kept her birthday a secret from me until today. When I found out, I insisted I be allowed to celebrate. I hope you don't mind." He knew he wasn't giving them a chance to mind, couching his insistence in the utmost politeness.

"No, no of course. Wonderful," her father said. "I'm Francis Murphy. My wife Caroline."

Caroline Murphy smiled. She seemed amiable enough as she shook his hand.

"So pleased to meet you both," Charlie said as they took their seats.

"Are you Tory's boyfriend?" Caroline Murphy asked bluntly.

Charlie coughed to hide his laughter. He glanced at Tory, who blushed lightly. "I'm not," he said. "We—my sister, Tory, and I—we're good friends. I figure you'd know if Tory had a boyfriend, right?" Actually, Charlie figured no such thing based on what he'd learned from Tory about her parents.

"Right, of course we would." Caroline Murphy picked up a menu.

Charlie and Tory did the same.

Charlie asked Tory, loud enough for her parents to hear, "What's your favorite thing here?"

"Francis and I enjoy the duck soup," Caroline said before Tory could speak.

Tory met Charlie's eyes. She looked…not miserable, but not happy either. No. She looked resigned. Her eyes, less bright. Even her hair looked less shiny.

Charlie didn't like anything about what was happening at this dinner table. "Duck, huh?" He let his southern accent come on a little more thick. "I thought this was a vegetarian kind of restaurant."

"Vegan." Caroline rapped the menu with her fingertips. "The duck is made of tempeh."

Charlie smiled. "You don't say." He set down his menu. "Sounds delicious. I'll have a bowl of that myself."

Tory stepped on his foot under the table. Glancing at her, he saw that the twinkle had returned to her eyes. In fact, it looked like she was suppressing laughter.

"What about you?" he asked her. "Do you want some fake duck soup?"

Tory quickly covered her face with her napkin and pretended to blow her nose to hide her laughter. From behind the napkin she said, her voice wheezy, "Yes, please."

"Tory, are you all right?" her father asked without looking up from a text message he'd just received.

"Fine, Dad," she said from behind the napkin. "I've had a cold lately." She dabbed at her eyes to catch the tears.

"Oh dear," Caroline said, pulling her hands into her lap. "Please try to contain the germs. We have an important presentation in Vienna in two weeks, and we're waiting on very important news right now."

At Caroline's words, Charlie took Tory's hand in his own and squeezed it, in plain view of her parents. "Will y'all let me buy a bottle of wine to celebrate Tory's birthday?"

Francis was still looking at his phone, so Charlie looked away from him and to Caroline, waiting for her to reply. She didn't.

"Mom, Dad." Tory's voice was sharp. "Do you want wine?"

Francis looked up from his phone. "What?"

"Charlie offered to buy a bottle of wine."

"Great, yes," Francis said, nodding.

"We're waiting on very important news," Caroline said. She sounded like a kid on Christmas Eve. "We've been here for fifteen minutes because we wanted to be settled in case we need to make an important call."

Charlie nodded. "That makes complete sense."

Tory pressed on his foot again. When he glanced at her, she mouthed, *Thank you.*

A few minutes later, Francis received another text message. After reading it, he stepped away from the table and didn't return. Shortly after his departure, four bowls of fake duck soup arrived, along with the bottle of wine and four glasses. Charlie didn't bother waiting for Francis to return to start eating, and after a moment, Tory started eating too.

Glancing at Tory, he noticed how much more relaxed she seemed than when they first came in, and he wanted to think her contentedness was due in part to his presence. But his happy thoughts were interrupted when he remembered her after-dinner date with Quentin. Charlie choked down his mouthful of soup—it wasn't bad—but thinking of Tory on a date with anyone else, even Quentin, whom Charlie actually thought was cool—made him unable to function.

After another five minutes, Francis Murphy returned to the table, an excited look on his face. Turning to his wife, he started speaking so quickly Charlie could barely follow his words. "Finalists for the grant were just announced. That was the chair. She called me personally to let us know that we made it. We have to go in and put together our finalist packet."

Caroline stood. "This is fantastic news."

"Fantastic," Francis said, nodding. "We have a lot of work to do if we're going to win."

They both looked at Tory, who seemed completely unsurprised by this turn of events.

"Good luck, guys," she said.

"Thank you," Francis said.

"We love you, Tory." Caroline said.

And then they walked toward the exit, elbow to elbow, talking nonstop, planning, apparently, and completely consumed by their success.

The server returned. She looked worried. "Were they unhappy with the food?"

Tory smiled reassuringly. "No, the food is delicious."

Charlie thought that *delicious* was a stretch.

Still uncertain, the server said, "Do you…want the check?"

Tory nodded. "That would be great. And I guess you could cork the wine. They didn't touch theirs."

"Sure thing." A few minutes later, she returned with the bottle in a paper bag, and the check.

Tory reached for her wallet, and Charlie placed his hand on hers, stilling it. "Do they even know that they left you with the bill?"

Tory laughed. "Nope. It happens all the time."

Charlie took the check, set his card on top, and handed it to the server. Before this moment, the dinner had been funny, and a little sad. Now, he was feeling angry. "They didn't even say happy birthday to you."

She tilted her head, thinking back. "You're right. Not this year."

Charlie held up his wine glass. "Happy birthday, Tory."

She tapped hers against his. "Thanks, Charlie." She took a sip. "I'm really glad you came."

He wanted to say that he would always be there for her. That he would go to every awful dinner with her parents. That he would walk Daisy for her every day. That he would personally repaint the exterior of Infinity Women's Health. Anything—if she would only give him another chance.

He didn't say any of those things. She had a date with Quentin, and Quentin, as he himself had said, was solid.

They finished their glasses of wine. Charlie signed the check, picked up the corked bottle, and stood. "Let's go, ma'am. I believe you have plans this evening."

Tory looked at him for a moment too long, as though she were about to go on a long journey, and then she nodded. "I need to run to the bathroom before we leave. I'll meet you by the door."

He watched her weave between the tables to the back of the restaurant, her skinny jeans hugging her hips and her black sweater falling off one shoulder. She made his head spin. He really didn't know how he was going to let her go.

But letting her go was what she wanted. And so he would.

Chapter Twenty

As Tory drove south toward Venice, she considered how she'd just had the best birthday dinner with her parents, ever. Charlie's responses had been perfect. *Fake duck soup.* Playing stupid? Charlie George? She snorted.

"What?" he asked from the passenger seat.

"I appreciate everything you did for me tonight."

He shifted in his seat. "It was my pleasure."

"Regardless, let me know if I can help you with something in the future. I know you won't be having any parental meals, but I have other skills."

Charlie sighed. "If we're trading favors, I think you're still in the black." He waved his hand in the air. "I ran up my tab pretty high after the third or fourth night at your house. And after you saw me in the emergency *department*." He whistled. "I'm sure I still owe you at least five more awkward family dinners."

Reaching over, she squeezed his hand. "Thank you. I mean it. I owe you one." When she started to pull her hand back, he kept hold of it.

"Well, if you insist. I'll take my return favor now."

"Now?" She laughed. "What on earth do you want?"

Charlie was quiet for a moment too long, so long that she wondered whether she'd asked a question she really didn't want the answer to. Finally, he said, "I'd like an answer to a question."

"Just one?"

He nodded. "Why are you so accustomed to your parents not noticing you? It's not like you fade into the background. There's a reason you and my sister are friends—she doesn't do wallflower." He shook his head. "You stand out like a supernova."

"That's a gross overstatement."

"It really isn't."

"I'm accustomed to it because it doesn't matter. Like I told you, they've never seen me."

"Then make them see you!"

"It's not that easy, Charlie. I hate it. But it's a battle I don't want to bother to fight. Don't you see? It just isn't worth it."

He sat back in his seat, taking in her words.

"When I was seven—second grade—my parents and I were having dinner at home like we usually did. Dinner growing up was a lot like dinner tonight. I mean, hardly anything has changed. I'm larger, but that's about it." As she neared her house, she slowed, pulling over to the side of the road to park. "That night, my parents were wrapped up in a project they were working on. Not a grant like tonight, but some sort of research. I don't remember what exactly because I didn't understand all of the words." She put the car in park, then turned to face Charlie.

"Because you were seven," he said.

She nodded. "I asked to be excused from the table, but they didn't hear me, so I asked again. But they didn't hear me the second time, either. Or, maybe they did, but they didn't answer me. I really had to go to the bathroom, so I finally just got up and went. When I came back to the doorway to the dining room, they were still talking to each other. They hadn't even noticed I'd left the room."

He began to speak, and she held up her hand to stop him.

"Our house is just off campus, and there was an ice cream and candy shop walking distance from us. I loved to go there with my babysitters, so I knew how to walk there. While they were still at the table, I went into my mom's purse—I'd never done that before, but I'd seen her get money out—and I took a twenty dollar bill. I left the house and walked to the ice cream shop."

"You got chocolate chip," he said. "Your favorite."

She smiled. "I got a double-scoop chocolate chip ice cream cone. I'd only ever been allowed to get one scoop before. Then I sat on a bench and took my time eating it. By the time I finished it, the sky was dark, and I had no idea what time it was. Worried I'd be in trouble, I ran all the way home. The walk was probably twenty minutes for me, since I was small, but the run took maybe half that time. By the time I got home, the front door was locked. I thought maybe they were worried about me and had left to go find me." She laughed, remembering how wrong she'd been. "But no. The car was in the carport. So I fished the hidden key out of the hose reel and let myself into the house. I snuck down the hall and found them both asleep in their room. They'd gone to bed never even noticing I was gone."

"What about bedtime? Didn't they tuck you in? I had nannies and housekeepers, but my mom always tucked us in if she could."

"Sometimes one of them would tuck me in. Usually I put myself to bed."

Charlie nodded, thoughtful. "They don't sound like parents. They sound like really weird college roommates."

Tory snorted a little, but she also felt tears prick her eyes. "After that, I think I stopped expecting much from them. Not consciously, you know."

"Because you were seven." He gave her a sad smile, his eyes crinkling at the corners, and she wanted to trace her fingertips down his cheek.

"Right." Tory took a deep breath. "Does that answer your question?"

Charlie nodded. "It does." He glanced out the windshield. "We're at your place. I guess I'll walk home. But to be honest, I figured my diverting company tonight would have earned me a ride."

"It earned you more than that, if you'd like." Suddenly, she felt nervous. What if she'd been reading his signals wrong? *Courage, Doctor Murphy.* "Would you like to eat ice cream on Ms. Honey's balcony?"

Charlie looked at her, and she couldn't read him. "What will you tell Quentin when he shows up?"

Suddenly, faced with this inscrutable Charlie George, who'd been so kind to her tonight, but whom she hadn't seen in weeks, she doubted herself. "Back at the restaurant, before we left, I called him and cancelled."

Charlie nodded. "Did you give him a reason?"

"I did." She felt her temper rise. "And no, you do not get to ask what it was. You don't get to be jealous or judgmental. You get to say, *Yes, Tory, I'd be delighted to have ice cream with you on your landlady's swanky ocean-view Venice Beach balcony.*"

Charlie leaned over the center console, his eyes on fire, and said in a husky voice. "Yes, Tory, I would love to have ice cream with you."

Oh, Jesus. "Great. Come on then." As she led him through the gate, she took some calming breaths. "Ms. Honey isn't home," she said. "And when she's out she lets me use her balcony. We can sit up there and eat your ice cream. I need to let Daisy out." She opened the door to her apartment and held it open. Daisy went flying out into the yard to run around and do her business. She left the door open and headed into the kitchen to grab the ice cream. When she didn't hear Charlie, she looked over her shoulder.

He stood frozen, staring at the patch of rug where Tory had found him with Regina.

Tory remembered the pain of that night like it was happening to her all over again.

His eyes met hers, and she saw the guilt there.

He gave her a sad smile, then walked back out of her apartment and into the dark evening.

As Tory watched him turn around, the pain still lingering inside her ribcage, she wondered whether it wasn't the right thing to let him go.

———

There is no way.

There was no way she'd forgive him after everything he'd done. And he didn't deserve her forgiveness.

He didn't forgive himself, not for this.

Standing in her yard, he checked the time on his watch. It was only seven-thirty.

Tory could have been having a great time with a guy who did deserve her, but she'd cancelled those plans for him, the asshole who'd done everything he could to shred her heart.

He should call Miranda to come over in his stead. Miranda could make it here in time to celebrate with Tory. Miranda was her real friend—loyal and honest.

Charlie was a scumbag piece of shit.

Daisy trotted over to him and sniffed his hand. He opened his fingers and scratched her ears. She sat, looking up at him, hopeful.

"The thing about dogs is, they don't know any better." Tory knelt down next to him to pet Daisy. "They love you anyway."

Looking down at Tory's dark hair, Charlie felt an ache in his chest as though every rib had been broken. How was he going to make it through so much pain? Swallowing hard, he said, "Why'd you come after me?"

"Finding you with that woman that day—it was the worst that I have ever felt in my life. I honestly didn't know I could hurt like that." She looked up at him as she spoke, her fingers still buried in Daisy's fur.

Charlie did not enjoy being told about how much pain he'd caused Tory, but he wasn't a coward. He knew he needed to hear it, and to apologize for it. "I'm sorry I did that to you. I don't expect you to ever forgive me." He toed the grass. "That's why I just left."

"I came after you because I needed you to know that you hurt me. But I also want to hear from you why you did it."

Charlie rocked back on his heels. He should have been expecting this question. "I'm not going to try to shine a pretty light on myself here. There isn't any way to do that."

Tory nodded, standing up to look him in the eye. Daisy romped off across the yard.

"That first night at your place, when we made our deal to wait for each other, I believed in it. At first. But then the days went by, and every day you came home from work you were getting brighter and brighter, like the damned sun. But I..." He took a deep breath. "Everything around me was getting darker. We said *not yet*, Tory. We said we could be together when I was better. But I *knew* that day would never come. I felt hopeless, and I hated myself for it." He rubbed his hand across his face. "Even remembering what it felt like hurts. And then—I don't think I did this consciously at the time—I brought her here to make sure I wrecked things with you. That way, there was no more promise for me to keep." He looked up at the sky, hoping some kind of answer might be there. "I broke it but good, didn't I."

"You did." At her words, his heart hurt even more. But he needed to hear her say it, to know things were truly over.

"After that day, there wasn't any more pressure for me to try. I could sink as low as I wanted. I could disappear. You weren't waiting for me anymore. Bringing her here broke my last anchor."

Tory nodded. "I see. What's her name?"

Shocked a bit by the question, Charlie said, "Regina. She's an ICU nurse."

"That's a tough job." Tory nodded. "I heard her ream you out. You hurt her too, you know."

He huffed a laugh at the memory of Regina's righteous rage. "Yes, I know."

Tory walked to the fence line where Daisy was sniffing something interesting. "After a couple of weeks, when I'd had time to reflect on things, I figured that was why you did it." Her voice came to him across the dark yard. "It still hurt though."

"I'm so sorry, Tory. I'm never going to stop being sorry."

"I believe you."

She knelt to the ground near Daisy's nose, and quickly reached out with two hands. She held them close to her body and came back to Charlie. She held out her hands to him.

"Is that a toad?" Charlie said.

"It is." The toad was small, about two inches long, gray, covered in darker gray spots. "Daisy was getting too interested, so I'm going to turn it loose outside the fence."

"What if something happens to it out there?" Charlie asked.

"Out there, that's beyond my control. Here, I've done what I can do. Can you help me?" She nodded at the gate.

He opened it, and she passed through, setting the toad down under a bush in Ms. Honey's front yard.

"When I saw you at the hospital, I was still so angry. I'd given you everything, and you smashed it."

"I did."

"But even worse, I couldn't hate you because I knew why you did it. I wanted to just write you off as some asshole, but I couldn't do that." She stepped up to him. "I couldn't just let you go. Because you're not just some asshole."

"The whole 'best-friend's-brother' thing is kind of a pain in the ass."

She poked him in the chest. "That's not why, you idiot."

"It isn't?" He didn't dare feel hope.

"I've known you for years. I know what you're like on a good day and a bad day. I know you, Charlie. And I know that what you did sent you to rock bottom. Am I wrong?"

Charlie shook his head, remembering how it felt to pack up and leave that day, feeling utterly and truly lost.

"What I'm saying is, I know it wasn't about me. As much as it hurt me, and as much as you were a royal fucking dick, what you did wasn't about me. It was about you trying to screw up your life." She poked him in the chest again. "And that is why I can forgive you."

Charlie's eyebrows shot up, and he felt hope prick his heart. "You can?"

"Time to eat ice cream," Tory said. "It's my birthday, so you have to do what I say. Go pack it up and meet me up on the deck."

"All right," he said, sounding way too peppy and not caring one whit. "See you up there."

Inside her apartment, he repacked the cooler with the Moët and ice cream. He followed her up the outside steps that led to Ms. Honey's balcony. Daisy trotted up and plopped down onto the smooth-sanded wood.

Ms. Honey kept her place nice. She had a pair of Adirondack chairs that matched the ones in the yard, and a small table between them. Charlie pulled out the pints of ice cream and two spoons from his hotel's kitchen, setting them on the table. Then he pulled out a bottle of Champagne and two plastic cups.

Tory's brows drew together as she eyed the Champagne. "What's that for?"

"Your birthday." He smiled.

"But you said you didn't know it was my birthday." She paused, frowning. "You lied!"

"I misled."

"No, sir. You lied."

"Fibbed?" He unwrapped the foil top and removed the wire from around the cork.

"I can't believe what an excellent liar you are."

"Really?" he scoffed. "Have you even met Miranda? I'm junior varsity compared to her." He took hold of the cork. "Ready?"

"But you don't lie to me," she grumbled.

He yanked the cork, and it made a satisfying pop. He poured them each a healthy cup full. "Drink it. Harangue me later."

"I'm not haranguing." She took a large swallow.

He smiled, glad that he brought a second bottle.

"Well, maybe I am a little. But you deserve it."

He shrugged. "Maybe a little."

He could handle her haranguing. It meant she hadn't given up on him.

He sipped from his cup and looked toward the water. Although Ms. Honey did not have an ocean-front house, she still had a view between two houses. He could see the grassy green hill, the tall palm trees, and the sandy beach beyond. And beyond all of that, the endless, glimmering ocean.

He glanced to his side to where Tory sat, her feet tucked up on the edge of her seat, holding her cup near her lips.

Her freckles scattered across her nose drew his eye, and her brown eyes, and her tall forehead. Her loose hair scattered across her shoulders, as dark as the night sky.

He thought about what it would be like to sit with her like this every evening, watching the sunset on a balcony, maybe in a building like Miranda's, or heading to work together and coming home together. Eating ice cream.

He shook his head. She might have forgiven him. But she wasn't taking him back, not like that. That was a dream for a different lifetime.

But he wanted tell her how much she'd helped him. He could give her that much. He held up his glass. "I'd like to propose a toast to myself."

Tory scoffed. "Not to me? After you lied about knowing it was my birthday?"

"To Charlie George, founder of George Law, west-coast edition. It's basically the opposite of the east-coast edition." He rested his hand on his chest. "I plan on making very little money."

Tory's brows drew down. "You founded a law firm? When?"

"The papers came through last week. I leased a space not far from your clinic, actually."

"But you hate that neighborhood."

"It's grown on me. I don't want you to think I'm crowding your space, though—it's just that it's the best place to reach my demographic. Like, for example, the women at your clinic."

She drew her brows together. "What kind of firm is this?"

"For anyone who can't afford to pay me, pretty much. In legal circles, we call it 'public interest law.' Say, if a woman needs a restraining order against an abuser. Or, if she were to fight back against an abuser and need a criminal defense attorney. Maybe you can refer some clients my way."

Tory, shocked, asked the obvious question. "How will you make money?"

He looked out at the water, thinking of his mother and the day she died, of the mansion she died in, of his father and the thousands of dollars he deposited in Charlie's bank account every quarter.

She didn't need to know about any of that. "I'll bill on a sliding scale."

"Cheers to you, then." She sipped from her glass and then set it down, picking up her pint of ice cream.

"I wanted to tell you myself," he said. "Miranda already knows. Daphne too. Creating the practice is what I've been doing since I saw you in the hospital."

She glanced at him, licking her spoon of ice cream, once, twice. Then a third time.

He had to tear his eyes away from that spoon.

"You wanted to tell me yourself?" she asked, interrupting his thoughts.

He met her eyes, and the twinkle there informed him that she'd known what he'd been thinking about the spoon. She'd been licking the spoon on purpose.

"I wanted you to know how much you helped me. I did everything you said. The medicine, the referral—everything. But more than that, you inspired me to create a good thing and leave behind my old firm."

"You know, sometimes women kill their abusers." She paused. "They often go to jail for it because they can't get a good attorney. It's hard for people to understand why a person might kill someone they love. But you understand that better than anyone."

Charlie nodded, his emotions tightening in his chest. "I do. And… so did my mom. She represented cases, what my dad would call *total losers*, all the time. Except she never lost."

"You admired her so much."

Charlie, his throat closing, could only nod.

"Did you move back home with Miranda?"

"I couldn't." He held up a hand when Tory tried to interrupt. "Not because of some complex about letting her down. I really do want her and John to have some privacy. I have a temporary place at a long-term hotel. I didn't want to sign a lease on a new apartment until I knew where my work would be."

Tory nodded, scooping out another spoon of ice cream and licking it.

Charlie took a deep breath. "Can't you eat it like a normal person?"

She shook her head.

He rolled his eyes skyward, taking in the glowing moon.

She spoke. "I think it's great. Really."

"I hear a *but*."

"So long as you did it all for you. Not for anyone else."

Charlie laughed. "Haven't you heard? I'm a selfish prick. I only do things for myself."

Tory put the ice cream on the table. "Don't duck the question."

Rubbing his hand on the back of his head, he said, "I did it for myself. But like I said, you inspired me—I can't lie about that."

Nodding, Tory picked up her cup of Champagne again,

swallowing the rest and holding it out for a refill. "I'm okay with being your inspiration. I just didn't want to be the reason."

Against his better judgment, Charlie wrapped his hand around her wrist as he refilled her cup. He took his time letting her go, feeling the soft skin of the inside of her arm as he pulled his fingers away. When he met her eyes, she was staring at him, and the heat in her eyes matched his own.

She took another sip of Champagne. "This tastes expensive," she said. "This is not pro bono bubbly."

"No, it is not."

"We should probably enjoy it while it lasts." She drained her cup.

"Probably."

She stood. "Come on. It's getting cold out here." Grabbing the bottle, she led him into her apartment.

Following her inside, he set the cooler on the kitchen counter, then starting loading the items in the refrigerator. Tory pulled the second bottle from the cooler, giving him a look that suggested she had thoughts about what a guy and girl might get into with that much wine, and tucked it into the fridge.

Then she poured the rest of the open bottle of Champagne in her cup and drank it down like it was a glass of water. "That was delicious. A perfect birthday gift." She licked her lips.

She was taunting him.

"You're, ah, welcome?"

Leaning in, she kissed him on the cheek. "I think I still have your toothbrush."

He leaned back, taking in her playful expression. "You didn't toss it in the toilet?"

"I'll never tell." She held out her hand to him. "Come on."

He let her lead him into her bedroom. He'd only passed through her room on his way to use her shower. Now, she stopped him by her bed.

"Tory," he said, taking her hands before she could tug his shirt up. "I didn't come here for this."

A frown marred her face, pain pulling lines around her perfect mouth. She thought he didn't want her.

"No," he said, "don't think that." He pulled her to him, wrapping his arms around her. "Never think that."

"Why not, then?"

"I don't deserve it."

Pulling away from him, she held her arms out wide in frustration. "This," she said, pointing at him, then at herself, "is not about deserving. Haven't you learned anything?" She poked his chest with her pointer finger again, so hard that it hurt. "Do you think the women I take care of deserve to be abused? Do you think you deserve to be rich as hell? Did you and Miranda deserve to have your mother hold a gun on you? Did I deserve to be neglected as a child and to have idiotic space-cadet parents who can't remember how old I am?"

"Um. No?"

"No! We all deserve to be cared for." She pointed at herself. "To have good healthcare." She pointed at him. "To have good legal representation." She grabbed his shoulders. "To have someone to love and to have them love you back."

Charlie was fairly sure somewhere in Tory's angry speech she'd just said that she loved him. And he was definitely sure that he felt the same way about her.

Bliss, true bliss, settled over him. "I'm sorry."

"What for? I'm the one yelling." She was, and she was so adorable, with her cheeks flushed red, eyes bright.

"You mentioned a toothbrush?" he said.

"I thought you didn't *come here for this*."

"Well," he said, and he truly believed he deserved a sainthood, "We could snuggle?"

She picked up a pillow from her bed and threw it at him in frustration, then she barged into the bathroom.

Leaning in the bathroom doorway, he watched her as she set out not only his toothbrush, but also his deodorant, razor, and shaving cream. She'd saved it all.

She brushed her teeth, scooting over so that he had room to brush his, too. She washed her face, and then returned to the bedroom. He heard the drawers of her dresser open and close, and he fought hard to keep his eyes away from her while she changed clothes.

He lost the fight. Glancing in the mirror, he watched her change into a long nightshirt. He only caught the rear view, but it was as delicious as he remembered. Resting his hands on the counter, he dropped his head and took a deep breath.

He hadn't come here for this. He hadn't. Tory had said that love wasn't about what a person deserved. Fine. But love was about trust, and he hadn't earned hers. She might care about him—only the Lord knew why—but she had no reason to trust him.

He stepped out of the bathroom while she was tugging the comforter down. Unbuttoning his jeans, he felt her eyes on him. He'd sleep in boxers and a t-shirt. Everything would be fine. He could keep his hands off of Tory for one night. Then he'd set about making her his.

She knelt on the bed and put the pillow she'd thrown back in place, her hair tumbling over one shoulder.

Actually, no. He should leave. Right now.

She slid under the comforter.

Correction. He wasn't going anywhere. "The nightmares are better," he said, climbing into bed. "But they're not gone, not entirely."

"That's okay," she said. "I'll wake you if it gets bad." She scooted closer to him.

He leaned back against the pillow, tucking her head against his shoulder.

He slept. The nightmares didn't come.

Chapter Twenty-One

Charlie woke early Friday morning to a torrent of text messages.

Miranda: **Wake up**.

Miranda: **You need to wake your ass up**.

Miranda: **Call me right now**.

Miranda: **Get your ass to my place right now**.

Miranda: **911**.

"What the hell, Charlie?" Tory said as his phone beeped over and over. "My alarm doesn't go off for another fifteen minutes."

"Something's wrong with Miranda," he said. "I need to call her."

Sitting up, concerned, Tory rested a hand on his arm. "Let me know how I can help, okay?"

He nodded, setting his feet on the floor. He dialed, and Miranda answered after the first ring.

"Charles Senior is here." Miranda's voice was hard.

For a moment, Charlie couldn't breathe. All of the awful gut-ripping fear of the past weeks returned in that second after Miranda spoke.

And then, it was gone. He exhaled. He recognized his reaction for what it was—a chemical reaction to a traumatic event. His father wasn't a boogeyman, he was just an ass. He took another breath, and he found himself again. Familiar words came, the ones he and

Miranda tossed back and forth so easily when they had a difficult problem to solve. "Location?"

"Ritz. Arriving at my place in fifteen."

"I'll be there in ten."

"I'll be ready."

Yanking on his jeans, he said to Tory, "Babe, I'm so sorry. I need a ride, right now."

Tory, he noticed, was already dressed. He admired the fact that she knew how to act in an emergency. Of course she did.

"Miranda's?"

He nodded. Then he used his toothbrush and deodorant. He glanced at his razor, wished he had time to use it, and knew he did not.

By the time he was slipping on his flip-flops, she was ready to leave.

He wished he could have had more time to say all of the things that should have been said on a morning like this one.

But, like he always did, his father destroyed everything he came near.

In the car, Charlie racked his brain for reasons why his father would have arrived now, after all these years. The timing was too coincidental. Charlie had been trained to doubt all coincidences. No, Charles Senior was here for a reason, and the only reason Charlie could think of was Charlie himself.

Tory came to a stop outside of Miranda's building. Turning to her, Charlie said, "I wish we'd had more time. There are so many more things I want to tell you."

"You can say them later, can't you?"

Charlie paused, considering his father's presence, and the reasons why he might have come. "I don't know." He touched her cheek. "You say it's not about deserving. But all I want is to be good enough for you." He kissed her, taking his time, savoring what might be the last chance he had to touch her. He pulled back and studied her face. "I have to go now, or I might never be able to leave." So he did.

———

WHEN HE OPENED THE DOOR TO MIRANDA'S APARTMENT, CHARLES Senior was standing in the kitchen, watching Miranda pour him a glass of orange juice.

"It's not fresh-squeezed," Miranda said. "I don't know why you're even asking for a glass." Miranda's voice expressed just how she felt about her father's presence in her apartment.

Displeased.

"Don't be rude," Charles Senior said, taking the glass from her. "You could at least try to be welcoming."

"Why? You're an uninvited guest."

Charlie took in his father. He looked…older. Charlie expected him to look the same, even though three years had passed since he'd seen him, and even more years since he'd spent any length of time living in his house. Charles Senior's hair had gone completely gray. He was still tall, of course, but he was thinner now, less broad, less imposing.

Or maybe the change was in Charlie's perspective.

Interesting.

Charles Senior turned to face Charlie. "Son."

Charlie snorted at the moniker. "Dad."

Miranda nearly spat out her coffee. Charles Senior never called Charlie "Son," and they certainly never called Charles Senior "Dad."

"Brother," Miranda said to Charlie solemnly.

"Jesus Christ," Charles Senior said. He moved to the dining area and sat at the head of the table.

Of course he sat at the head of the table. He didn't care that he wasn't in his own home. Charles Senior dominated whatever space he was in.

Miranda sat to one side of him, and Charlie sat on the other side, facing her.

Thoughtfully, she'd brought Charlie a mug of coffee, too. She pushed it to him across the table.

"So, *Dad*," she said, still chuckling. She was going to call him "dad" for the rest of the day, and she would laugh the entire time. "What brings you to our fair city?"

"I might as well cut to the chase," he said.

"You always do," Miranda said sweetly.

No one was better at getting under their father's skin than Miranda. Charlie just let her work her magic.

Charles Senior took a deep breath, visibly suppressing his annoyance. "I've received lots of interesting news about Charlie."

Miranda raised an eyebrow at Charlie while sipping her coffee. The message was clear. They were going to offer him no information. The children of Sorcha George knew the first rule of interrogation: *Keep your mouth shut.*

Turning to Charlie, their father said, "I got notice that you filed papers to form your own law firm here in L.A. True?"

"True," Charlie said.

"I also spoke with Romeo Birch. He said he let you go weeks ago."

"Also true," Charlie said.

"Said you bungled a case. An easy case, some pro bono defense with a gimme plea bargain."

Charlie gritted his teeth, thinking of the Dunworth kids. Nothing about that case had been easy.

"Is that what Birch told you?" Miranda said before Charlie could speak. "Interesting."

Charles Senior turned to her. "You have something to add?"

"I thought Birch was a good attorney." She sniffed, letting their father know she thought Birch's lawyering ability was lacking.

Charles Senior leveled a glare at her. "He is."

"Not if he thought that case had a gimme plea bargain. That would make him a dope."

"Does your disrespect have no limit?"

Miranda smiled. "I've yet to hit it."

"You have now," he said, slamming his hand on the table. "I'm cutting you both off."

As the words echoed throughout the room, Charlie stood. "You can't do that."

His father stood as well. "I can. I already have."

Miranda continued to lounge in her seat, apparently unconcerned by their father's threat. But Charlie felt panic rising. Once again, his actions had caused unintended pain to the people he loved most.

Charlie shook his head. "Why are you punishing Miranda for what I've done?"

She spoke. "Because he has no other leverage, Charlie. But don't worry about it. I never wanted his smelly money anyway."

"Shut up, Miranda!" Charles Senior had finally lost his temper.

Score a point for Miranda, who still sat at the table sipping her coffee as though her father hadn't bellowed in her ear.

"What do you want?" Charlie asked.

"Birch said he'll take you back. You will go back to respectable work, and you will stop it with this small-firm low-bono/pro-bono law nonsense. Then I'll reinstate your stipend and your sister's."

Miranda snorted at the word *stipend*.

"I'll have your answer by tomorrow morning. Nine a.m. You'll both join me for breakfast at the hotel."

When neither of them answered, he left.

After the door shut behind him, Miranda said, "He hasn't changed a bit." Then she tilted her head. "Actually, he looks older."

Charlie, shaken from his shock by her calm words, said, "I thought so, too."

"They say men age quickly when they no longer have a woman around to take care of them." She tapped her chin. "There's also a statistic that widowers die within a certain amount of time after losing their wives." She sipped her coffee. "We weren't so lucky on that front."

"No we were not." He looked at her. "What are we going to do?"

"I don't care if he cuts me off after I graduate. If you move back in here with me, we'll figure out how to make everything else work. You don't have to pay rent, and you'll have the world's best paralegal and soon-to-be law partner." She pointed at herself. "So our firm will do fine."

"I don't want to move in here. You have your happy little love nest with John."

Miranda frowned, glancing around her spacious home. "It's not exactly a nest."

Charlie felt despair threaten to drown him. Despite his sister's bravado, he knew he was going to have to yield to his father. "Give me some time to think about it. I'll call you later."

Miranda looked at him sideways. She could always sense when he was lying. "I'll give you exactly one hour. Then I'm hunting you down."

———

CHARLIE STARTED WALKING, THE HOPELESSNESS OF HIS SITUATION DIGGING into his bones. He'd come so far. He'd thought he could make it.

What had he been thinking? He walked for nearly an hour, turning the problem over in his mind, trying to find a way through that didn't require him to give up his newfound freedom from his past, his newfound dream for the future. His father wasn't stupid—he'd set his trap well. Charlie would never sacrifice his sister's future just so he could chase a pipe dream. Charlie would never be so selfish, even if he was a shallow prick. Miranda meant everything to him. For so much of his life, she was the only person who'd meant anything at all.

He would have to go back to the firm, back to Birch, back to whomever they'd hired to replace Chalk, a person who'd likely be just another Chalk, and there'd be another and another and another. How had Charlie never seen, before now, just how much he'd been one more asshole in a long line of assholes maintaining a broken system?

What had Tory said to him when he'd driven her to her new job? When he'd scoffed at the rough neighborhood and dinginess of the clinic? She'd said, *Why is it so hard for you to understand the desire to help people who need your help the most?*

He'd had no answer for her then, but he had an answer now. It had to do with needing help himself and not realizing he needed it at all, with having had people stand by him these past weeks, even when he'd done everything he could to alienate them. When he'd needed help the most, they'd been there, even though he hadn't deserved it.

Because it wasn't about what he deserved.

He didn't want to go back to the firm, where they'd expect him to plea the Michael Dunworths to murder two and call it a day. He didn't know how he would live with himself.

He glanced at his father's watch on his wrist. Weeks ago, when he'd taken off his mother's watch, he'd thought he was taking off the burden of her death. But it hadn't been that easy.

He'd worked so hard to hide his pain he'd carried alone for years. He'd thought he was supposed to suffer for what he'd done. And now, just as he was beginning to understand that his mother's dying wasn't his fault, and that he might, just might, be able to have something good in his life, his father had shown up and destroyed all of his hopes.

The first thing he would do was put her watch back on. He could wear it now without shame. Her memory would keep him together while he worked for Romeo Birch and tried to do some good in a place where doing good wasn't easy.

It was eleven a.m. He stood in a familiar spot, outside of the Typhoon. His feet had brought him here while his mind had wandered. Sighing, he stepped inside.

He sat in a booth in the corner with his back to the door. He very much did not want company today. Lala came over, took one look at his face, then came back with a double gin and tonic in a pint glass.

Over the past few weeks, while he'd been apologizing to the people who mattered most to him, he'd included Lala. He'd taken her out for fish tacos during her lunch break, and he'd told her some of what had been going on—only some, because she didn't need to bear all of his burden. But he wanted her to know that he respected her, that he cared, and that he was sorry.

After setting down the glass, she said, "Miranda texted me. She wanted me to let her know if you came here. I just wanted to tell you that."

"Yeah, okay. I'll text her too."

"Charlie. Babe. You look miserable."

He gave her a half-hearted smile. "My life just fell apart."

"Again?" She mussed his hair. "I'm sorry."

"It'll be all right. I think. Eventually." He gestured at his glass. "Maybe after a couple more of these."

"You are allowed to have two, and then you will eat something. I don't feel like cleaning up barf this morning."

"I love you, Lala."

"You and everyone else." She headed back behind the bar, her perfect legs displayed by painted-on jeans.

Charlie was on his second double gin when a woman he didn't recognize sat down across from him. "Hi," she said. Her wavy blond hair hung nearly to her waist.

He racked his brain—had he met her before? He hoped not—he couldn't remember her at all.

"I'm Bonnie."

He leaned back in his seat, relieved. He definitely didn't know a Bonnie.

"I go to Southern Cal. I'm getting my MBA."

Charlie nodded, sipping his drink.

"How about you?"

Charlie looked at her sideways. "Do you want the truth? Or would you prefer a good story to tell your friends?"

Bonnie's eyes widened. "Well, with words like that, I've already got a good story, and you haven't even answered the question yet."

Charlie smiled despite himself. He let his eyes drift down to her bright blue halter top and her perfectly round C-cups. She was like a cupcake in his favorite flavor.

His *former* favorite flavor.

He thought of Tory, of her sculpted shoulders, her strong legs, her thick black hair and freckles.

He thought of the disappointment he would see on her face when he told her he'd be going back to the firm, giving up his public interest law practice before it even opened.

Bonnie leaned forward, putting her breasts on display. "How about a mixture of both?"

"All right." Charlie took a sip of his drink. "I'm a down-on-his-luck attorney, former millionaire, living out of a small hotel room, waiting for the love of my life to walk through that door behind me."

Bonnie smiled. "That's a great story."

Charlie finished his drink, realizing he felt tipsy. He wished any part of the story were a lie.

Bonnie stood, and Charlie noted that her miniskirt matched her top, and that her tanned legs were as luscious as her breasts. *Cupcake, indeed.*

She slid into the booth next to him, tucking his hair behind his ear. "You're hot," she said.

Charlie smiled so Bonnie wouldn't feel bad. But what he really needed was lunch. Lala had been right that he needed food. He leaned forward to signal Lala for a menu, and that's when Bonnie made her move.

When she kissed him, his eyes opened in surprise. He put his hands on her shoulders. "Wait." He backed away.

And that's when he saw that standing behind Bonnie was Tory.

———

Tory knew her mouth was hanging open, but she couldn't seem to close it. Or care to close it. At this point, what did it matter that she was making stupid faces around Charlie George? How many times was she going to humiliate herself in front of him?

She stepped backwards and tripped over a barstool, catching herself on the edge of the bar before she fell down.

Four times, apparently. She was going to do it four times.

Charlie stood from the booth, nearly tipping the woman sitting with him onto the floor. "Tory, wait."

She shook her head, feeling angry now. "No way am I waiting for you." She strode toward the exit, trying to erase from her mind the picture of Charlie with yet another perfect woman.

"Damn it," she heard him say as she passed through the doorway, but when she glanced over her shoulder, he wasn't behind her.

She wasn't even worth following from the bar.

She was half-way down the block when he called out to her. "Tory, stop!"

She didn't want to. She knew that looking at Charlie would cause her physical pain. As a doctor, she knew that the pain made no sense, but neither did love.

She took a deep breath and turned to face him. He approached, carrying what looked like half of a baguette in his hand, more of it stuffed in his mouth. "Why are you eating bread?"

Swallowing, he said in a pleading voice, "That wasn't what it looked like. Please, listen to me."

"You weren't making out with a gorgeous woman in front of me? Again?" She tapped her foot. "I don't have time for your bullshit. I'm on my lunch break."

He stuffed some more bread in his mouth, chewed, and swallowed. "I went to the bar alone. I wanted to be alone after..." he paused, his brows drawing together, lips pursing. "After what happened this morning. Then she sat down and kissed me."

"Only you, Charlie. Women just throwing themselves at your mouth."

"Please, Tory. I wasn't interested."

"That's not what I saw." Tory thought back to what she'd seen, exactly—Charlie, his hands on the woman's shoulders while they kissed. But then Charlie stuffed another piece of bread in his mouth, and she was distracted from her memory. "What are you eating?"

"Lala gave it to me. I haven't eaten anything today."

"Day-drinking on an empty stomach?" She scoffed. "Keeping it classy." She looked up at the sky, feeling tears prick her eyes. Trying to hang onto her anger, she refused to cry in front of him. "Charlie, I'm only here because Miranda called me and asked me to come over. I don't even know why she did that. I should have expected to get kicked in the teeth again."

Chewing on another piece of bread, he winced. "I didn't kiss her, I promise." He held out his hands, the gesture comical because one held the remaining baguette and the other held the piece he was about to eat. "I wasn't interested."

"Why not?" she asked, her voice rising, the tears coming again. "She's gorgeous. And going by what I've seen over the past years— and *weeks*—she's completely your type." Unlike Tory herself, apparently, no matter how much she'd allowed herself to believe otherwise.

She was so stupid.

Charlie pitched the rest of the bread toward a group of seagulls gathered near a trash can. "I wasn't interested, and I didn't kiss her." He ran his hand through his hair, obviously frustrated. "Please Tory, think about what you saw just now. Not what you saw," he paused, "last time."

Tory shut her eyes, and all she could see was the last time. She opened them and saw Charlie's pleading eyes. She closed them again and did what he asked.

She'd walked into the Typhoon. Charlie had been sitting in the booth. As Tory had neared them, the woman had touched his hair. Then, the woman had kissed him, and Charlie had pushed her away.

He'd pushed her away.

She exhaled. "You weren't interested."

"Right before you came in, all I could think about was you."

"I thought you were saying good-bye to me this morning."

Charlie nodded. "I thought I might have been, but not because of you." He reached out for her hand. "Come on."

He led her to an empty bench near the boardwalk, where they sat facing the ocean. "My father is here. He came to Miranda's this morning. That's why I had to leave so quickly."

"He's here? Why?"

"I have to go back to the firm, or he's cutting us both off."

She tried to meet his eyes, but he kept looking away from her. "What does Miranda have to say about this?"

"Miranda said to tell him to piss off."

"You don't agree with her?"

"I can't let him do that to her. Not after she's done so much for me. Besides, how can I make it work at my firm without funding? What am I going to live on?"

Tory laughed. "Charlie. Don't be a baby. You've already won, can't you see?" She grabbed his wrist, pointed at his fancy watch. "Right here—this watch would pay your firm's rent for five years!" She dropped his arm, frustrated. "What are you afraid of losing if you let go of your parents' legacy?"

"It wouldn't pay rent for five years. Maybe one."

"A year? *A year?*" She wanted to slap him. "Who even has watches that expensive?"

"This one was my father's. I don't like it very much." He sounded less defeated, now.

She looked him over. "You really weren't interested?"

He shook his head. "I told her I was hoping my dream girl would walk through the door. It's not my fault she thought I was talking about her."

When he said *dream girl,* Tory couldn't stop her chest from squeezing tight.

The afternoon was warm, and Tory had to get back to work. But she knew now why Miranda had called her to find Charlie. "You should listen to your sister. She wouldn't lie to you about how she was feeling. If she says she doesn't care about the money, she doesn't care about the money. As I recall, she has *never* cared about the money."

Charlie nodded. "You're right. That was always my problem."

"What are you going to do?"

He reached over and picked up her hand. "The right thing. For once."

And then he pulled her to him and kissed her deeply. He pulled back, examining her face, running his hand over her hair, smoothing it back. She'd have to redo her ponytail before she went back to work, but she did not care.

"I'm really interested," he said. "Really, really interested."

Chapter Twenty-Two

After saying good-bye to Tory, and promising to call her to say good-night, Charlie strolled back to Miranda's building. He needed to talk to Miranda—to tell her he'd decided to turn their father down. Although she'd sworn she didn't care about losing their father's money, he needed to see her face when he told her so he could be sure.

The only person who could tell if Miranda was lying was Charlie.

He sent her a text: **I'm coming up**.

Miranda: **K. Did T find u?**

Charlie: **Yes. Thx for sending her.**

Miranda: **I'm a genius I know I know. C u in a min.**

As Charlie stepped off the elevator on Miranda's floor, he thought of the question Tory asked, the one question that finally changed his perspective: *What are you afraid of losing if you let go of your parents' legacy?*

He'd been afraid of losing what made him Charlie George. But then he'd realized that what made him Charlie had nothing to do with his father, or his mother, or how his mother died, or all of the trappings of success and wealth that he'd pulled around himself to hide the ugliness that lurked beneath his façade.

Now he could look that ugliness in the face and let it go.

Sorcha's legacy was the only legacy that mattered. Her legacy was what he wanted to carry on with his new firm. Sorcha had always made time for pro bono cases when she'd been alive. She'd abhorred injustice.

That was Sorcha's legacy.

He stopped short in the hallway of Miranda's building. *Sorcha's legacy.* It hit him.

More secrets. More lies.

Damn. The answer had been in front of them the entire time.

His hands shook as he tried to insert his key into Miranda's door. Finally, he flung the door open, calling out, "Miranda! Get your butt out here!"

She came out of her bedroom in a t-shirt and underpants. "What's got bees in your bonnet?"

"No, yuck." He held his hands over his eyes. "Put on some pants."

She looked down, seeming surprised by her state of undress. "I was about to, but you barged in like an elephant."

John came out behind her, smoothing down his hair. "What's the emergency?"

"Oh man," Charlie said, turning to face the window. "I don't need to see all of this."

"All of what?" Miranda said. "You've seen me in underwear four million times."

John laughed. "I think he means that you're breaking the cardinal rule."

Charlie kept his eyes glued to the window. "We can bring down Charles Senior, but I refuse to talk about it while you're half-naked in front of your boyfriend."

"What's the cardinal rule?" Miranda said to John.

Patiently, John explained. "You can't be naked in front of your brother and your boyfriend at the same time."

"That's a rule?"

"How do you not know the rule?" John asked.

Miranda harrumphed.

"She hasn't had many boyfriends," Charlie explained to John. To Miranda he said, "Hurry up! This is important."

"This better be worth all of this hubbub," she muttered.

After she pulled on some cut-off sweat pants that had obviously belonged to John before Miranda had attacked them with scissors, she sat with him on the couch.

"You had some sort of epiphany?" She didn't sound convinced.

"We need John in here for this." John had followed Miranda into the bedroom, but he hadn't come out again.

"John!" Miranda hollered.

"You are so loud," Charlie said, amazed. "How are you still so loud?"

"Did you expect me to mellow with age?"

Charlie shook his head. "No, not really."

John emerged. "You called, dear?"

"Charlie says he has breaking news. He wants you here, too. Something about bringing down Charles Senior."

After John sat down, Charlie continued. "Something Tory said when I saw her earlier tripped a wire in my brain. She talked about our family legacy. And I remembered something that happened after mom died." Charlie paused, and he realized that, for the first time, that phrase—his *mom died*—felt right to him. He no longer thought in terms of what he'd done to her, drowning in his guilt. She'd *died*. The guilt was finally, *finally*, slipping away.

"Well?" Miranda said, as impatient as ever. "What did you remember?"

"After mom died, you were sick. And then you got better and you moved here and then," he waved his hand in the air.

"I acted like a total diva."

"Okay, I was going to say you had a medical crisis, but you can call it what you want. In any event, in all that time, we never saw her will. Her *legacy*, Miranda. What was it?"

Miranda's eyebrows shot up. "We never saw her estate documents."

"No, we didn't."

Hopping up, Miranda grabbed her laptop, then sat down next to Charlie so he could watch her work. She entered a legal database, going back a few years. "I'm going to pull up the probate court docket for the year mom died. I don't know if the will went into probate, but just in case…Whoa. The documents are sealed," she said. "Weird."

"Not too weird, considering Charles Senior."

"No, I mean, I can't see anything at all. I don't even know who the judge was. Nothing. Just the date of probate."

"Is this why you wanted me out here?" John said. "You want me to hack a court database? That's super over the line, even for me. There has to be a better way."

Smiling, Charlie shook his head. "I wanted you out here because Miranda would want you to know all of this."

John leaned back in his seat, giving Charlie an assessing look. "Involving me in family matters? That's new, coming from you."

Charlie nodded. "I'm sorry it took me so long to treat you like I should have. You deserved better."

There was that word again. *Deserved.*

"We could call her attorney," Miranda said. "Paul Barrow. He'd have a copy of her documents on file."

"What would we tell him?" Charlie asked.

Miranda tapped her lip. "The truth?"

Charlie chuckled. "That would be an interesting change for us."

Miranda pulled up Barrow's information on his firm's website. "I hope he's still in the office. We're cutting it close. With the time difference, he's probably out of the office by now."

John pulled out his laptop. "You need a cell phone number? That's something I can get you."

Twenty minutes later, Miranda was dialing the mobile number of her mother's estate attorney.

"Mr. Barrow? This is Miranda George, Sorcha's daughter. My brother and I have a very important question to ask you." She set the phone to speaker and laid it on the table so everyone could hear.

———

Tory only had one more patient to see before she headed home Friday afternoon. It was three-thirty, and she was grateful she could leave early. She wanted to call Charlie and see how he'd fared after their talk, if he'd taken her words to heart and told his father to shove off.

She entered through the yellow door of the exam room and

stopped short. Sitting on the table was Amanda Dunworth, the little sister of Charlie's client, Matthew Dunworth. No, Michael.

Tory shut the door and stepped into the room. Amanda followed her movement with her too-big eyes.

"I'm Dr. Murphy," Tory said, keeping things as normal as possible. "What can I help you with today?"

"I called the hospital number on your card. They said you worked here now. Do you remember me?"

Nodding, Tory said, "I do."

"Is it true what that lawyer said?" Amanda's voice sounded scared but hopeful.

"Which part?"

"Can he get my brother out of prison?"

Tory didn't know the right answer. Could Charlie have gotten a good outcome for Michael Dunworth weeks ago? Probably. Now? "Truthfully, I don't know if too much time has passed. And Charlie—the lawyer you met—he isn't your brother's lawyer anymore."

Amanda put her face in her hands, then looked up again. "When Michael first killed our parents, the case attracted so much attention. Everyone wanted to know every detail about what happened to me to figure out if they believed me or not. At first, I shared everything with the police to prove that my story was true."

"I'm so sorry. That must have been so hard."

Nodding, Amanda said, "But, when the police interviewed me, they made me feel...dirty. The first two detectives, they kept asking questions about what my dad did to me. They wanted to hear the details about what he liked. They didn't ask questions to learn about the shooting. They asked because they wanted to have stories to tell at work. I could tell." She sniffed, holding back tears. "They'd already arrested Michael. They didn't care that he was defending me." She fisted her hands over her face. "They were disgusting. And then they leaked it to the press."

Tory had heard plenty of stories about police who victimized women, who didn't care about the crimes committed against vulnerable victims—prostitutes, addicts. These cops believed the women deserved to be hurt. Tory had even met a few in the emergency department when they brought the women in for medical care before taking them in on charges.

She'd hated them all.

Tory kept her face placid. "I'm sorry. The police are supposed to protect you. But sometimes they aren't trustworthy."

Amanda shook her head. "Eventually, I refused to talk about what happened to me anymore. And Michael told me he didn't mind. He said he hadn't protected me from our parents just to put me in harm's way all over again. He told me to hide and to refuse to talk to anyone. So I found that apartment where no one would look for me, and everything was quiet for months."

"And then we came," Tory said.

Amanda nodded. "After you came, I called Michael. I was just so upset. I didn't know what he would do."

She started crying in earnest, and Tory held her hand. The crying turned to sobs.

"And yesterday, he told me that he's about to be sentenced. The minimum is thirty years. He could get life in prison, and I'm never going to see him again."

When Amanda finished crying, Tory said, "How can I help you, Amanda?"

"I want to help him. I want to talk to the lawyer. Your friend. Can you call him for me?"

"I can. But like I said, he's not your brother's lawyer anymore."

"He will be. Michael told me he will take him back."

Tory raised her brows. "Does Michael know you came here to meet me?"

Amanda nodded. "Can you call the lawyer?"

"I think it's best if you do it." Tory pulled her prescription pad out of her pocket and wrote down Charlie's name and number. Handing it over, she said, "I'll step out while you call him. When you're ready, open the door. Okay?"

Amanda took the paper, pulling her phone from her purse. "Okay."

In the hall, Tory texted Miranda: **Charlie is about to get a call. He must answer**.

Miranda: **Done. Can you tell me more?**

Tory: **I can't. Just wait.**

A few minutes later, Tory received another text from Miranda: **We're on our way now. Tell Amanda. If you have a conference room, we need it.**

———

Charlie sat across from Amanda Dunworth in the conference room of Infinity Women's Health. Miranda sat to his side. Tory sat next to Amanda. On his way over, he'd called Sunita and told her to put a hold on the sentencing because Michael Dunworth wanted to change his plea due to new evidence.

It was time to talk to Amanda, who looked like she'd been crying, but who also looked like her spine had turned to steel since the last time he'd seen her.

He glanced at Tory—his dream girl. He gave her a small smile. She nodded at him and smiled back, and he felt like maybe he could finally do right by Amanda Dunworth.

He took a breath, then dived in. "Amanda. First—I want to apologize for the last time I saw you. I pressed you to testify when it clearly upset you. I'm deeply sorry."

Amanda looked surprised. "Thank you. I know you were trying to help."

"Regardless, I made a mistake. Please forgive me."

She nodded. That was enough.

He moved on to official business. "We're going to record your statement. Is that okay?"

Amanda nodded.

"When I turn on the recorder, I'm going to ask that question again, and I need you to say out loud that you agree." He nodded at Miranda, who pressed the button to start the recorder.

"Amanda Dunworth, do you consent to have this interview recorded?"

"I do."

"Also present are Charles George, Jr., attorney for Michael Dunworth, Miranda George, my paralegal, and Dr. Tory Murphy, as assistant to the witness. We're here to interview you about the events that occurred the morning your parents died. Do you agree to this interview?"

"I do."

"Let's begin."

While Amanda gave her testimony, Charlie listened to the memories she recounted—including the abuse by her father stretching back so many years. Then she detailed what happened the night before her parents died, and the following morning when her brother shot her parents because there was nothing else he could do to make her father stop hurting her.

"He said he would never stop. He said there was nothing we could do to stop him. That no one could stop him." Amanda was weeping, and Tory had her arm around her shoulders. "Michael had no choice."

Charlie couldn't speak. He'd known this was coming, and he'd figured he'd react this way. He'd prepared himself.

That's why he'd brought Miranda.

"I understand," Miranda said. "I really do."

"You couldn't," Amanda said. "No one could."

Miranda smiled, but the smile was painful. "But I could, more than you know."

After they wrapped up the interview, Charlie and Miranda stepped out of the room. A nurse escorted them from the building via the back entrance. Once they were in Charlie's car, Charlie dialed Sunita on the phone, putting it on speaker.

"My client will plea to voluntary manslaughter."

"You have witness testimony to back that up?"

"We have the sister's. Recorded, and she'll come in and give it to you as well."

"You know I never liked this case. But the defendant didn't give me a choice. He insisted."

"We know," Miranda said.

"We'll accept his plea," said Sunita.

Charlie met Miranda's eyes, and the relief on her face matched what he was feeling. She smiled, squeezing his arm.

Once Charlie hung up with Sunita, he gripped the steering wheel of his car and rested his head on his fists. Miranda mussed his hair.

"Do you feel redeemed, Little B?"

He glanced at her. "That's what this case was about at first. But now, I just wanted to do the right thing after messing up so badly."

"That's fair."

"I feel like I have so much I need to set straight."

"Not so much anymore, though."

He leaned back in his seat. "No, not so much anymore."

———

THAT EVENING, ON THE FARTHEST TIP OF THE FARTHEST DOCK OF THE marina, Charlie stared out at the ocean, Miranda by his side.

"Is this why we live out here?" he asked. "Because it feels like the edge of the world?"

"Probably," Miranda said. "Georges are highly bred misanthropists."

"We like Lala," Charlie said.

"Lala is also a misanthropist."

"But she runs a bar."

"That doesn't mean she likes people," Miranda said. "That means she likes bossing them around and taking their money."

"God, she's fantastic."

"She really is."

Charlie's phone beeped, and he fished it out of his pocket. Surprised, he said, "It's Birch."

"What does that asshole want?"

Charlie read the text aloud: **I heard about your win today. I knew you could do it.**

"Seriously?" Miranda said. "He's taking credit for your success? I hate this guy."

Another text came through, and Charlie read it to Miranda: **Let's grab a beer and talk about getting you reinstated. Perhaps it's time to talk promotion. Partner isn't far off.**

Miranda made gagging sounds.

Charlie stared at the words. Promotion? And partnership? These were the dreams he'd been chasing his entire adult life.

Miranda cut into his thoughts. "That jackwacker wants to give you a promotion? He just fired you."

Shaking his head, Charlie said, "Perhaps Charles Senior talked him into texting me this."

"Or, you just won an unwinnable case at the eleventh hour. They'd be lucky to have you back."

Charlie smiled. No one would ever doubt Miranda's loyalty. "Or that."

Charlie reread Birch's text one more time, and then he chucked the phone into the water.

Miranda cracked up. "That was firm property!"

Charlie watched the splash dissipate. "Yep."

"Cool. Let's go get you a new phone."

Chapter Twenty-Three

Saturday morning, at nine-o-two, Charlie and Miranda slid into their chairs in the breakfast room at the Ritz.

Their father didn't look up from his paper. "You two are cutting it close."

Miranda slid a file folder across the white linen tablecloth, then pulled their father's newspaper out of the way, rumpling it beyond readability.

Charles Senior looked up, aggravated. "What is this?"

Miranda rested her chin on her folded hands. "Open it and see."

He opened the folder. Inside was a faxed copy of their mother's will.

In a quiet voice, Miranda said, "Don't make a scene. Keep smiling. In fact, don't even talk."

Charlie chimed in. "We had a great conversation with Paul Barrow. Imagine how horrified he was when he learned that you encouraged him to unwittingly commit malpractice. He wanted to report everything to the state bar ethics committee. We said that getting you sanctioned wasn't necessary."

Charles Senior's eyes tightened, the only evidence that he was furious.

"You lied to him. He's on our side." Miranda kept her voice light, as though they were discussing the weather, or sports. "Think of Barrow as our pocket aces. You understand poker."

Actually, Miranda understood poker better than anyone in their family.

Charlie couldn't keep the anger out of his voice. "Mom left us our money in trusts. You're the trustee. That money is ours, and you've been stealing."

Charles Senior cut in. "Stealing is an overstatement."

"I said to shut up." Miranda's voice turned to steel. "I will cut you down like a weed."

For the first time in his life, Charlie saw fear in his father's eyes. But he didn't want Miranda to have to fight their father. She'd left Charles Senior behind to start a new life. This fight was his own.

Charlie stepped in. "Here's what we want."

Taking a deep breath, Miranda said, "Buy Charlie a condo in my building. There's one coming available on the floor just below mine."

Charlie nodded. "It's a very nice unit. And," he met his father's eyes, adding some of the steel his sister had shown, "you're going to endow our law firm with all of the money you've stolen from us over the past two and a half years."

"That's more than—" Charles Senior began.

"Do you really want to finish that sentence?" Miranda said. "Do you want to announce to everyone in here how much you've stolen from our trusts?"

Charles Senior stopped arguing.

Miranda delivered the final blow. "Finally, you're going to make Barrow the trustee of our trusts, and we're never going to hear from you again. Unless you grow a conscience and feel like acting like a human being, in which case you can start by apologizing and sending birthday cards or something." Miranda drew her brows together in thought. "Although that might be weird, so we'll cross that bridge later."

Charlie added, "And if you don't do these things, we're going to sue you for fraud and mismanagement of funds. Barrow has a guy all lined up for us."

Charles Senior nodded once. Then he dropped his napkin on his seat and left.

A moment later a server arrived. He glanced at Charles Senior's empty seat. "Eggs Benedict with Alaskan crab?"

Miranda held up her hand. "That's for me." The server set the plate in front of her. She rubbed her hands together like a small child before taking a fork and shoving a big bite into her mouth. Even when things were tense, Miranda never lost her appetite.

After swallowing, she asked Charlie, "So. Has Tory taken you back or what?"

———

BEFORE GOING TO TORY'S, CHARLIE HAD AN ERRAND TO RUN. HE KNEW where to go because he'd looked it up after he'd spoken to Tory the day before, before his mad dash to the clinic to interview Amanda. The errand took two hours. When he was done, Tory's birthday card lay on the passenger seat beside him with a gift tucked inside.

He parked outside her house, took a deep breath, then pulled out his new phone.

Charlie: **Hey, this is Charlie. I got a new phone.**

Tory: **Charlie who?**

Feeling a flare of jealousy, he didn't know what to write. How many Charlies did she hang out with on a regular basis?

Tory: **Just kidding. I'll save your new number.**

He took a deep breath, letting out a laugh. He'd just survived the Valley of Death, and Tory was going to break him in half with her hilariousness.

He took another a deep breath and texted: **Do you have time to talk?**

Tory: **Sure. When?**

Charlie: **Now?**

Tory: **If you insist. Look up.**

She was leaning in her open gateway, watching him. Her hair was sleep-mussed and loose around her shoulders. She wore the long t-shirt she'd slept in when he'd stayed over two nights ago with baggy sweatpants underneath.

He wanted to pick her up and take her straight back to bed.

Climbing out of his car, he brought her birthday card with him. He held it up to show her. "I brought you a birthday present."

She motioned for him to follow, leading him into her apartment. "You already got me a present."

"Ice cream is hardly a present."

"Don't forget the Champagne."

How could he forget the Champagne? And holding her all night after?

"Can we sit?" he asked.

She sat on the couch, and he followed, tugging on his wool dress pants.

"Why are you all dressed up?" she asked.

"Miranda and I had a fancy brunch."

"Is that something you do a lot?"

"We used to, when we were younger."

"Why today?"

"We had to say good-bye to our father. For good."

Tory nodded, thoughtful. "Are you happy about that?"

Charlie smiled. "More than I can possibly explain."

"Can I have my present now?" she said, reaching to take it from him.

He held it high above his head, out of her reach. "Not yet. I need to tell you a story first."

She crossed her arms over her chest. "Fine. Make me wait." She leaned forward so her nose nearly touched his. "I hate waiting."

He swallowed, and reminded himself that he wasn't going to kiss her. Nope. Not yet. Later.

He could wait till later.

Tory raised her brows and smiled as though she could read his thoughts. "You were going to tell me a story?"

Charlie cleared his throat. "Have I told you that my sister is better than me at tennis?"

"I know you two play a lot."

"She always was better, even when we were kids. I thought for sure I would start beating her once I got bigger—she's so much smaller than me, plus she's a girl."

Tory snorted. "She's not that small."

"I can hit it harder, serve harder, but none of that matters. We'll be neck and neck for a few games, but then she'll wear me down and get in my head. And then she wins the set. It's so annoying."

"Miranda definitely can be annoying."

"That's not why she wins, though. It's because she's more consistent, and she has more shot variety. She can return anything I hit at her—my power's not a problem for her—and then she'll murder me with a drop shot from six feet behind the baseline."

Tory's eyes were serious. "Charlie, dude, I don't know what any of that means."

He laughed. "It means I only know one way to be good at things —I only know one way to win. And if I can't win that way, I don't know what to do."

Understanding lit in Tory's eyes.

"These past few weeks, I've been telling myself there had to be another way to save Miranda and my mom that awful day. Over and over—I've been blaming myself because I couldn't save them both. And then with the Dunworth case—that kid almost went to jail forever because I dragged you to his sister's house. I couldn't figure out another way to save him besides going against his wishes and getting his sister's statement—even though he explicitly told me not to."

Tory cut in, "But you did save him. Dragging me along was really smart, actually. And I don't know what anyone would have done in your situation with your mom. She was trying to kill your sister, and she had a gun on you, and she was out of her mind. She might have had a knife, too, or something else. You couldn't have known everything that was happening."

Charlie held up his hand, asking for her to wait. "And then yesterday, my father came, and there seemed to be only one way to solve that problem, too. I had to do what he said and go back to the firm. I couldn't see another way despite what Miranda said. Despite the obvious answers in front of my face." He handed her the envelope.

She opened it, pulling out the folded paper inside. "What the heck is this?"

It was a check, made out to Infinity, for one hundred and fifty thousand dollars. On the memo line it said the gift was made in honor of Sorcha George.

"I used to have three watches." He held up his wrist to show her the one he wore. "Now I only have this one, the one my mother got me. When I was assigned the Dunworth case, and things got hard, I couldn't wear it because it reminded me too much of the day she died. So I wore my father's watch instead. But then you said something about letting go of my father's legacy, and you were right. So I sold his watch this morning and the one from my grandfather, too."

She glared at him. "Who even has watches this expensive?"

He smiled. "Not me."

"But you can't give this money to Infinity. You need it for your firm."

"My firm has recently received an endowment. We'll be all right."

"So you've decided then? You're not going back to your old job?"

"I'm not going back. Everything you just said—you're right. I couldn't save my mom—I had no other choice. I could have done things differently with Michael Dunworth's case, but it turned out all right, and I'll do better next time." He nodded at the check. "And the most important parts of my family's legacy have nothing to do with fancy watches. Even though making it through the day could be the hardest thing in the world for her, my mother still loved me. The least I could do is not throw my life in the garbage."

Tory smiled. "Yes, that's probably the least you could do."

He reached out, tucking her hair behind her ear. "I'm so sorry I hurt you."

"You've said that already."

"I'm going to say it over and over until you believe that I'll never hurt you again."

"Women are never going to stop throwing themselves at you. You're way too charming."

"I can become gruff and rude like Marlon." Marlon was Daphne's fiancé. He and Charlie tolerated each other—most of the time.

"Don't. I like you the way you are." She held her palm against his cheek.

"You're my only type."

She snorted.

"You don't believe me?" He stood, pulling her to her feet. He scooped her up in his arms and carried her to her bedroom.

She looked at him, eyes wide. "No one has ever picked me up like this before."

"Their loss." He nuzzled her ear before laying her down on the bed. He knelt on the floor beside her, taking her hand in both of his. "There are two things I'm going to do with you for as long as you will let me. I will earn your trust, every single day. And I will show you that you are the sexiest, smartest, most beautiful woman I've ever seen."

Tory pushed up on her elbows. "Take off all your clothes."

"Wait a minute. I'm trying to be sincere."

"Yeah, okay," she waved at him with her hand. "Get naked, big boy."

Grinning, Charlie unbuttoned the top two buttons on his shirt and then yanked it over his head.

"Better," Tory said. "Now your pants."

When he was down to his boxers, he said, "What about you, Doc?"

"I trust you will undress me next."

He crawled up the bed until he was propped over her. "Trust?" He traced his finger along her jaw. "You trust me?"

"I do trust you, Charlie George."

He dropped his face to her neck, resting there, relieved. "Thank God. Through all of this, you've become everything to me." He met her eyes, and they glowed in the afternoon light pouring through the window.

"Whatever, you've been hot for me for years."

Charlie chuckled, nuzzling her neck. "You're right. I just never thought I deserved anything this good until now."

"Me neither." She wrapped her arms around his neck and pulled him close. "I'm glad we came to our senses."

Want More of the George Siblings?

You can read more about Miranda and Charlie in *Fallout Girl*, which tells the story of when Miranda first ran away to Los Angeles—lost, prickly, alone—and terrified. Don't worry, there's a happy ending.

And be sure to catch the rest of the IPPY-Gold-Winning Hollywood Lights series, which is now complete, starting with *Entanglement*.

To learn about my books and writing life, subcribe to my Substack at pryalnews.com.

Acknowledgments

It's hard to believe that the Hollywood Lights Series is coming to an end.

I began writing these novels so many years ago that I can't remember precisely when I started. *Entanglement* was published in 2015 by a small publisher called Velvet Morning Press (now shuttered), and they also published *Love and Entropy* and *Chasing Chaos* (2016).

I thought I was done with the series after *Chasing Chaos*, but a certain character kept nagging me—Miranda George—as did a certain author friend of mine. Lauren Faulkenberry, who has been by my side throughout my entire publishing career, urged me to write another story with the characters from Hollywood Lights. That book became the novella *How to Stay*, which I wrote in 2016, and soon after I wrote that story, Lauren and I founded Blue Crow Publishing.

The rest is history.

Blue Crow Publishing published dozens of titles by award-winning authors. And as a small press and a cooperative, we have accomplished so much. I couldn't be more proud to have Lauren at my side through all of these years. We've built something out of nothing, and it is truly hard to believe. If not for Lauren, none of the *Hollywood Lights* books would be here.

Also, if you like the book's title, she gets the credit for that, too.

I also want to thank two authors who've fiercely stood by my side, despite our long-distance relationship, Camille Pagán and Kelly Harms.

Other friends and fellow authors have been crucial to the success of this book and to the series: Alexa Z. Chew, Eileen Goudge, Sonja Yoerg, Erin Celello, Amy Sue Nathan, Diane Haeger, Kimberly Brock,

Orly Konig Lopez, and Tina Ann Forkner. All of you know what you mean to me. Thank you for being a part of my life.

And lastly, my family: my sister and frequent early reader Chris Guest Adigun; my cousin, proofreader, and Los Angeles fact-checker Janet Angela Linnane; Karen Alvarez, who cares for my home and my children with love; my Aunt Carol, an incredible teacher and also a fine early reader; my parents who *mostly* know what I do for a living; my husband, who *does* know what I do for a living and who does everything he can to support it; and finally, A. and E., my two brilliant quasars, who illuminate space, time, and everything in between.

About the Author

Katie Rose Pryal, J.D., Ph.D., tells stories about the outsiders, the misfits, and the beautifully complicated. She is a Bipolar-AuDHD author of many books of fiction, nonfiction, and memoir.

Her books include *Your Kid Belongs Here: An Insider's Guide to Parenting Neurodiverse Children* (Johns Hopkins, 2025), *Life of the Mind Interrupted: Essays on Mental Health and Disability in Higher Education* (Blue Osprey, 2017), the IPPY-Gold-winning *Even If You're Broken: Bodies, Boundaries, and Mental Health* (Blue Osprey, 2019), and the IPPY-Bronze-Winning *A Light in the Tower: A New Reckoning with Mental Health in Higher Education* (Kansas, 2024).

Her Hollywood Lights romance series includes *Entanglement* and the IPPY-Gold-winning *Take Your Charming Somewhere Else*. Like all of Katie Pryal's writing, the series centers neurodiversity, in addition to angsty romance, star-crossed lovers, sexy woodworkers, movie stars, and happily-ever-afters.

She lives in Chapel Hill, North Carolina, with her spouse, children, and many, many animals. Subscribe to her monthly letter at pryalnews.com.